PRAISE FOR

GODS OF GLENHAVEN

"Fans and sufferers of Greek myths, rock 'n' roll, and middle-age crises will take great comfort and joy from this hilarious novel. Stephen Statler's wit and charm are on full display in *Gods of Glenhaven*."

—**CHRIS MONKS**, editor of *McSweeney's Internet Tendency*

"A rollicking good time. And not just fun but also serious, asking us what it might mean to be 'heroic' today. I can't recommend this highly enough. Percy Jackson for adults!"

—**JOHN ZILCOSKY**, author of *Kafka's Travels*

"A raucous comedy grounded in relatable characters. A hilarious exploration of how we react in the face of absurdity and terror. Stephen Statler has created a joyous, bawdy world in which the question 'Is a dashiki the most appropriate way to cover a permanent erection when you've made an unwise deal with Dionysus?' is absolutely reasonable.

"Statler has managed to weave together the suburban and the supernatural in a wonderful story of an Everyman trying to find meaning at midlife. With a wickedly sharp pen, Statler tells the tale of Christian, a man beset by woes around marriage, parenting, and work. He clings to his polite habits and mores even as the world, and a cast of wonderfully delineated characters, begin to throw supernatural events his way. Statler pushes his protagonist to the brink, asking the question 'What happens when our habits of being in the world no longer work?' Can we turn chaos into joy? Is there room for fulfillment when you've lost everything you thought mattered? *Gods of Glenhaven* is at once a funny, laugh-out-loud joyride and a thoughtful meditation on what it means to be forced out of our comfort zone into the Dionysian, the absurd, and the unpredictable."

—**ALFREDO BOTELLO**, author of *Spin Cycle*

"Stephen Statler's *Gods of Glenhaven* has managed to not just open Pandora's box but also create an entirely new structure for those vices to spill forth. Bawdy, intelligent, and hauntingly accurate in its investigation of suburban mores, Statler's illustrated novel takes the best that Greek mythology has to offer and infuses it with modern wisdom and wit. The cast of characters, from Christian and Sloan to Francesca and 'Dee,' are crafted meticulously with Statler's trademark precision, casting us as a willing chorus to their collective sorrows and triumphs. Quick-paced and accentuated with illustrations by Vasylyna Tumanova, Statler's prose sets a new bar that Dionysus himself would approve of and applaud."

—**KATIE ZIEGLER**, author of *The Last of the Cursive Writers*

GODS OF GLENHAVEN

Gods of Glenhaven

by Stephen Statler

Illustrations by Vasylyna Tumanova

Cover design by Lauren Sheldon

Published by

◤köehlerbooks™

3705 Shore Drive
Virginia Beach, VA 23455
800-435-4811
www.koehlerbooks.com

GODS OF GLENHAVEN

A NOVEL

STEPHEN STATLER

VIRGINIA BEACH
CAPE CHARLES

For Kelly, Nina, and Collin.

MY BOOK REPORT

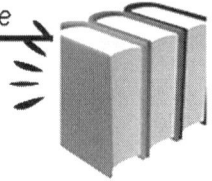

Francesca Orr/World Studies/6th Grade/Burke 6S

Chapter Title: "Greek Gods: Dionysus"

Review Title: "Sex, Drugs, and Tumescent Members: The Story of Dionysus"

Dionysus was the Greek god of sex, drugs, and rock and roll. Actually, he was the god of wine and religious ecstasy, but he was definitely like a rock star.

He drove everybody crazy with his good looks and his ability to make people do weird things.

He had long hair and was called "slim-hipped" and a "beautiful youth."

Statues of Dionysus often depict him with an erect penis ("tumescent member," if you prefer).

I would be remiss if I didn't mention this hilarious thing called priapism.

Dionysus could make men have erections that wouldn't go away. Can you imagine men with erections that won't go away?

Dionysus had a sidekick, Silenus, who famously said, "Better not to be born. Once born, better to die as soon as possible." What a guy!

Even though he was a cynic, Silenus helped Dionysus do their important work to make people happier (see below).

Dionysus had a wife, Ariadne, who was as awesome as he was. And they had a son named Maron, who was gorgeous and immortal just like his dad and mom.

Dionysus could do many things, including turning regular women into raving lunatics called "bacchantes" who would follow him everywhere he went. They would start out as regular women, and then, under the spell of Dionysus, they would tear wild animals apart, drink wine, and have sex with everything that moved. They were just like groupies!

MY BOOK REPORT

But Dionysus wasn't just about fun. His serious goal was to get people out of their humdrum lives and accept terrible things like aging and death.

Dionysus and Silenus would bring people into their rites of initiation where people "died" to their old selves and were reborn in some way. And everybody came out happier, but nobody knows why, because everyone who did the ceremonies was sworn to secrecy. Amazingly, no one ever blabbed!

Scholars think people were given a weird drink called kykeon that caused them to have an acid trip.

Dionysus eventually faded away as a major god because he ended up in competition with Jesus Christ, and we all know who won that battle. Boo!

Scholars say there were similarities between the two gods, so that the image that everybody has of Jesus, with the rock-star long hair, actually comes from Dionysus. Can you imagine a statue of Jesus on the cross with an erect phallus?

In summary, Dionysus was a very important god for a long time, but then he faded away, before being totally defeated by Jesus.

But since he's immortal, he could still be out there, so keep your eyes open for goats and bulls, especially ones with tumescent members. They might just be Dionysus in disguise!

NOTE: SLOAN AND CHRISTIAN—NOT OFFENDED IN ANY WAY, AND I LOVE FRANCESCA DEARLY, BUT DOES IT SEEM LIKE MAYBE SHE'S TRYING TO SHOCK/OFFEND HERE A BIT? SHE MENTIONED THAT THINGS HAVE BEEN A LITTLE CRAZY AT HOME. EMAIL ME IF YOU WANT TO DISCUSS -- NATALIE BURKE, GLENHAVEN, 6S

"You have innervation all the way to the glans
of your penis. A good sign!"

CHAPTER ONE

Christian Orr, thirty-nine and thin but with the paunch of a man who doesn't exercise, sits on an exam table holding a clipboard.

How do you rate your confidence that you can get and keep an erection? Moderate/low/very low.

Christian sighs and, with a trembling hand, circles LOW on the questionnaire. His feet dangle over the edge of the table like a child on a swing. The gown he wears crinkles as he squirms to find a position that doesn't expose his bare ass.

During sexual intercourse, how often are you able to maintain an erection after you enter your partner? A few times/almost never/never.

"Assumes facts not in evidence," Christian says aloud, using a legal objection he's heard from his wife. "No intercourse with partner, so no erection to maintain."

Before Christian can answer the next question, Dr. Daniel Fuchs enters. The first thing Christian notices about the silver-haired urologist is his fire-engine-red glasses. When Fuchs smiles and displays his recently bleached teeth, Christian recalls that this man will soon be touching his penis.

"Oh no," Fuchs says, taking the clipboard from Christian's hands. "You've only answered two of the questions."

"With all due respect," Christian replies, aware that he's using another of his wife's lawyerly phrases, "I'm taking time off from some very important meetings, so the sooner we can complete this, the better."

"Certainly," Fuchs says. "But I can't begin your examination until the questionnaire is complete."

"Wow, okay." Christian sighs heavily. "FYI, as you can imagine, this is awkward for me. This is the first time I've had issues with . . . And not to overshare, but my wife cheated on me with my daughter's swim coach, and my entire workplace found out about it, so that might have something to do with this."

Fuchs nods as if waiting for an interpreter to finish translating Christian's words. "Swimming!" he says. "Not just a sport, a *life skill*." Fuchs gestures with the clipboard. "Let's finish this together: 'During sexual intercourse, how difficult is it to maintain your erection to the completion of intercourse?'"

Christian sighs again. "As with the first question, there's an assumption of sexual intercourse. But that stopped the night she told me about her affair. Since then, I've only been able to achieve something like half-mast, nothing full, and all on my own. Honestly, it's more like quarter-mast, to beat the sailing metaphor to death. Is that enough detail for your questionnaire?" Christian flushes red.

Fuchs, abruptly resolute, sets the clipboard down on his desk. "Okay, hop down," he says. "Let's have a look at the gear."

Cowed by the doctor's sudden professionalism, Christian dutifully slides off the exam table and tugs up his hospital gown. Fuchs drops to his knees in full fellatio pose and palpates Christian's flaccid penis and shriveled testicles.

"It's too soon to say for sure," Fuchs begins, "but experience tells me that your problem is likely psychological in nature. But we do need to cover"—Fuchs squeezes first one testicle, then the other—"all of our bases. This might hurt a touch." Fuchs squeezes the head of Christian's penis.

"Ow!" Christian yelps.

"Good," Fuchs says. "You have innervation all the way to the glans of your penis. A good sign!"

Fuchs moves his hands up and down Christian's genitalia like a blind man reading Braille. "At this point, I would normally run a battery of tests," he murmurs.

"If we could avoid the battery of tests," Christian interjects. "I'm trying to get off my wife's insurance, and so depending on when things get billed, I might have to pay out of pocket, which I can't afford, so please, no tests."

Fuchs rises to his feet and frowns. "There is a test you can run at home with an NPT monitor, but those are also quite expensive."

"NPT?" Christian says.

"Nocturnal penile tumescence test," Fuchs replies. "A normal man will have three to five erections during sleep per night. An NPT monitor records these events electronically. However, there is a more economical, old-school way of determining the occurrence of tumescences. Involving stamps."

"Stamps?"

"Postage stamps," Fuchs says. "Placed on the penis before bedtime."

Christian presses a hand to his forehead and slumps back onto the exam table. "I'm feeling lightheaded," he says. "Do you have anything to eat? Any of those . . . doctor crackers? Animal crackers?"

"Animal crackers?"

"I just need to lie down for a minute." Christian lies down.

Fuchs squints at his watch. "I do have another patient in fifteen minutes."

"I'll be out before then," Christian says, letting his gaze dissolve in the fluorescent lights above. "I just need a minute, I promise."

Two months ago, I would have
fucked you at a hotel.

CHAPTER TWO

Sloan Green sits alone at her desk on the thirty-fifth floor of an office building overlooking the San Francisco Bay, drinking green tea and flexing first one butt cheek and then the other. This independent cheek flexing is usually a point of pride for Sloan—because how many other women her age can do this?—but today, as she thinks about the failure of her marriage to Christian, she can't help but feel that her obsession with glutes and pecs and VO_2 max might have caused her to miss the more important aspects of human life. And not just any human's life, Sloan hears the voice of her therapist telling her, but *her* life.

Sloan dials her daughter, Francesca, remembers that she's in school, and hangs up and texts her.

COFFEE LATER?

Immediately, Francesca texts back.

CAN'T DO LATER, MAYBE TOMORROW. AREN'T YOU WORKING?

Sloan types back with her thumbs: I'M TAKING A MEDITATION BREAK.

Sloan waits for a response to her meditation text, but it never comes. She wants her daughter to be impressed by the wholesale changes she believes herself to be making, including meditation. Since her separation from Christian, Sloan has begun therapy and has uncovered feelings of guilt surrounding the long work schedule she maintained throughout

Francesca's childhood. Most recently, she realized that she could easily have made time to breastfeed her daughter but didn't.

One of Sloan's junior associates, an eager whelp named Parker Fanning, knocks and enters.

"I hear you're thinking about settling with the electrocution guy's family?" Parker says.

"Actually," Sloan replies, wheeling around in her chair, "I'm thinking about killing myself and giving you all my cases."

Parker shoves his hands in his pockets. "Ha! You know I could never replace you, because you say shit like that."

"You should replace me," Sloan says with a sigh. "You're young, you have no family, and all you want to do is win."

"Yeah, but you're Sloan Green; you're the bomb," Parker responds brightly, making the explosion gesture. "I'd rather replace Kelly or Borton."

"You don't have to replace anybody, Parker. You don't have to work here. You don't have to make a living screwing people who can't afford to fight back."

Parker shrugs. "I know they'd do the same to me if they could."

"Is that what you'll tell yourself every morning for the next thirty years?"

"I'll tell myself that I have two hundred and fifty thousand dollars in loans."

Sloan turns her chair again toward the window.

"Sit," she says. Parker sits, staring at the back of Sloan's head.

"Ten years ago . . ." Sloan lowers her head. "Maybe even two years ago. Maybe two months ago. At any rate," she says, finally turning. "I would have taken you out for a cocktail and fucked you at a hotel."

Parker nods quickly, his shoulders hunched high.

Sloan sighs. "But I'm not going to do that now."

"No," Parker says. "Of course not."

"My problem was," Sloan continues, "that the only thing I could imagine doing with somebody like you outside of work was fucking you. Any other thing, like this, chatting, would bore me. Does that make sense?"

"Sure, absolutely."

"Just like everything would bore me." Sloan stands and again turns toward the window. "Which, I realize now, was my problem, not anyone else's."

"I don't know why it's a problem," Parker says. "People are boring. And why should you care about me beyond what I can do for you?"

Sloan sits back down and leans toward him. "Why should I? Because you're a human being and you matter."

"Sure," Parker replies. "I mean, yeah, everybody matters, insofar as every human life matters."

"Every human life does matter."

"Yeah, but if you're gonna go there, then you've got to worry about every person in the world and the effect that anything you do might have on every one of them," Parker says quietly.

"That's right," Sloan says. "That's right."

There's a long silence. Sloan perceives that she is now only a half step from crying and wonders how she got there.

After a long pause, Parker leans forward. "I mean, we could just go get a drink if you want?"

"And fuck?" Sloan looks at him, her eyes suddenly hard.

"No," Parker says. "Or yes, sure. Either way. I'm easy."

"Don't be easy, Parker. Easy is for losers." Sloan rises. "I need to get back to work."

Parker stands quickly. "Okay. I'll go now."

Sloan doesn't respond. Parker gives a weak salute and stumbles toward the door.

Sloan drops into her large leather chair. She looks out at the white sailboats slicing through the green water in front of the East Bay hills. She holds her head in her hands. The vine-of-grapes tattoo carved into her right shoulder dances as Sloan sobs, her broad *latissimus dorsi* expanding and contracting beneath her dress.

Outside the office, Parker cups his ear to the door, presses down on his erection, and scoots quickly down the hall.

CHAPTER THREE

It's been two months since Sloan's one-night stand with Stu Sherwater, Francesca's high school swim coach, which took place inside Stu's 1999 Honda Odyssey and lasted no more than fifteen minutes. This happened after a twenties-themed auction at Glenhaven High, Francesca's school, where Christian had been working recently as a part-time guidance counselor. Sloan dressed that night in a flapper number with sparkles that showed off her broad back. Big Stu, as he was known, wore his purple 2016 Ridge County Swim Conference windbreaker and jeans that didn't quite zip all the way up. Christian had on his blue TJ Maxx blazer, black dress pants, and brown loafers but left early due to Alfredo-sauce-related stomach pain.

Stu Sherwater, who had been the high school swim coach for as long as anyone could remember, was a large man with clam-colored skin and huge tufts of knuckle hair. The blond hair on his head was tinted green from four decades of steady chlorination. He spoke little, though his narrow eyes hinted at a distant, aqueous pain that could never be expressed above water. Francesca had been a lower-tier swimmer on Stu's team for two years, showing up each day primarily to placate her athletic mom, who occasionally hinted that Francesca might be growing fat, or at least soft like her father.

Sloan had flirted the entire night of the auction with teachers, school board members, and even a few neighbors. Her daughter was nearly a senior, so what did the potential petty gossip matter to her? She was drunk on red wine and turned a bare shoulder to nearly every man she encountered. However, she had somehow missed Stu, who tended to lurk in the shadows, right up until the end of the evening.

By the time the lights went up, Sloan had decided that she would wake her husband and try to cajole him into having sex. Though sex between them had never been frequent, Christian had until recently been a willing participant. However, lately he would roll away from her in bed. But that night Sloan found her way into Stu's bleached arms and back into the realm of anonymous late-night sex where she had always felt unusually comfortable.

Sloan also had sex with Stu that night because she sensed that he wouldn't talk before, during, or after sex. In fact, Stu left on his windbreaker as he slammed Sloan repeatedly against the inside of his Odyssey. She enjoyed the slight dashing of her skull and shoulders against the metal, as she once enjoyed fighting with boys as a child. Sloan's love of vigorous, even rough sex, had never, not even once, found expression in her relationship with Christian.

Sloan chose to tell the entire Big Stu story honestly to Christian, though only after rumors had begun to fly around the school. She said that she didn't like Stu particularly. He was an idiot; also, sex with Stu didn't make her love Christian any less. It was simply about fucking a man who could fuck her hard and about whom she didn't have to "worry." Christian averred that worrying about one's spouse is an inherent aspect of marriage and that he had, by the way, fucked her hard in the past, which made Sloan drop to the couch with laughter.

Christian felt the urge to spit in his wife's face at that moment. But Sloan waved her hands and said, "You've obviously already made your decision to move out," and Christian said "How could I not move out when you're fucking one of my colleagues and you're not even sorry about it," and Sloan said, "I'm not sorry," and then Christian said, "I hate you" and handed Sloan a copy of the lease, which she needed to cosign because Christian didn't make enough money to secure an apartment on his own.

CHAPTER FOUR

Christian paces the floor of his apartment, a one-bedroom by the freeway in a building known by the local teenagers as the "Divorced Dads Apartment Complex." This was the only apartment Christian looked at, given that the process of credit checks and rental applications triggered both headaches and feelings of shame within him. The canned overhead lighting in the unit immediately reminded Christian of an operating room, but he took it anyway.

Christian plucks a tennis ball from one of the many open moving boxes strewn across the floor and tosses it weakly against the wall. He grabs his laptop from the kitchen table, pecks out a URL, presses play on a YouTube video, and stands in front of a floor mirror.

An internet baseball coach barks out commands as Christian raises the tennis ball and checks his profile in the mirror.

"Feet, ninety degrees!"

"Right arm back and up!"

"Left leg forward!"

"Elbow up!"

"Step forward!"

"Release the ball!"

As Christian steps forward to release the ball, his right elbow drops, and the ball leaves his hand more like a shot put than a baseball. He sighs.

As a child, Christian spent hours in his bedroom studying his throwing motion in a mirror, trying to achieve the fluid, whiplike delivery he saw the other boys manage effortlessly. Now, as then, Christian somehow believes that fixing his throwing motion will solve all his problems at once.

He carries his laptop to his tiny kitchen table, types out another URL on the computer, sits down, and unbuttons his pants.

To avoid further urology costs, Christian has been employing his favorite porn videos from the internet in an attempt to activate his dormant penis. One video tells the story of an unhappy bride-to-be who has a case of cold feet on the eve of her wedding. Her fiancé is a kind man, she tells her buxom maid of honor, but he can never satisfy her. Her friend commiserates, saying that she, too, has never found a man who could satisfy her.

In the video, a handsome preacher with big hair enters the bride's changing room.

"What is it, my child?" says the preacher. *"Are you experiencing cold feet?"*

"Oh, Father O'Rourke," the bride-to-be replies. *"I'm so ashamed."*

"God doesn't want you to be ashamed of your feelings." Father O'Rourke smiles as he places a hand on the bride's shoulder. *"Or your body."*

"Oh, Father!" the bride says, ripping off her bodice.

As Father O'Rourke pulls the blushing bride toward him, Christian feels a slight increase in his heart rate that used to be accompanied by an erection. But as the video continues, with its tinny moans and groans, Christian discovers that no amount of manipulation will summon a response from his penis. He whimpers, looks briefly at the unopened penis pump on his kitchen table, and then opens his briefcase. From the briefcase he removes a roll of stamps and a pamphlet given to him by Dr. Fuchs entitled *Nocturnal Penile Tumescence: A Guide to Home Testing.* A Post-it note from the doctor attached to the pamphlet reads: NO NEED TO BREAK THE BANK. 2-CENT STAMPS WORK JUST FINE :)

CHAPTER FIVE

Christian was first an undergraduate, then a graduate, and finally a teaching assistant at Santa Clara University during the mid-nineties. It was during the first year of his master's program in psychology that he met Sloan, who was then a second-year student at the law school. That was when Christian—clinging to the academic world as a means of avoiding the working world—grabbed hold of Sloan's coattails, hitched his wobbly wagon to her golden chariot, and jumped into his new life as a househusband.

While at Santa Clara, Christian had chosen for his thesis subject the psychologist-cum-mystic Wilhelm Reich. Christian fell in love with Reich's concept of character armor, the theory that one's personality is the expression of one's neurosis. "My personality *is* my problem," Christian would say avidly after a few drinks at department parties. He spoke less candidly about Reich's theories of sexual armoring and UFOs, as well as orgone, a mysterious chi-like substance that Reich believed pervaded the universe. Above all, Christian identified with the persecution Reich endured throughout his career.

Sloan first met Christian at a holiday party, on a night when he was drunk enough to be mostly relieved of his usual anxieties. Sloan found Christian warm, funny, and, unlike nearly everyone else at the university, unpretentious. At two in the morning, Christian's play-by-play of their sexual congress made Sloan laugh. The next morning, as she watched him sleep, mouth agape, in her bed, she was surprised to have a vision of the two of them married in a house with children.

Christian and Sloan married and settled, along with their baby daughter, Francesca, in the East Bay suburb of Glenhaven. The structure of their daily lives was established early. Sloan went from work at her law firm in the city to a nearby gym every other weeknight. She stayed home on the weekends but often worked in the home office and usually went for a run before dinner. During this period, Sloan felt no guilt or concern about leaving Christian to care for Francesca. She not only trusted but was proud of Christian as Francesca's primary caregiver. She did not dislike her daughter (or children), but she always enjoyed Francesca more after an obliterating workout.

On weekdays, Christian took his young daughter to the local playground. He took great pride in his playground parenting and always made a point to include those children who were being ignored by their parents or nannies. Christian fancied that he could easily parent more children and once broached the subject to Sloan, who laughed heartily until she recognized that Christian was serious and then simply shook her head and said no.

One way of describing what happened to Sloan and Christian's marriage was that Francesca became a teenager and Christian became less relevant—to Francesca, to Sloan, and to himself. In dark moments, Christian realized that he resented Francesca for growing up.

"So, anything you want to say to me?

CHAPTER SIX

Christian has passed Stu Sherwater many times in the hallway at Glenhaven High since rumors of Sloan's tryst began to spread throughout the school. Prior to the scandal, Christian gave Stu the greeting he gives all teachers and staff: a half smile, along with a slight head tilt and the beginnings of a wave. Since the scandal, Christian has resorted to his favorite method of social avoidance to avoid eye contact with almost everyone: He frowns at his cell phone as if deeply considering a newly arrived text.

Today, however, as Stu approaches from the east wing, Christian—burning with rage over his erectile dysfunction—vows not to lower his gaze. He clenches his phone in his pocket but refrains from looking at it. As the two men near each other, Christian fancies he sees a smirk pass across Stu's face, a perception which, right or wrong, triggers his next move.

"Hey, Stu!" Christian blurts out, stepping forward and extending his hand, which Stu is forced to shake. "How're you doing?"

"I'm okay," Stu says quizzically.

"Just wondering," Christian begins, unaware that he is nearly shouting, "since you and I pass each other in the hallway like it's no big deal. I'm wondering if maybe you have something you want to say to me?" He continues to clench Stu's hand, as if the whole enterprise might collapse if he let go.

"You're the guidance counselor, right?" Stu says.

"Yes, I am the guidance counselor," Christian responds crisply. "Part-time. I imagined you'd know this since we've been colleagues for a year now and I played right field on your softball team at the faculty mixer last fall."

A few students stop and gather in the hallway.

Christian continues, "Not only do we know each other, we also have one *very* significant acquaintance in common. Am I ringing any bells yet?" He again squeezes Stu's hand.

"No." Stu shakes his head.

"You're kidding me, right?" Christian says. "Fuck off!" He squeezes Stu's hand once more as hard as he can and lets go. "Fuck off for you cheating on me with my wife. I mean, for cheating on me with you. I mean—"

Stu grabs Christian by his shirt collar and hustles him into a nearby restroom, closing the bathroom door behind him with his foot.

"What the hell are you doing out there dropping the f-bomb," Stu says. "There are kids out there."

A toilet flushes. A wiry boy scoots out of a stall and exits, returning momentarily for the briefest of hand washes. Christian smells Stu's breath, as well as urine and bleach, and the fact that he's not sure what's coming from where renders him dizzy and weak. Christian imagines himself fainting and Stu carrying him like a wounded soldier to the nurse's office, where he is revived with smelling salts.

"What's this all about?" Stu says.

"My wife!" Christian shouts. "You fucked my wife!"

"Who?" Stu says.

Enraged, Christian throws a weak punch at Stu. Stu parries Christian's right cross with one hand and grabs his shirt with the other.

"Stop it," Stu says, not entirely without sympathy. "You can't do this here. We work here. Who's your wife?"

"What do you mean?!" Christian's chin quivers, and tears well in his eyes. "Sloan! You had sex with her after the auction, and it's ruined our marriage!"

Stu finally lets go of Christian. "Oh."

"It's actually ruined my life," Christian sputters.

"Okay," Stu says. He sighs and looks at his watch. "I have class in five minutes, and I only came this way because I really have to pee. Hold on."

Turning toward the urinal, he unzips his pants. Christian shuffles into a stall and covers his ears as the pressure-washed din of Stu's powerful urination fills the room.

"I'm glad to talk about this later," Stu yells to him over the sound of his peeing. "But like I say, I've got weight-training in five."

Outside the boys' room, ten or twelve students look up as Stu emerges. He looks squarely at two or three in the front and points. "Nobody goes in there, do you hear? Go to class."

Inside the bathroom, Christian attempts to compose himself. He fixes his wispy hair, breathes on his glasses and wipes them with his tie. He removes his cell phone from his pocket and makes his way toward the door.

As the door opens, Christian already has the phone to his ear. "The refi is pending," he says, "so I need an appraisal on the property ASAP." He flashes an all-business smile at the gaggle of gawking teens. "If you can't get it done by Thursday, I definitely need it done by Friday EOD, okay?"

Christian picks up his pace and eventually lowers his phone as he finally sprints down the hallway.

A fifteen-year-old boy who was first on the scene and who has been clinically observing the proceedings turns to his friend. "He wasn't talking to anyone, you know."

The friend shrugs. "C'mon, everyone fake-talks into their phone."

Ari puts the cigarette out on her forearm.

CHAPTER SEVEN

Still shaking after his dustup with Stu Sherwater, Christian sits in his office and fidgets with the levers of his flimsy ergonomic chair. Despite the relative wealth of the district, Glenhaven High has not been fully upgraded since it was built in the seventies, and Christian's tiny office is cluttered with broken chairs, printers, and monitors.

Christian takes a deep breath, closes his eyes, and recalls a self-help book he read recently that reminded him to fill his mind with champion thoughts in order to become a champion human, just as champion athletes fill their bodies with champion food.

Christian struggles for a long while to retrieve a champion memory and finally recalls his recent performance at the karaoke bar. His "Come as You Are" by Nirvana was good, possibly even excellent. Granted, he could have quit while he was ahead and skipped his herky-jerky cover of Devo's cover of "Satisfaction," which drew snickers, but all in all it was a successful night. People enjoyed him. People applauded. He felt a little like a champion.

Building on this positivity, Christian closes his eyes and catalogs his achievements as guidance counselor. There was the goth girl who walked into his office holding up both middle fingers but who, within moments, told Christian about her rigid parents and her eating disorder. There was the lacrosse player struggling with his sexuality who left Christian's office assured that his true orientation would reveal itself eventually.

Most recently, there was Evan, whose parents had called Christian to tell him that their son's suicidal tendencies had become dangerously intractable. The parents told Christian that Evan mentioned his name repeatedly and asked if he would be willing to meet with the boy. After humbly warning Evan's parents that he was not a licensed therapist and that his job was to refer teens to professional help and not offer it himself, Christian agreed to three meetings in his cramped school office.

During those meetings, Evan opened up to Christian. He complained about mean jocks, mean girls, mean adults, and the overall meanness of the world. Christian listened as the boy played Norwegian death metal music from his phone. Christian told Evan of his foibles on the karaoke circuit and recited, with a sense of humor, humiliations from his own adolescence, which made the boy laugh.

At their third and final session, Christian pitched Evan his version of the "It gets better" speech, elevating the concept by first mocking it as a cliché, then digging deeper into the notion that a person at fifteen is not at all the same person at twenty, even at the cellular level. If your twenty-year-old self will be a *biologically* different person, Christian asked the boy, isn't it possible that the *you* defined by that new biology will also feel differently? Maybe, Christian continued, twenty-year-old Evan might be happy when he wakes up, might have a girlfriend, might be a music producer of California death metal, might want to be a father someday—a better father than his own.

Then Christian leaned forward, like a salesman closing the deal, and asked Evan whether he would be willing to hang around to see what those future versions of himself, the ones with entirely new cells, might feel like when they woke up every day. And if all those future selves were also miserable, Christian said, the two of them could definitely reconvene and discuss whether life was worth living.

"Is that really true about the new cells?" Evan asked as he looked at Christian with hope in his eyes.

But those successes were in the past, before Stu Sherwater and the ED and the Divorced Dads Apartment Complex. Before Christian gave up working on his Reich dissertation, without which his PhD would remain incomplete. Without the PhD, Christian knew that he would not gain full-time employment at Glenhaven, primarily because of the competition for the job with the highly qualified Laura Hartwood.

Christian opens his eyes and raises them toward the fluorescent lights, allowing them to remain open until they sting. He offers up a silent prayer for something to happen, something to lift him out of his inertia and despair.

And then, something does.

A slender, middle-aged woman with dark hair and olive skin enters Christian's office hurriedly. She slams her right knee against a chair and curses.

"Fuck me."

The woman has a sharp yet delicate nose and long arms that end in regal fingers. She wears gold bracelets and gold rings with red and green stones in them. Christian involuntarily sniffs the air as he catches the woman's scent, which is like fresh mud.

"Maron!" the woman shouts, turning toward the door. "In here!"

Maron enters. The boy is a seventeen-year-old male version of his mother.

The woman sits, then Maron sits. Christian suddenly remembers that this is the intake interview he thought was tomorrow, that Maron is the new student with a record of disciplinary problems from his previous school. The mother's name, if Christian recalls correctly, is Ari.

"You must be Ari," Christian ventures, extending his hand. "It's a pleasure to meet you. My name is Christian Orr."

"Christian or what?" Ari says. He wonders if her accent is Italian, Greek, or perhaps Arabic.

"Orr," Christian says, blushing. "O-R-R."

"I'm sorry to bother you, Mr. Orr," Ari says with a smile. "I'm told you are the one who decides whether my son gets to come to this school?"

Christian laughs. "No, no! My job is simply to welcome you both to Glenhaven and to answer any questions you may have."

"Well, I have no questions. Do you, Maron?" Ari says. "I guess we're done here then?"

Christian laughs again and turns toward Maron. "Maron, good to see you. So, what brings you to Glenhaven? You and your . . . mom, I assume?" Christian turns toward Ari, barely refraining from adding, "Unless this is your sister?"

"I know you've heard that Maron had disciplinary problems at his previous school," Ari says immediately. "I know your job is to advise the administration on whether you think he'll be a problem here, so I just wanted to clarify a few things."

Ari rises and walks toward the only window in Christian's office, removes a cigarette from her purse, and lights it. Speechless at the sight of the glowing cigarette, Christian raises his hands in front of him like a meerkat. His wild eyes dart from the No Smoking sign above the door to the No Smoking sign above the window.

"Ma'am . . ." Christian says.

"It's true, Maron was expelled from his last school for fighting," Ari continues. "But it wasn't his fault. Of course, every mother will say that, but in this case it's true." She takes a long drag on her cigarette. "We had to leave anyway because his father had just bought a house across the street from us."

"Miss . . . Ma'am!" Christian says.

Ari picks a piece of tobacco from her lips. "Actually, if I'm not mistaken, his father is currently buying a house in *this* neighborhood as well." She turns to her son with the lit cigarette in her hand. "But we're not running this time, are we, Maron?"

Christian's secretary, the ancient, legally blind Joyce Wilcox, staggers into the room, sniffing the air. Joyce grunts and points at Christian. Then she grunts and points at Ari.

Christian says, "I think Joyce, my secretary, is reminding us that there's no smoking anywhere on school grounds. It's been that way for the last fifty years or so, give or take."

Ari takes one last drag on the cigarette, searches in vain for an ashtray, then moves toward the window as if to throw the butt outside.

"Fire season!" Christian paws at his desk, looking for a mug in which to extinguish the cigarette.

Ari too looks around the room and, finding nothing, stubs the cigarette out on her forearm.

"Miss!" Christian yelps.

"The fact is your own football coach emailed him last year." Ari drops the extinguished cigarette into the trash. "So he obviously wants him on the team. And Maron needs an activity that keeps him busy and away from his father."

She pulls a folded manila envelope from her purse. "This is a recommendation from his previous coach and an affidavit that he had no disciplinary problems on the team. The fights happened in school, not on the field. Also, it says here that he rushed for a thousand meters."

Maron finally speaks as he stares absently out the window. "Yards."

"Yards." Ari hands Christian the envelope. "Look."

Christian takes the envelope and sits back at his desk, unable to remove his gaze from the black burn on Ari's arm, which appears to be fading before his eyes. He inadvertently touches his computer mouse and lights up a Viagra web page on his monitor.

"Football," Christian begins, methodically closing the Viagra window as if it were part of his train of thought, "and all sports are a great outlet, although personally I never played," he continues as two more pop-up windows open, each displaying a giant penis. "Mostly I didn't like showering with other boys."

Maron laughs.

Christian struggles to recall whether he actually spoke those last words aloud. He glances at Ari's arm and sees no trace of the burn.

"I know that fighting is wrong, sir," Maron says. "I promise it won't happen at this school."

"Okay then." Christian steadies himself with both hands on his desk as he takes one more glance at Ari's now-pristine skin. "No fighting would be . . . good." He is fiddling with papers beside his keyboard when the smoke alarm goes off. "Okay, well, that's the smoke alarm, a little late. We may have to evacuate, but we can move this meeting outside or resume here in a few minutes."

"It's fine," Ari says, rising from her chair. "Can you please just tell the administration that Maron is a good person? And show them this letter?"

"Of course," Christian says. The smoke alarms stops, leaving a pregnant silence in the room.

Ari moves close to Christian. "Our family is a broken family," she says. "Maron and I need help; it's as simple as that. You understand, don't you?"

Christian inhales Ari's scent, which renders him somewhat dizzy as he responds. "Yes, I know a thing or two about broken families."

Ari kisses Christian on the cheek and heads toward the door.

"One more thing," she says, turning. "What do the women do around here? If I wanted to make friends, where would I find them? Is there a Daughters of the American Revolution or a Tupperware group?"

Christian holds two fingers against the spot on his cheek where Ari kissed him. "I don't know if we have a DAR, but the principal's wife hosts a bunco game, and he did say they were looking for new members. I can ask him about it."

"What's bunco?" Ari says, before waving her question away. "Doesn't matter. I would love to. Maron, shake the man's hand and let's go."

Maron extends his hand. "Thank you for meeting with me and my mother," he says politely. "I promise you, sir, I won't be any trouble here."

"Don't call me sir; I work for a living!" Christian snorts.

As mother and son leave, Christian catches a whiff of lingering cigarette smoke and marvels again at the rapid disappearance of the burn on Ari's arm.

"Good god, Orr. Let the girl go!"

CHAPTER EIGHT

Francesca Orr, seventeen, can't recall a time when she wasn't belittled by the girls in power.

In elementary school there were popular and unpopular girls, but for the most part the atmosphere lacked malice. It was in middle school that cruelty began to grow exponentially, like a virus. Middle school was also the period when Francesca became aware that she had inherited her father's nearsightedness, his wispy red hair, and what looked like the beginnings of his rosacea. One night during this period she overheard her father say to her mother that Francesca might be half bald like him by the time she was thirty. Francesca went to her room and cried then. Her father was always kind to her. Why would he say something like that?

Christian described middle school to Francesca as a time when nothing is more important than fitting in—when kids will do anything, even awful things, to survive. This instinct, he said, explained the barbarism Francesca perceived from the moment she began sixth grade.

"Tween girls are desperate not to be at the bottom of the ladder," Christian said.

"But why do we need ladders?" Francesca replied. "Why do we have to climb all over each other? Why can't we climb side by side?"

Christian smiled and patted his daughter's head. "That's a great question, honey. You'll have to ask Jesus or Gandhi that one. Or maybe you'll answer it yourself someday."

Five years later, as Francesca stands at her locker, she notes that her interactions with her father have grown more businesslike. Perhaps, due to Christian's recent troubles, he simply has less to give. Perhaps empathy, like everything else, is a zero-sum game.

As she steps away from her locker, Francesca raises her phone to her ear and begins talking into it. Like her father, she has become adept at using her phone as a prop, pecking out texts and having conversations with no one to maintain a barrier between herself and the world. "I can't do three o'clock," Francesca says to no one. "Let's meet at four. Starbucks? By the door? See you there, okay? Okay!"

She steps to one side of the busy hallway to get a glimpse into her father's office—and promptly collides, face-to-chest, with a large boy.

The first thing Francesca notices about the boy is his breath, which is sweet like oranges. Their eyes meet, and she quickly registers two more things: The boy's eyes are somehow green and brown and blue all at once; and they are profoundly sad, with an old-soul quality she always hopes her own eyes display. After what seems like minutes but is only seconds, the boy's expression changes to one of concern. Francesca wonders if he has just perceived some mortifying truth about her.

"I'm so sorry," she says. "I was on my . . ." She raises her phone. Instead of responding, the boy continues to search her eyes with ever greater intent and concern, as if data about her were flowing into his mind at high speed.

"It's okay. I'm not hurt," the boy says finally, before laughing at the possibility. Francesca responds with one of her horsey, snorting laughs. She has learned to treat this laugh like a medical condition—one she can manage but not cure. She believes she contracted this laugh during the terrible days of middle school, although her father says she's always had it and that he's always adored it.

Francesca hears her father's voice behind her.

"Francesca, hi! *Quelle coincidence*, it looks like you've met our new student, Maron."

"Hi, Dad," Francesca says, wincing at her infantile use of the term. "I just ran into him. But he's not hurt. You're not hurt, right?" She smiles at Maron, who smiles back with an easy warmth that makes her blush.

"Great," Christian says tightly, clapping his hands once. "Glad no one is hurt." He turns his body toward Francesca as if onstage, performing a scripted scene.

"He's a football player," Christian continues, still in theatrical mode. "And apparently a good one, so he's going to have a great football year this year, right, Maron?" He pats Maron once on his muscular back. "And this," Christian says, gesturing toward Francesca as if she were a used car, "is my daughter, Francesca. Francesca, Maron. Maron, Francesca."

The two teenagers laugh and smile at each other. "Great to meet you," Maron says. "Your father has been very kind to me. Thank you, sir." Maron nods to Christian, who nods back, blushing. A long and pointless silence ensues. "Well," Maron says finally. "I don't want to be late for my first class." He extends his hand toward Francesca, who shakes it. "Great to meet you."

"Great to meet you! Sorry to bowl you over like that! Bye!" Francesca says sprightly. Maron nods once more and leaves.

"What?" she says, blushing, at her father's look.

"Nothing!" Christian says. "Nice kid. I just met him and his mom. Good mom. Broken family, but nice people."

Francesca snorts. "So what? Everybody's from a broken family. I'm from a broken family."

Christian half waves at a passing faculty member. "I would say your family is bent at the moment, not broken," he says. "Remember, the strongest trees bend in the breeze."

"Really, Dad?" Francesca looks at her father. "You think our family is bending in the breeze?"

"I'm only saying we're not broken," he replies, scanning the horizon. Towering above the throng of students, Stu Sherwater approaches.

"Honey, turn this way." Christian grabs Francesca's shoulders and changes positions with her.

"Are you trying to avoid Sherwater?" Francesca looks past her father at her swim coach. "Dad, I don't even think he knows who you are."

"He does," Christian replies, lowering his gaze and muttering as though speaking to Francesca as Sherwater finally passes.

"Fuck Stu Sherwater," Francesca says. "He's a home-wrecker and shitty swim coach. What that guy needs from you is a right cross to the jaw!" She raises her right arm to throw a fake punch and accidentally elbows a tiny girl behind her, hard, in the nose. The girl covers her face and, like a toddler, is silent for a moment before she begins to cry.

"Oh my god!" Francesca turns to the girl. "I'm so sorry!" The girl begins throwing wild punches. "I'm sorry!" Francesca yells, trying to keep the girl at arm's length. "Dad, what do I do?"

"Bella!" Christian steps toward the slight but furious girl. "It was an accident! She didn't mean to!" One of Bella's errant punches lands on the bridge of Christian's nose, splitting his wire-rimmed glasses in half and drawing blood.

"Shh, calm down, Bella, calm down," Christian whispers, moving behind and bear-hugging the girl to protect himself from the punches as a rivulet of blood runs down his cheek. His rear embrace of the tiny girl draws laughter and finger-pointing from passing students. To avoid touching the girl's chest, Christian crouches down further, making his posture look even more inappropriate.

"Dad, let her go!" Francesca cries. "Oh my god!" She turns and covers her face with both hands.

Just then, Mark Apple, former school athletic director turned principal, arrives on the scene. He stares open-mouthed at Christian, who is whispering softly into the girl's ear, "Shh, shh."

"Good god, Orr. Let the girl go!"

CHAPTER NINE

Christian winds a piece of Scotch tape around the bridge of his glasses as he sits in Mark Apple's office. At his desk, Apple sits with his head bowed, massaging his brow with both hands before raising his eyes to Christian with a forced smile.

"You seem like a good guy," Apple begins. "In fact, I know you're a good guy. So let's just dispense with the formalities and speak man to man. Sound like a plan?"

"Sure," Christian says, crossing his eyes to see whether blood is still flowing down his nose.

Apple continues, "So, as you know, I'm an athletics guy by trade and only principal because of Rankin's illness and because our superintendent likes to promote from within. Though I've dealt with plenty of conflicts on the sports side, I don't yet have a lot of cred on the boundary-crossing-weird-stuff side. Whereas you seem like a guy with a lot of psych credentials but maybe not a lot of real-world experience; am I right?"

"Well," Christian says. "I am a father."

"Right, and that was your daughter you were having a private conversation with during school hours in the hallway before the incident with Bella Buell?" Apple replies in a friendly tone.

"It wasn't private," Christian says petulantly. "I just came across her in the hall."

"Of course," Apple says, waving his hand, "and not a big deal. Big deal, though, that when I approached, it looked a lot like you were dry-humping a ninety-pound junior in front of twenty students. Huge deal, actually, depending on what kind of attack Bella's parents mount. In six months, I could be sitting through a three-hour deposition trying to defend your character and my negligence, and neither of us wants that, do we?"

"Mark," Christian says. "I was just trying to calm the girl down. She was screaming and punching me. She broke my glasses and drew blood."

Apple winces. "I'm not a lawyer, but I'm going to say self-defense isn't the way to go here."

"I just wanted to keep the situation from escalating. She was freaking out."

Apple sighs. "Listen, I know that's all true. But what if Bella goes home and tells her parents that you were shoving your erection up against her?"

"Ha!" Christian snorts, expelling a small amount of snot from his nose, which he wipes away with the back of his hand. "If she happens to say that, I happen to have a perfectly good response!"

"Which is?"

Christian looks down at the floor, reconsidering his perfectly good response. "Which is that I am currently seeing a specialist for erectile dysfunction and am incapable of having an erection," he says quietly.

Apple takes a deep breath and exhales. "Okay, that . . ." He raises his hands into a time-out gesture. "Look, all I'm saying is that Bella could tell her parents you had an erection whether you had one or not."

"Then I would subpoena my urologist, Dr. Kevin Fuchs, MD," Christian says primly, "and he would testify that an erection would be a medically impossible event for me."

Apple gets up and paces. "I gotta tell ya, this is not the conversation I thought I'd be having this afternoon." He stops and looks gloomily out the window. "Then again, I've had a lot of conversations lately I never thought I'd have."

He bows his head, his still-athletic figure silhouetted against the window. To Christian, it seems as though Apple has left the room and is now far away. After a long silence, Apple claps his hands.

"Fuck it, I'm not even gonna worry about this. Why would I worry about this?" He rushes to Christian and places his hand on his shoulder. "We both know you weren't trying to dry-hump the girl, Chris; everybody knows that. And you've obviously got enough problems already. Don't we all!"

Apple grins and pats Christian's back forcefully, and Christian coughs in response.

"What a world, eh?" Apple turns again, with undue animation, toward the window. "Misunderstandings, people getting fucked from every direction. And then you die!" He wheels around. "I'm aware that you're in line for that full-time counseling job, and I want to see you get it. I don't like Laura Hartwood and her flowing dresses one fucking bit. You're already part-time. You just need to finish your PhD, and the board will rubber-stamp your application. How's that coming, anyway?"

"The PhD?" Christian says, his voice faltering. "It's coming."

"I'll take the temperature of the Bella Buell thing. I know a guy who plays golf with Bella's dad. If things look like they could go south, I can talk to him. But for now, don't worry about it. Enjoy your life! Spend time with your daughter—outside of school, preferably."

"Oh crap!" Christian says, looking at his phone. "I forgot my daughter has a swim meet right now. Can we discuss this—"

"Go, go!" Apple says, waving Christian to his feet.

"I didn't hump Bella. I was just trying to help," Christian pleads and moves toward the door. He catches his broken glasses as they fall from his face.

"I know," Apple says, grabbing Christian by the shoulder at the threshold. "So, ED, huh? That one I never had. I see ads for it everywhere. Could be worse. ED can't kill you."

A thin tear trickles down Apple's smiling face.

"Mark, everything okay?" Christian says.

"Yes, sure," Apple says. "Have *fun* with your daughter. Enjoy every moment."

"You crushed that girl!"

CHAPTER TEN

Since he was a child, Christian has had difficulty anticipating the movements of approaching pedestrians. He never understood how his schoolmates (the same ones who threw baseballs effortlessly) could carry on conversations while walking through crowded hallways. Today, after numerous bumps and apologies, Christian finally manages to exit the building and jogs toward the outdoor pool area.

As Christian reaches the pool deck, he hears the starter's voice over the loudspeaker: *"Women's fifty-yard freestyle. Heat eight of eight!"*

Traditionally, there are no cuts from the Glenhaven swim team. To accommodate slower swimmers like Francesca, heats are simply added until everyone has had a chance to swim. The local athletic conference has also long encouraged swimmers with physical disabilities to participate, and today there are several disabled swimmers in attendance.

Raising his phone, Christian presses the video record button and hustles toward the pool's edge. "Go, Francesca, go!" he shouts as he searches for her with his phone. "I'm here, honey!"

From her block, Francesca assesses her competition, which includes a one-armed girl from the San Tomas Sharks team.

"Let's go, honey!" Christian shouts. He locates Francesca and frames her in his phone.

As the starter horn sounds, Christian sees that the entire San Tomas team has gathered at the far end of the pool, whereas no one from the Glenhaven team is at the end of Francesca's lane. He glares at Stu Sherwater and edges closer toward the finish line.

Christian screams encouragement at his daughter with a stridency and violence of which he is completely unaware and which draws stares from the parents.

"C'mon, Francesca, kick!" he shouts. "You got this! Push, push!"

As if responding to her father's entreaties, Francesca kicks a little harder and draws even with the one-armed girl. At twenty yards it is a two-girl race. The San Tomas teammates increase the volume and pitch of their cheering. The other swimmers have all turned to watch the race.

"C'mon, Francesca!" Christian snarls. "Kick, dammit!"

It's a sea of foam at the wall, but Francesca out-touches her opponent. A collective groan rises from the San Tomas fans, followed by a cheer for their girl's effort.

Francesca raises her foggy goggles and extends a handshake toward the one-armed girl, who has already been hoisted out of the pool by her teammates.

Christian arrives at the pool's edge, holding a towel he's plucked off a chair.

"Hell yeah!" he shouts. "You crushed that girl! Nice!" He raises Francesca's hand in victory.

"Dad!" she cries, jerking her hand away. It's only now that Christian notices the San Tomas swimmer has only one arm. "Oh," he says. Christian stands and backs away from the pool as if someone were pointing a gun at his belly. He bumps into a very large male swimmer, loses his balance completely, and falls face-first into the warm-up pool.

Underwater, as his tie floats up and touches his nose, Christian wonders what might happen if he never surfaced. No more ED, no more divorced dads building, no more humiliation of any kind. Then he thinks of Francesca, imagines her grief at the loss of her father, and kicks his way up. As he breaks the surface of the water, Christian is relieved to find that there is surprisingly little laughter and no finger-pointing. Stu Sherwater approaches the edge of the pool and extends his right hand.

"I got ya," Stu says.

"I'm good!" Christian shouts back. "I'm good!"

Stu retreats a couple of steps and hovers as Christian struggles to remove himself from the pool. Due to a combination of weak arms, soaked clothing, and waterlogged shoes, Christian can't summon the upper-body strength to pull himself out of the pool. Finally Christian extends a hand, and Stu quickly yanks him up.

"Here are your glasses," Stu says. "You all right?"

"Excellent!" Christian says with a strange grin, grabbing his broken glasses and shoving them onto his face, from which they immediately fall to the ground.

"I'm sorry about how things went down today," Stu says as he picks up Christian's glasses. "We'll talk."

"Of course!" Christian shouts stridently. "Of course we will!"

As Christian begins the long, wet, squeaky walk toward the pool's exit, he hears some titters. As he nears the gate, he turns to see one or two phones raised, recording him. When he scowls at these phones, more phones appear in response, and with them more laughter.

Safely outside the gate, Christian turns one last time to peer at his daughter, who is still seated poolside with her head in her hands. He hurries to the parking lot, shaking his phone in a futile attempt to dry it out.

———————————

Christian opens his wallet and lays out credit cards and dollar bills on the hood of his rusting Ford Fiesta.

"Christian!"

He lifts his head to see Laura Hartwood standing two cars away from him, wearing an expensive floral-print dress and elegant, Navajo-themed jewelry. She presses a key fob, and the BMW X5 next to her lights up. Christian gulps, unprepared for an apparently inescapable conversation with his archrival.

"You look really wet," Laura laughs with an empathy she seems to exude naturally. Christian recalls that she has never been anything but kind to him. "Are you okay?"

"There was a drowning," Christian says quickly. "A near drowning. I had to save somebody. It was a student. Not a student. A visitor. A visitor was drowning."

"Wow," Laura says, wide-eyed. Christian studies her face until he feels certain that she believes him. "That's incredible," she continues." Are you all right? Is the visitor all right? Who was it?"

"Ted, I think was his name they said," Christian responds sharply. "Ted Kascinski." It quickly dawns on him that he's just given the name of the Unabomber. "Or maybe Kablowski, Kirlowski, not sure. Ted something-Polish. A visitor. He's gone now. He went home. He's better now."

"Wow, good work. Way to go!" Laura raises her fist in a display of triumph. "Hey, by the way . . ." She takes a step toward Christian, who fights an impulse to step backward. "I know it's been awkward lately, with all this talk about the full-time position. But I just want you to know that I think you're super smart and competent and you'd be excellent at the job."

"Well," Christian says with sudden bitterness. "You're way more qualified than I am. I mean a hundred percent. You have a master's, everybody loves you—you're basically a perfect person." Christian finds himself unable to stop. "My only advantage is that I'm occupying the office already, which only gives me squatter's rights, I suppose. But you're much more qualified. Much more everything."

To have something to do, Christian shakes out one of his wet dollar bills. "Soggy wallet!" he says with an odd laugh.

"Sure," Laura says, evidently uncertain how to respond. "I'm just glad you were here to save that visitor today, and congrats on being a hero. That's got to feel good. Okay, Christian. I'll see you around."

Christian looks up and smiles quickly at Laura before continuing to fiddle with the contents of his wallet. Laura beeps her BMW again and gets into the car. After what seems like an eternity, the BMW leaves. Christian picks up a wet ten-dollar bill, sets it down, picks up a one-dollar bill, tears it in half, tears those halves in half, and then throws all the pieces at the ground.

"You'll be bald and impotent!"

CHAPTER ELEVEN

Sloan has finally gotten her date with Francesca at a local café. She vowed to herself on the drive over to listen more than talk, identify with her daughter's point of view, and be only kind and uncritical. However, as they sit at their table, she finds herself haranguing Francesca for helping Christian with his dissertation.

"Why would you waste your term paper on the same subject as his?" Sloan asks. "He's never going to finish it. It's his problem, not yours. Plus, Wilhelm Reich is a freak."

Francesca, her hair still wet from the pool, smiles. "Actually, Reich was a total genius. He was Freud's favorite pupil and influenced a ton of modern psychologists, including your therapist, most likely."

"The way your father talks about him," Sloan muses, "Reich always struck me as a sexually frustrated nerd. Sort of like, you know . . ." She rolls her eyes.

"Right!" Francesca responds. "For sure, Reich and Dad aren't the liberated kind of guys that screw married women in a van. No sir! That's next-level enlightenment."

Sloan sighs. "You have every right to be angry right at me."

"Oh, thanks!" Francesca smiles mockingly. "Did your therapist give you that line? Or did you get it from Oprah on the closed captioning at the gym while you were on the whirligig or the cyclotron or whatever?"

Francesca, noticing the volume of her own voice, catches eyes with a middle-aged woman at a nearby table who has apparently been listening. Sloan turns her head toward the woman, displaying what Francesca has long recognized as her mother's animal instinct for conflict. The woman stares at her coffee as Sloan fixes her gaze. Finally, the woman has no choice but to look up. Sloan continues to stare at her, not angrily, not even menacingly, but in a powerful manner that Francesca recognizes as distinctly Sloan.

"Mom, over here?" Francesca says. "Have you seen Dad's apartment? It's pretty frickin' sad. There are no lamps, and there's like a twelve-pack of Coors Light and some jelly in the fridge. He's got cable, but all he plays is the nineties rock channel."

"I'll get him a lamp," Sloan says, checking her phone and then putting it away. "Is he playing his guitar?"

"He plugs it into headphones so the neighbors won't hear. He's painfully polite," Francesca says.

"I'll get him a lamp," Sloan says.

"So, are you guys done now?" Francesca says. "Divorce coming soon to a theater near me?"

Sloan sighs. "I don't know."

"All this for sex with Stu Sherwater in the back of his van." Francesca shrugs. "Seems worth it to me."

"How does anyone know about the van?" Sloan sighs. "Who's disseminating these details anyway?"

Francesca waves her hands. "Please don't say disseminating. It sounds like semen. And you can't be surprised. It's a frickin' suburban high school. Everybody knows everything about everybody."

Three teenage boys tumble through the front door of the café, laughing and backslapping. One of them spies Francesca and makes a neighing noise.

"Hey, Franny, whassup? Hawnh, hawnh!"

"Who are they?" Sloan asks.

"Nothing," says Francesca, sinking in her chair.

"Franny, hee-haaw! Whassup?"

Sloan turns. "Are they . . . ?" She rises from the table.

"They're not!" Francesca yells. "Mom!"

Sloan moves quickly across the room until she is within six inches of the loudest boy. "Who are you?"

"No one, ma'am," the boy laughs, while behind him another boy mumbles, "Bitch."

Sloan grabs the mumbling boy by his jacket collar and slams him hard against the wall. "What did you say?" She cocks her head as her right bicep bulges.

"I said 'Stitch," the boy laughs. "Mitch."

"I remember punks like you from high school," Sloan says. "Think you're big men." She squeezes the boy's collar in her fist and gets within an inch of his face. "You'll be bald and impotent by the time you're forty, junior. Women are going to laugh at you forever. I can tell by looking at you."

At the counter, a barista smiles and lowers her head.

"Get out of here," Sloan says, letting go of the boy's jacket and shoving him. "Now."

The boys tumble over one another back out the door, one of them squealing, "Whattabout my Frappuccino?"

At the table, Francesca rests her face in her hands. Sloan sits and sighs. She looks past her daughter out the window. "You can't let assholes be assholes," she says finally. "They just keep doing it if you don't stop them."

After a long pause, Francesca looks up. "People didn't pick on you when you were a kid, did they?"

Sloan shrugs. "There was a boy in the neighborhood. He tried to pull down my pants, and I punched him in the face. Blood and snot came out of his nose. I had to walk him home because he was crying and he couldn't see."

"That's disgusting," Francesca says.

"What's disgusting"—Sloan narrows her eyes—"is that he attacked me and thought he could get away with it."

As Sloan leaves to take a call, Francesca wonders if she's been fair to her mother over the years. Isn't Sloan, in addition to being a woman who cheats on her husband, also a feminist warrior? A defender of the abused? A role model for women and young girls everywhere?

""Thunderer! Thunderer!"

CHAPTER TWELVE

The new klieg lights purchased by the Booster Club shine celestially over Glenhaven High's football field. The sky is cloudless, and the metal bleachers are crowded with students and parents eagerly anticipating the first home game of the season.

Having showered and changed into dry clothes after the swimming pool incident, Christian leans against the fence that borders the field, glad to have his back to the large crowd, a few of whom, he guesses, probably witnessed his tumble into the pool.

From the far end zone, the Glenhaven football team bursts through a paper banner reading GO, SPARTANS! and rushes toward midfield. The cheerleaders pick up the torn paper like dutiful housewives and return, fist-pumping and high-kicking, to their station on the sidelines. The younger cheerleaders wrestle the paper into garbage cans.

Francesca sits on the upper deck of the bleachers, clutching a notebook. She has a camera around her neck and a pencil behind her ear. She wears a black beanie over her red hair. She feels proud at this moment to be representing the class of nerdy cub reporters who don't participate in the orgy of vanities that is high school but simply document it. It's her second year taking the media course and her third as a member of the Journalism Club.

Francesca can't take her eyes off Christian, who has just failed to affect a casual shift of position at the fence. Her heart sinks as she realizes that her father has never been capable of effortless acts of any kind. *Is it because he overthinks everything? Because he doesn't trust his body to do anything naturally, even shift his weight?* Francesca feels an urge to run down the stairs and hug her father.

On the field, Maron, in his first game as a Spartan, runs the opening kickoff back eighty yards for a touchdown. The field is littered with defenders who missed tackles or were simply bowled over by him. A roar goes up from the bleachers.

Christian claps and hoots like a man watching sports for the first time. He turns to gauge who might have noticed him cheering and happens to see Ari, Maron's mother, standing near the concession stand, smoking a cigarette and looking anxious.

A long-haired man approaches Ari. He is of indeterminate age but perhaps forty-five. His skin is leathery, and he wears billowy yoga pants, a purple tank top, and flip-flops. He moves languidly, apelike, with a broad smile that looks almost like a leer. The man shouts to Ari in the same foreign language that Christian heard Ari use with Maron. As the two meet, Ari shoves him backward. They argue briefly before Ari storms off.

The long-haired man starts to follow Ari but then spies Christian and shuffles happily toward him. Christian involuntarily clenches his anus, fists, and jaw.

"Good evening!" the man says in lightly accented English as he approaches. Christian normally responds eagerly to all salutations out of sheer politeness but at this moment finds himself mute.

"Ah, marriage!" the man says, shrugging. "You know how it is." Christian notices many scars across the man's arms and legs, like the skin of an old shark. "She just needs a whole lotta love, like all of us. You know the song?" The man commences dancing and singing the Led Zeppelin song. "Want a whole lotta love, duk-ah-doonk, duk-ah-doonk."

Christian looks around for any other witnesses to the scene before him. Suddenly, the man puts his arm around Christian and presses his face close enough that Christian can smell wine on his breath. Despite the smell of alcohol, the man's eyes are clear, and he doesn't seem intoxicated in the least.

"For better or worse, things are happening," the man whispers. "People are getting entangled. It raises questions that bore me but might interest you. Like, why you? Why Ari? Why is your cock soft and your wife so hard? I feel like the joke might be on me this time. Which is strange." The man looks at the sky and then smiles at Christian. "Because I'm supposed to be the funny guy."

Christian is barely breathing and wonders whether he could move if he tried.

The man pats Christian on the cheek, which causes Christian to exhale. "You're ready, right? You look ready," the man says. Then he shimmies away, once again singing the Led Zeppelin song.

As the man reaches the edge of the fence surrounding the football field, he wolf-whistles in the direction of the cheerleaders. A few of them approach. He speaks a few words, gives two thumbs-up, then turns and shimmies toward the far end of the stadium, continuing to sing: "Duk-ah-doonk, duk-ah-doonk."

Large purple clouds sweep in from the northeast. Rain begins to fall, first in a trickle, but the trickle quickly becomes a downpour. Fans scatter for cover.

Oblivious to the rain, the cheerleaders stand in military formation, their chins high. They begin to chant in unison. Their voices are both unusually deep and loud.

"Thunderer! Thunderer! VoHe! Vohe!"

As if in response, thunder booms from the clouds overhead.

All at once, the cheerleaders run like Pickett's brigade toward the middle of the field, where a play is in progress. As they approach the line of scrimmage, the cheerleaders begin to high-kick and cheer, and Christian wonders if he is witnessing some kind of new opening-game tradition.

Then Caitlin Sharpe leaps onto the shoulders of offensive tackle Matt Stephens and howls at the sky. Ally Baum grabs Tim Knight's hips and, with a wink toward the crowd, pantomimes rear-entry coitus. Kara Sims twirls an imaginary lasso and then jumps onto Hayden Findlay's back. Kavita Kaur rips off John Boucher's helmet while another girl steps forward and kisses the boy.

Players on both teams are initially too stunned to mount a defense. Some of the cheerleaders begin to ululate. The referees circle the action, arms outstretched, but none seem ready to intervene.

Finally, one of the visiting team's players, noticing a cut on his cheek, shoves a cheerleader to the ground. This triggers an all-out brawl in which the teams begin fighting each other.

Amid the chaos, Christian's eyes land on number 34, who alone walks slowly off the field, shaking his head. As the boy takes off his helmet, Christian recognizes Maron.

"Maron!" Christian hears his daughter's voice from behind him. He watches, jaw agape, as Francesca runs past him and leaps the fence directly onto the field.

As the football players toss one another around like WWE wrestlers, Francesca makes a beeline for Maron. One tossed player sails toward Francesca, and Maron swoops in and gently tackles her to the ground. He whispers something in her ear.

Cheerleader Alyssa Phipps leaps onto Maron's back and begins pulling his hair. Maron gently guides Alyssa over his shoulders and lays her on the ground. He whispers a few words into Alyssa's ear, and she appears to fall asleep.

At the sight of his cheerleader daughter being taken down, Ken Phipps, local realtor, leaps the fence, catches his toe, and falls onto his face. Rising, red-faced, he rushes to Maron and gives him a hard but ineffectual shove.

"I'm sorry, sir," Maron says politely to Ken. "She'll be fine."

Ken Phipps harrumphs and shakes his daughter, who slowly rouses.

Parents and spectators have by now filled the field. The cheer coach, Melanie Stark, with shocking strength pulls one huge football player after another off her girls.

Christian watches Maron jog toward the bleachers, where Ari stands smoking a cigarette. Mother and son appear to argue for a moment and then hug.

At midfield, the skirmish gradually comes to an end. The cheerleaders are guided off the field, some in the arms of their parents. The scuffles among the opposing football players die down. The officials gather in a huddle.

Christian looks up and notices that the rain has stopped. The purple clouds have retreated with unnatural speed to the east. Francesca approaches him, breathless.

"Wow," she says. "That was frickin' weird. Cheerleaders gone wild! And rain in September?"

Christian meets his excited daughter's gaze. "What did he say to you? Maron. He just said something to you."

Francesca shakes her head uncertainly. "I don't know. Nothing. He just said it would be fine."

"What would be fine?"

"The cheerleaders, I guess," Francesca replies. "He said everything would be fine."

Christian turns again toward the gate and sees Ari and Maron leaving together.

"Maybe keep your distance from that kid," Christian says gravely to Francesca.

"I don't think so," Francesca says. "He's the coolest thing to happen to this school in years."

"VoHe! VoHe!"

CHAPTER THIRTEEN

Francesca's instinct to tail Emma Lancaster and Caitlin Sharpe after the game turns out to have been a wise one, as a small group of the cheerleaders managed to rid themselves of their parents and drive to Lime Ridge State Park, a traditional drinking and necking location for students.

Francesca huffs and puffs along the moonlit trail up Lime Ridge Hill. She stops to admire the gibbous moon in the night sky and wonders about the random rain shower earlier in the evening. She can't recall ever seeing rain in September in Glenhaven. As she nears the peak of the ridge, Francesca hears laughter and the beating of a drum coming from the valley below.

She nestles behind a large oak tree. On a plateau in the valley below, six cheerleaders, still in uniform, dance around a fire. A large bass marching drum hangs around the neck of Alyssa Phipps, who beats it in four-four time. The girls dance in a spasmodic way that looks to Francesca like a slow-motion seizure. They fling their heads backward on the first beat of the drum, then take slow steps forward on the second, third, and fourth beats, then throw their heads back once again on the next downbeat. Francesca feels her body grow cold.

Removing the camera from her bag, she attaches the zoom lens to get a closer look. Though the light is dim, through the lens she can see Emma Lancaster slamming what looks like a large wooden pole into the earth as she dances in time to the drum.

From the east, purple clouds roll back in. They hover over the plateau below, and once again rain falls. Raising their faces to the falling rain, the girls resume chanting, quietly at first, then louder.

"*Thunderer! Thunderer! VoHe! VoHe!*"

Francesca feels like the large oak she hides behind is shrinking, and panic swirls from her belly toward her throat.

Around the fire, which crackles in the rain, the cheerleaders laugh, shouting and ululating.

"*Ichos! Ichos! VoHe! VoHe!*"

A brown deer with a white tail bobs across the plateau toward a ravine. All six girls turn their heads at once like startled dogs and take off at frightening speed in pursuit of the deer. They ululate as they disappear into the darkness.

Francesca carefully descends the rocky slope toward the deserted campfire. Around the fire, cell phones, purses, and pom-poms are carelessly strewn. The heavy wooden pole recently held by Emma Lancaster lies halfway in the fire. Francesca shoves it away with her foot.

Next to a pom-pom, Francesca sees what looks like the severed head of a ground squirrel. Next to the head is what appears to be a half-eaten body of the same squirrel. She raises her camera and takes a picture.

———————————————

"That does look like the head of a squirrel," Christian says, yawning as he looks at his daughter's camera. It's 11 p.m., and Christian was just awakened by a knock on the door from his excited daughter.

"And this pole," Francesca says, pointing at another image on her camera. "They were slamming it into the ground."

"That stick, yes, I see that," Christian says. He is abruptly aware of the bright overhead lights in his apartment. "Your mother texted me and said I need a lamp in here. How does she know about the lighting?"

"Dad, those girls were acting like they were possessed," Francesca says. "I'm sending you a link." She follows her father into the kitchen, pecking at her phone. "There was this case of mass hysteria among girls from a cheerleading team in Upstate New York in the nineties. They all developed tics, like Tourette's. They were cursing, acting out, and exhibiting bizarre sexual behavior. Just like these girls."

"I don't know about mass hysteria," Christian replies, yawning as he wanders over to his empty refrigerator and peers into it. "What I do know is that girls experiment with rebellion, sexuality, anything that's taboo, because it's taboo. They do what they can to separate themselves from their parents. It's developmentally appropriate."

"But, Dad, these are cheerleaders. They don't want to separate from their parents. They want to be just like them. They never want to leave Glenhaven."

"That's a broad generalization," Christian says, cracking open a Coors Light. "But maybe true. So, what's up with Maron? You said he's the best thing to happen to the school?"

Francesca blushes. "Why are you changing the subject? There's nothing up with Maron."

"It seems like there was some . . . something going on between the two of you."

"There was no something," Francesca replies. "I know you think he's a bad boy because his parents are fucked up. But you should be happy; his parents make you and Mom seem normal."

She picks up her camera and shoves it into her bag. "I have to go. Please, just read that mass-hysteria article I sent. The parents blamed the water, the chemical plant, Satan, you name it. These parents are definitely going to blame the school. I guarantee it. Since you're the guidance counselor, you should be ready."

As Francesca nears the door, Christian suddenly feels his heart being pulled from his chest. He rushes after his daughter. "'Cesca, I know I've said this before. But I apologize again for everything your mother and I have put you through."

Francesca nods. "Gotcha. Are you going to remind me that none of this is my fault? Mom gave me that old chestnut the other day."

"I'm not going to tell you that," Christian says. "But it isn't your fault. Any of it."

Francesca laughs and throws her backpack over her shoulder. "You should have married someone neurotic and polite like yourself instead of Mom. I'm pretty sure that two neurotic parents would have faked it out of guilt and got divorced *after* I left for college." She opens the door and turns. "But you got close. Oh well! G'night!"

CHAPTER FOURTEEN

Behind the closed curtains of her 1950s-era California ranch home, Sloan meditates alone on a Saturday morning. Outside lawn mowers hum, dogs bark, and children squeal. Muted voices from the neighborhood flutter against the double-pane windows of the living room, but the noise doesn't bother her, a fact she notes with pride as she breathes deeply, remembering to exhale for one second longer than her inhale.

Sloan's therapist gave her a simple meditation instruction: to watch her thoughts float by like puffy white clouds without chasing them. As she meditates, fragments of arguments with Christian appear and disappear in her mind like fireflies on a summer night.

"*You think everyone's lazy,*" Christian says in one memory.

"*No, I don't,*" Sloan responds. "*Those Mexicans who dug our drainage ditch weren't lazy.*"

"*Yeah, but it's not like you gave a shit,*" Christian responds. "*I brought the fat one lemonade when he looked like he was going to die.*"

"*You don't care one way or the other about people,*" Christian says in another fragment. "*Which wouldn't be so bad if those people didn't include your husband and your daughter.*"

A strident male voice pierces Sloan's meditation. She opens her eyes, pads toward the door, and peers through the sidelight.

Ken Phipps, the local realtor, stands in the weed-strewn front yard of the empty house across the street, laughing and gesturing toward a figure who remains unseen behind a hedge. Ken wears his signature green Izod shirt, the same shirt he wears on billboards, For Sale signs, and on the advertising pages of high school yearbooks.

Sloan notices a red Prius parked behind Ken's BMW in the driveway.

Soon, a bearded man emerges from behind the hedge, as calm as Ken is squirmy. He is probably in his late fifties but could be as old as seventy. He has a wild, graying beard that obscures his mouth. He sports one of those large bellies that seem to contain only muscle. Most improbably, the man wears cut-off blue jean shorts, Doc Martens boots, and a black leather vest. He looks to Sloan like a Castro Street bear. Around his neck is what appears to be a rabbit's foot necklace, except that the foot seems to be from a much larger animal. Sloan pulls over an ottoman and sits by the sidelight to watch.

Another man emerges from the house. He is thin and wiry, wearing purple shorts and a ripped T-shirt. His long, stringy hair falls onto his muscular shoulders. Sloan's first thought is that this is a gay couple fleeing San Francisco. *But why move here? Perhaps they have kids*, she thinks, *but why the Prius then and not a minivan?* The thin man squats on the porch to pet a black cat.

In the yard, the fat man laughs, Santa Claus-like, at some bon mot from Ken's obsequious pitch. Ken pulls a phone from his pocket and nervously drops it. He picks up the phone and drops it again.

Sloan's landline rings.

"Sloan? Craig Entwerp. Pardon my French, but are you watching this shit?"

Sloan carries the phone toward the kitchen window and peers at Craig's house, which sits diagonally from the foreclosure. "No. What's up, Craig?"

"Is Ken Phipps really about to sell this piece-of-shit foreclosure to a couple of I-don't-know-whats from the city?"

"I don't know, Craig. What do you mean by 'I-don't-know-whats'?"

"Ach, C'mon, Sloan. You know what I mean."

"Well, look at that. I think Ken just picked up the For Sale sign," Sloan says, moving back toward her front door. "It looks like the I-don't-know-whats are about to become our new neighbors."

"Whatever. I'm a big-tent guy."

"Big-tent guy is not what I think of when I think of you, Craig," says Sloan. "But maybe we can have a block party. Cheers." She hangs up.

In the front yard, Ken, using a signature gesture Sloan has seen on his billboard, raises the For Sale sign above his head like a victorious warrior.

Sloan watches the skinny man get into the red Prius with the fat man. For reasons she cannot even later identify, she rushes out the door into her front yard. There, she pretends to inspect a Japanese maple while making sure she is in view of the inhabitants of the Prius.

As the car backs out into the street, the tinted passenger-side window of the Prius lowers. The thin man leans his head out and rests it on his forearm.

"Hello," he says, smiling at Sloan.

Sloan affects as casual an air as she can muster. "Welcome to the neighborhood," she says.

The thin man smiles. "Now that we will be neighbors, may I borrow sugar from you?"

"You may," Sloan says.

"And will you come to our fondue parties?" the man continues.

"I will," Sloan responds.

From the driver's side, the fat man leans toward the open window. "Hello, neighbor!" he shouts. "My name is Lenny, and this is Dee."

"I'm Sloan." Sloan waves back.

"An honor to meet you," the fat man says earnestly.

There is a long silence as the Prius idles silently in the street. The thin man studies Sloan intently.

"How can we be sure it's her, Lenny?" The thin man speaks quietly and plaintively to Lenny but loud enough for Sloan to hear.

"Nice again to meet you, my dear!" Lenny shouts as he places the car in drive.

Sloan notices a tear roll down the thin man's face as the car pulls away.

CHAPTER FIFTEEN

All weekend, Francesca feared arriving at school and encountering the mean boys from the coffee shop. She imagined fanciful retribution scenarios in which the boys were sexually humiliated: getting "pantsed," girls laughing at their small penises, etc. But ultimately this only made her feel worse.

The better part of Francesca's weekend was spent researching mass hysteria, teenage psychokinesis, and viewing the original *Carrie*. On Saturday night, while her peers were out partying, Francesca downloaded a free PDF of the famous *Extraordinary Popular Delusions and the Madness of Crowds* and devoured it in one sitting. On Sunday, she tracked a couple of the Glenhaven cheerleaders on social media and found they had made another trip to Lime Ridge. She sent her father links to articles on conversion disorder and dissociation and felt good when Christian responded that she was a born researcher and should consider putting this work on her college resumé.

As Francesca arrives at her locker Monday morning, she catches a glimpse of Maron crossing a hallway perpendicular to hers. He has the look of someone hurrying to get to someplace private. A gaggle of popular girls standing in the intersection point as he passes. They bite their knuckles, giggle, and slap one another on the shoulders.

Narrowing her eyes, Francesca pushes through the crowd and catches up to Maron. With a sharp exhale, she taps him on the shoulder. "Hey!" she says, loudly.

"Hey," Maron says, turning.

"How are you?" Francesca says.

"Good," Maron laughs. Francesca's heart pounds as she forces herself to smile. There's a long silence during which she realizes she hasn't prepared any talking points. Maron rescues her.

"You ran off so quickly the other night," he says.

"Well, after I rescued you from the insane cheerleaders," Francesca begins, "I felt like my work was done."

"Thank you. I'm guessing you never wanted to be a cheerleader?"

"Many are called, few are chosen," Francesca says, speaking quickly. "I happen to prefer activities that don't involve pom-poms and squealing."

Maron laughs again, this time a more high-pitched and spontaneous laugh. Involuntarily, Francesca responds with her own horsey laugh, only to hear it echoed a moment later.

"Hyannnhaaw! Hyannaahw!"

It's Dylan Kanter and Brian Agee, two of the jerks from the coffee shop.

"Oh Jesus," Francesca says, lowering her head.

"Who are they?" Maron asks.

"No one. Nothing."

"Franny, where's your kick-ass mom?" Dylan says. "She was so frickin' hot. I wanted her to kick my ass." The boy juts out his butt and slaps it.

"Excuse me?" Maron politely approaches the boys. "Can I help you?"

"No, and we can't help you if you're with her!" the other boy sputters, making the horsey laugh again.

"I don't understand," Maron says, his accent thicker now. Francesca recalls reading that people's accents grow more pronounced when they're under stress.

"I don't understand," says one of the boys, mocking Maron's accent.

Maron turns once again to Francesca, as if for final confirmation that what appears to be happening is actually happening.

Two boys from Maron's football team approach.

"What's going on here, Mor-on?" says Hayden Findlay, a broad boy with a square head and an incongruously soft jaw.

"Why are you picking on these guys?" the other teammate says with a smile. "They're half your size. I know you're the big new thing now, but . . ."

"I'm not picking on them," Maron says tersely.

As a third football player arrives, Francesca steps forward. "He was just trying to protect me from these dickwads," she says, immediately recognizing her mistake in speaking.

"Wait a minute. You're . . . with her?" Hayden Findlay says with an incredulity so exaggerated that his eyes bug out. "Franny the horse? Wow."

Francesca, with an angry impulsivity she's long recognized in her father, blurts out: "Fuck off, Hayden. You're just jealous because Maron took your starting spot and now you sit on the bench with your dick in your hand where you belong."

"Whoa!" A collective groan rises from the dozen or more students who've stopped in the hallway to watch the drama.

Hayden, whose face has turned a bright pink, searches in vain for a response before finally being rescued by his pal Dylan, who begins neighing. "Hyannnnahw, hyanhaww!"

Hayden grits his teeth and joins along with the other boys in the chant. "Hynannnnaw! Hynannnnaw!"

Maron turns to Francesca, who has lost all her courage and turned pale.

Clare O'Connell, a tiny senior from Francesca's journalism class, shoves through the crowd and grabs Francesca by the arm. "C'mon," she says, "this is not going to end well. Remember, your dad works here. Let's go."

Maron grabs Hayden's forearm. Hayden stares at Maron's hand

like it's an alien life form.

"I don't know what you're doing right now," Hayden says, "but you're going to want to stop."

"You should be nicer," Maron says evenly.

As Francesca leaves the scene, she turns to see Hayden Findlay's surprised face moving clockwise through the air as his body slams into the lockers on the opposite side of the hall. Crashing sounds multiply. Clare whisks Francesca around the corner.

CHAPTER SIXTEEN

Christian's first three Monday meetings following the bizarre events of the Friday-night football game have gone well. He empathized with the shaken quarterback, Liam McDade, telling him that assault is assault—it doesn't matter if it's a cheerleader or a mugger, and pom-poms are made of hard plastic, so you damn betcha they hurt.

At lunchtime, Mark Apple appears in Christian's doorway.

"Crazy night, I heard," Apple says. "I was home sick, so I missed it. Good news is everybody thinks they need counseling, so now's your time to shine. How's it going?"

"Good," Christian begins. "Are you feeling better?"

"Excellent." Apple wipes sweat from his brow. "Take advantage of this moment, Chris. You want kids and parents leaving these meetings saying what a great guy you are. You want Brandi Cooley to believe you're the only one who can help her traumatized daughter. See what I'm saying? Help them and they'll be your biggest advocates, and the school board will notice. Then you get your plum job with benefits and retire and die happy. Ish. Oh, I talked to Bella Buell's dad, and he's willing to let the dry-humping matter drop."

"There was no dry-humping," Christian says.

"Mike and I played club ball together," Apple says, wiping his forehead again. "Can you believe that shit still matters? Gotta go."

"Wait," Christian says. "Did you talk to Ellen about the new mom coming to their bunco game? I'm trying to help her, you know, get her footing in town."

"I'll bet you are," Apple says, winking. "She is definitely a yummy mummy."

"I'm not"—Christian blushes—"doing that . . ."

"Nothing to be ashamed of," Apple says. "You're a free agent now, right? Don't worry, I talked to Ellen. She's on the list. My wife will be glad to have new blood, believe me. Those ladies are a paddy wagon full of drunkards. Warn your girl that it's heavy on the drinking, light on the cards. They don't call it 'drunco' for nothing."

Diane Sharpe and her daughter, Caitlin, appear in the doorway. Apple points to his watch and slides past them.

"Whoa, look at the time. Diane, Caitlin. Mr. Orr will see you now."

"Come in, Diane," Christian says, checking his computer for Viagra ads.

Diane pulls up a chair for Caitlin. Christian notices a strange leer on the teenager's face, which makes him think briefly of the expression on Maron's father's face the night of the game.

"So," Christian begins. "Crazy weekend. How's everybody doing"?

"How are *you*?" Caitlin sneers, leaning forward in her chair.

"I'm okay," Christian says with a patient nod. "I'm really more interested in you."

"Well, I'm more interested in you," Caitlin replies. "After all, this is all your fault.".

"My fault?"

"Dickless couldn't satisfy his wife." She leans forward again and smiles at Christian. "And that's why we're here."

"Don't let her talk to you like that!" Diane slaps the back of Caitlin's head. "She's been like this all weekend! Completely insane."

"Limp dick means limp soul." Caitlin shrugs.

"Caitlin!" Diane slaps the back of her daughter's head again.

"Diane, please!" Christian says.

"In my opinion," Diane begins with breathless anger, "this event is without question caused by Glenhaven's pornographic sexual education classes. Teaching tenth graders about oral and anal sex. Gay sex! Bestiality!"

Christian sighs. "Diane, there's one human sexuality class taught by a very level-headed and kind instructor. The class is standard throughout the state, and Mrs. Fotouhi follows the book. The main point of the class is to make kids aware of safe sex practices."

Caitlin gets up and shuffles around the room. She sings the Led Zeppelin song: "Want a whole lotta love, duk-ah-doonk, duk-ah-doonk."

"Please don't gaslight me," Diane continues as Christian, awestruck, watches Caitlin dance and sing. "I've read the curriculum. The words 'oral sex' are in there four times. Are you even listening to me?"

"Yes, yes." Christian turns to Diane, shaken. "Look, we all want to know what happened Friday night and why. Based on some research I did over the weekend, it turns out there is a direct precedent for what happened to our cheer team. The technical term is 'conversion disorder.'"

"Psychobabble," Diane says.

Christian reaches for his phone, pokes at a few keys, and hands it to Diane. "Read this: In 2012, a group of cheerleaders in Western New York developed the same symptoms as our cheer squad: involuntary twitching, inappropriate outbursts. It was like a mild version of Tourette's, and they all had it together. But it wasn't Tourette's, it didn't last, and the New York girls got over it quickly."

"Why do you let your girlfriend smoke in here?" Caitlin says, moving toward the window and pantomiming smoking.

"Excuse me?" Christian says.

"Ignore her; she's babbling," Diane replies, handing Christian back his phone. "I can't read any of this. It's too small. What about the cheerleaders in New York?"

"The girls were subconsciously converting normal high school stress into physical symptoms," Christian says hurriedly. "They were doing it together, just like they were cheering together. There was a kind of social contagion effect."

"That's ridiculous," Diane snorts.

"It's not. Reich wrote about this kind of substitution frequently."

"Who's Reich?" Diane reaches into her handbag. "Did the New York girls send each other drawings like this?" She pulls out a hand drawing of a giant phallus sticking out the top of a mountain.

"Well." Christian nods, receiving the paper. "I don't know. I would have to check."

"Ichos, ichos, ichos," Caitlin sings as she moves away from the window, making the finger-in-the-hole sexual gesture.

"People are calling our girls a coven on Facebook." Diane looks severely at Christian. "A coven!"

"People say a lot of things. Words like coven are obviously not helpful," Christian says.

"You're just here to gaslight me until I leave." Diane surges to her feet. "Let's go, Caitlin!" She grabs her daughter and yanks her toward the door.

As mother and daughter leave, Caitlin turns toward Christian and sings, "You need cooling. Baby, I ain't fooling."

Finally, Christian stands alone in the middle of his office. After a long silence, he hears a chorus of teenage shouts rising from the hallway.

"You have to get out there!"

CHAPTER SEVENTEEN

Entering the hallway outside his office, Christian is nearly leveled by Trevor Pfister, one of the football players. Trevor's nose is bleeding, and his shirt is torn. He grabs Christian by the shoulders.

"He's beating us up! Kids are all over the floor in the hallway. You have to get out there!"

Christian doesn't want to get out there. As Trevor pulls him into the hallway, Christian imagines all the ways he might get hurt breaking up a fight among large teenage boys.

In the hall, three of the football players are piled atop another boy, who can be heard yelling beneath. The situation is actually fairly stable, Christian decides, and he instinctively turns toward his office. Suddenly, all three boys are tossed into the air toward the lockers.

"Look at that!" Trevor yelps, spinning Christian around. "Did you see that?"

"Maron?" Christian says.

From the floor, Maron sits up while around him the football players groan and rub their heads.

Christian steps forward. "Come to my office, please."

Maron slouches in a chair while Christian pretends to peck out an email on his computer. "It's always the same," Maron says, staring at his hands as if they might be to blame for what just happened. "Everyone turns on me, and then we have to leave."

"It doesn't have to be that way this time," Christian says. "And nobody's turning on you. I'm not turning on you."

Maron looks up at Christian, and the two smile briefly at each other.

As he turns again toward his blank computer screen, Christian wonders what kind of father he might have been to a young man like Maron. He certainly couldn't have taught him to throw, shoot, run, or dribble. But perhaps he could have taught him to be self-aware, to be kind to himself. But had Christian taught those lessons to Francesca? Or had he taught her to be a neurotic, self-loathing, excessively polite loser like him, destined to be miserable and to develop a succession of psychogenic problems such as impotence?

Ari enters Christian's office and smashes her knee against the same ill-placed chair. She curses and turns to Maron. Christian wonders if she is about to smack her son, but instead she gently kisses the top of his head.

"What now?" Ari says.

Maron raises his head. "Ask him. I was on a thirty-day probation. Expulsion, I guess."

"Whoa, whoa!" Christian protests. "No one expels anyone without my say-so."

"You're not the principal," Maron says bitterly. "You don't have any power."

"That's not true. I have advisory power."

Ari takes a cigarette from her purse.

"Ari, remember?" Christian says. "No smoking?"

"Right," Ari says, putting away her cigarette. "So many rules. I want to like it here," she continues, as if Maron's fight were of no importance. "Glenhaven, I mean. But everyone seems to have their lives all sorted out. They do things while I just sit at home and wait for Maron. Is this what suburban life is like?"

"It can be," Christian says. "But you'll be glad to learn that you have been cordially invited to tomorrow night's bunco game at the home of Ellen Apple, wife of principal, Mark Apple. Trust me, a night of bunco will plunge you deeper into Glenhaven society than you may like."

"Why don't you come with me?" Ari says.

"Ha!" Christian blushes. "Well. It's . . . generally for women only."

Ari laughs. "These people and their segregated activities. What do you do with your free time?"

Fighting off images of himself watching porn and practicing his throwing motion, Christian hears himself blurt out, "Well, I'm really good at karaoke, and I'm performing tonight."

"How wonderful!" Ari says, clapping her hands. "I'll come!"

"No!" Christian yells before softening his voice. "It's just that, well, it's a Tuesday, and I'm not sure exactly when I'll be going on. You'd have to wait around for hours. And a lot of the singers are terrible!"

"So what," Ari says. "I'll buy you a drink to thank you for all the help you've given me and Maron." She hands Christian her cell phone. "Put your number in my phone."

His hands shaking, Christian struggles with Ari's phone, making and correcting several mistakes. As he hands the phone back, Ari takes his hand. "I'm sure you're a wonderful singer," she says.

"I'm . . . okay," Christian says.

Maron rises from his chair. "Mr. Orr, if I'm still enrolled, I have class in five minutes. Can I tell you what happened in the hallway?"

"Yes, yes, of course!" Christian turns toward Maron. "What happened?"

"Well, I was in the hallway talking to your daughter, and a few boys came up and started making fun of her. I asked them to stop. They attacked me, and I fought back. That's basically it."

"My daughter?" Christian feels his mind stretch painfully.

"Yes," Maron says. "Remember, we met in the hall the other day, before—"

"Yes, yes, I remember," Christian says quickly, shooting a defensive glance toward Ari.

"Well, these guys were being mean to her," Maron says. "Like, for no reason, making fun of her laugh or something. All I know is it was hurting her. So, I asked them to stop."

"Well, there you go," Ari says. "He was protecting your daughter. What else would you have him do?"

"I . . ."

Maron bows his head. "I know I should have found another way, sir. But Francesca's a really nice person, and I felt like I had to do something."

"Right. I'm sure she appreciated your help. But . . ." Christian lowers his voice. "These boys are your teammates. You have to find a way to get along with them if you want to stay in school and keep playing football."

"I have to keep playing football," Maron says, his eyes watering. "It's all I have right now."

"I understand," Christian says. "So, find a way to turn down the temperature." He steals a glance at Ari and feels her approving gaze upon him. "There's a Booster party coming up. The players and their parents will be there. It'll be a good opportunity to start mending fences and rebuilding goodwill with the team."

Maron shakes Christian's hand firmly. "I will definitely do that, Mr. Orr," he says. "I promise, I will mend fences."

Christian turns to find Ari still looking at him lovingly.

"If only his own father could be like you," Ari says, taking Christian's hand in both of hers. "I'll see you tonight at karaoke."

Before Christian can object, Ari and Maron are gone.

"She just had surgery!"

CHAPTER EIGHTEEN

Two years earlier, local developers purchased Glenhaven's oldest pub, tore out the beer-soaked bar, added lights, mirrors, and a low stage, and opened a spiffy, nostalgia-soaked joint called Retro Junkie. The new club, which featured cover bands, karaoke, and trivia nights, was designed to cater to middle-aged people looking to cut loose on a Saturday night but still get home by 10:30 to pay the babysitter.

Christian attended karaoke nights at Retro Junkie on occasion while living at Sloan's house, telling her he was meeting colleagues for beers. Sloan knew he was lying but didn't wonder or care where Christian was really going. Since moving into the Divorced Dads Apartment Complex, Christian has become a regular on Tuesday nights, the first to arrive and the last to leave.

His preparation for karaoke night begins hours before showtime, as he kneels before his standing mirror. Here he applies makeup, tries on Roger Daltrey wigs to cover his thinning hair, and squeezes into satin pants and polyester tops that do not always succeed in covering his paunch. Just before departure, Christian spends twenty minutes warming up his voice with lip trills, fricatives, and two-octave vocal slides.

In high school, Christian imagined rock and roll as a path to the kind of power and success he felt he could never experience otherwise. As a sophomore, he read a biography of Led Zeppelin entitled *Hammer of the Gods*, which chronicles the excesses of the band on tour in the seventies. Brandishing "the Hammer," Zeppelin's members famously wrecked hotel rooms, concertgoers, critics, the music charts, your mom's sense of safety, and all things reasonable in the world. Zep had done this not out of malice but out of obligation to the immense power that fame and the public had given them; they were merely operating in service to the Hammer. It was this book that, even as an adult, Christian cherished more deeply than all the books by Freud, Adler, and even his hero, Wilhelm Reich.

At 5 p.m. Retro Junkie is empty except for the bartender and the emcee, Morris, a rotund man who looks like Wavy Gravy. Christian arrives early for what he calls sound check, even though he and Morris know there is no such thing. Morris has a soft spot for Christian, appreciating his commitment to Tuesday nights, which are generally so poorly attended that management discounts well drinks to bring people in.

"Morris!" Christian enters, flashing the devil's horn with his fingers. The afternoon sunlight reflects off Christian's gilt vest and pale arms as he leaps over one of the monitors and strides onto the stage. Morris smiles and raises his own devil's horn, a gesture he would have preferred to stop making years ago but realizes goes with the job.

Because there is no green room at Retro Junkie, Christian spends the long period before karaoke starts sitting to one side of the empty stage, hunched over a cranberry and vodka. Even at a discount, the well drinks are five dollars, so Christian has become adept at making each drink last.

As the un-rock-and-roll showtime of 7 p.m. nears, Christian reflexively turns toward the door each time it opens. He often fears that a ringer will show up, someone who trolls the karaoke circuit looking to humiliate other performers. But on this Tuesday night Christian is not anticipating a ringer. He is anticipating Ari.

At 6:55, Laura Hartwood enters, followed by an entourage of other attractive middle-aged women. Laura and her big smile find Christian immediately. She waves. Christian waves back, grinding his teeth. The bartender (who barely acknowledges Christian each week) kisses the back of Laura's hand as if she were a princess.

Christian has chosen the moody "Night Swimming" by REM as his warm-up to other, more complex numbers he plans to slay the crowd with later. But Laura Hartwood's arrival has changed everything. There can be no warm-ups now. As Laura heads for the sign-up sheet, Christian scurries toward the front door. From there, he hides in the shadows like Nosferatu, observing his rival as she approaches the table.

Morris, curious about Christian's sudden anxiety, joins him by the door. "Know her?" he says.

"No, no," Christian says dismissively. "I've seen her at school. I think she's a therapist of some kind. Actually, I'm theoretically in competition with her for this big position, but I don't really know her."

"So, whatcha singing tonight?" Morris asks as casually as he can, knowing that the significance of Christian's song choice rivals the words chosen by Churchill for his Dunkirk speech.

"Dunno, dunno, a little REM, maybe some Creedence," Christian says, trying to stuff his hands into nonexistent pockets. "Just gonna feel it out, see what strikes me when I get there."

When Laura finally returns to the bar, Christian rushes to the sign-in table and sees that Laura has written beside her name the words TBD -OK?

"TBD okay?" Christian mutters to himself. "TBD not okay. What, is Morris supposed to guess your song?"

With sudden decisiveness, he scratches out "Night Swimming" and writes in "Stairway to Heaven." He quickly returns to his seat and resumes slurping his glass of ice.

Morris grabs the sign-up sheet, leaps onto the stage, and, with a shocking lack of preamble, starts the show.

"Alright, first up is Christian, singing 'Stairway to Heaven.'"

There is a smattering of applause as Christian takes the stage. He scans the room for Ari and is relieved not to see her. He turns toward the karaoke screen and hears himself warbling out the first few words of the song as they appear.

"There's a lady who's sure all that glitters is gold . . ."

He remembers, bitterly, that although he practiced his fricatives and arpeggios, he did not prepare for falsetto. He had no *intention* of singing falsetto, but extreme measures have forced his hand.

"And she's buying a stairway to heaven."

Christian hears the first titter. He strains to discern if the laughter might be coming from Laura Hartwood's crew at the bar. He drops an octave to play it safe . . .

The octave drop does not work, as he now sounds like Barry White.

There is general laughter. Christian can see that Laura Hartwood is covering her mouth. Laura's friends are chuckling freely.

Christian decides to jump back to falsetto for the final line of the verse, a bold move that motivates a few people to clap spontaneously.

Feeling the support of the crowd now, he dances through the instrumental section. As Francesca has pointed out many times, Christian doesn't dance so much he boogies. According to his daughter, he pulls it off.

By the middle of the song, Christian's voice is finally warm, and he is prepared for falsetto. He feels the Hammer of the Gods firmly in his grasp. Approaching the climax, Christian feels sure enough of his voice that he twists his torso in a Robert Plant-style contortion of orgasmic agony.

"And she's buying a stairway to heaven."

If there are titters now, they are subsumed by the healthy though not overwhelming applause that rises along with the tinny karaoke cymbal that signals the end of the song.

Christian bows once, twice, three times. In the middle of the third bow, he realizes that all applause has stopped. So, with a friendly rock-star wave, he hurries offstage and quickly assumes his seat. To have something to do, he sucks at the newly melted ice in his glass.

"Next up," Morris reads from his sign-up sheet, "Laura Hartwood singing TBD OK? TBD OK? Is that Radiohead?" He winks at Christian.

As Laura reaches the stage, she grabs the microphone and with a room-quieting basso profundo declaims: "Maestro, if you please, I'd like to sing 'Bad Reputation' by Joan Jett."

The crowd cheers, and with a speed that makes Christian wonder whether Morris is somehow in cahoots with Laura, "Bad Reputation" is up on the screen and playing.

Christian clenches his glass with a force that threatens to crush it.

"I don't give a damn about my bad reputation."

Laura snarls the first line into the microphone, and the crowd cheers wildly.

Christian, his chair humiliatingly close to Laura and the stage, evinces a mocking, dismissive expression. "Bad Reputation" is a song that requires no singing ability, he muses. It's basically spoken. Degree of difficulty: zero.

"The world's gone to hell . . ."

"*Everything's* gone to hell," Christian corrects Laura under his breath. "'The world'!"

Laura's laughter as she mangles the lyrics only encourages the crowd to encourage her more. She firms her posture and steps forward, revealing some thigh as she slams her high heel into the stage like a flamenco dancer.

The entire crowd joins Laura for the *"Oh no, not me."* Even Christian finds himself singing along.

When the song ends, Laura steps off the stage and approaches him.

"You were great!" she shouts, raising her hand for a high-five. Christian raises his palm at the very moment he catches sight of Ari entering through the front door. Laura's face registers a look of concern as she sees that Christian's high-five is veering off course. She tries to compensate, but Christian's hand slams into her right breast.

Laura clutches at her chest and slumps into a chair. One of her friends from the bar rushes forward with the urgency of a wartime medic.

"Jesus Christ," the friend says to Christian as she arrives. "She just had surgery last month."

"I'm so sorry," Christian stammers as his eyes follow Ari, who hasn't seen him yet.

"It's okay, I'm fine." Laura looks up at Christian with a genuine smile. "Good job up there," she says earnestly. "You were great.

At this moment, Christian makes his boldest decision of the night—to run. He leaps onto the stage, drops to his knees, and crawls behind the karaoke screen. He smiles weakly at Morris before sliding off the back of the stage and scurrying toward the rear exit.

Emerging from the building, he inhales the fetid air beside the dumpster. His phone pings with a message from Sloan.

I NEED TO TALK TO YOU.

CHAPTER NINETEEN

During the bubble bath he prepared after returning from Retro Junkie, Christian apologized to Ari via text, telling her had a sudden migraine and had to leave.

At midnight, as Christian sits on the edge of his bed, he picks up the pamphlet given to him by Dr. Fuchs and stares with dismay at its title: *Nocturnal Penile Tumescence: A Guide to Home Testing*.

After many heavy sighs, Christian sets down the pamphlet and carefully maneuvers his flaccid penis through the opening in his boxer shorts. He unrolls four postage stamps, licks them all, and curls them snugly around his penis.

As Christian leans back onto his pillow, his weak core muscles quiver, and the stamps flutter away. He wonders as he lies on his back how a woman as elegant as Ari could ever be interested in a man who licks stamps and puts them on his penis.

On Christian's third try, the stamps remain in place, and he lowers his head back. He carefully places a lavender-scented eye pillow across his brow and takes a long, tremulous exhale. Suddenly, there is a voice outside his door.

"Christian, open up. It's me."

"Sloan?" Christian scrambles to his feet as the stamps fall to the floor. "It's midnight!" He quickly pulls on sweatpants and a T-shirt as he stumbles toward the door.

Sloan knocks again and enters, nearly knocking Christian over. "You don't lock your door?" she says blandly.

"You don't wait for a door to be opened?" Christian whines.

"I brought your rent check," Sloan continues, inspecting the apartment with disdain. She opens cabinet doors and sniffs the air. "Do these windows open?" She opens a window. "It smells like a dungeon in here."

"You came by at midnight to hand me a check?" Christian says.

"Francesca said she was worried about you, so I wanted to see you," Sloan says, opening another window."

"Francesca's not worried about me," Christian snorts. "And if she were, she'd tell me herself. We happen to have a great relationship."

"I know you do," Sloan says wistfully and then sits on Christian's sofa. "Can we sit for a minute?"

"No, I'd prefer to stand," Christian replies, suddenly aware of the penis stamps scattered on the floor between him and Sloan.

Sloan sighs. "I've been thinking a lot lately."

"Oh, really?" Christian says peevishly. "I thought you were worried about me and that's why you came. Don't you have a therapist you could think a lot to?"

Sloan nods. "I do."

"Maybe you just need to pay her a bit more to disabuse you of your guilt for fucking up your family," Christian says, picking up a few stamps. "I'm sure she has a price."

"He."

"He." Christian shakes his head. "Of course. Should I ask if you're fucking him or just assume it?"

Sloan smiles calmly. "One of the things I've been thinking about is how much I appreciate you and what you've done for Francesca," she begins. "You've been great to her, her whole life. And she's especially lucky to have you right now when things are chaotic."

"Well," Christian says, somewhat taken aback by Sloan's candor. "What do you want me to say? She's my daughter. Our daughter. I love her. Although it begs the question why you'd betray such a great husband to screw a moron like Stu Sherwater?"

"I didn't say you were a great husband," Sloan says. "Just that you're a great father. You're not a great husband. You never have been. And I don't want to talk about Stu Sherwater."

"Why not?" Christian says, his voice strengthening. "He's an endlessly fascinating character. The tufted nose hair. The soiled windbreaker he wears every day. By the way, do you really think I didn't know about your extracurricular activities in San Francisco? What CrossFit class lasts six hours? But I let it go for the sake of the marriage, for the sake of Francesca. But to screw a colleague of mine, in my own backyard, at your own daughter's high school? The only possible explanation is that you were trying to hurt me."

"No, I never wanted to hurt you," Sloan says firmly.

"Why then?"

Sloan looks at the ceiling and then at Christian. "I think I was just trying to find a way to end our marriage without actually ending it. Because I didn't have a good enough reason to end it. I just didn't want it anymore. I wanted something different."

"Stu Sherwater not different enough for you?"

"No," Sloan says. "I wanted . . . some purpose."

"You're the one who took a meaningless job defending evil corporations," Christian says. "Why wasn't being a mother and being part of a family purposeful?"

"It was," Sloan says. "It is."

"I'm not sensing great conviction."

Christian snorts and begins to pace the short distance from the living room to the kitchen. "I think I just realized why you're here," he says, finally. "You're here to get me to explain your selfish behavior to you. You've done this before. You're like a big dumb lioness who eats one of its young and wants the zookeeper to tell her it's okay, it's her nature, what else could she do?"

It occurs to Christian that he could stop ranting now, plant his flag on the moral high ground he's gained, and tell Sloan to leave. But he is also aware of feeling relieved to have someone, anyone, in his lonely apartment with him, so he keeps talking.

"I don't know if you've ever read John Locke," Christian continues. "But human life, he said famously, is nasty, brutish, and short. What he forgot to say is that it's also boring. When life is exciting, it's usually because something's gone bad. Feeling bored and purposeless means that things are going *well*, Sloan. You could have cancer; you could have a daughter who cuts herself in front of the mirror. Then life wouldn't be boring, would it? It might even feel purposeful, but at what cost? And let's say even if"—Christian lengthens his paces—"even if you could get above your malaise and ennui or whatever the fuck it is you think is bothering you, you would never get there by fucking strangers or ruining your family."

"How would you do it then?" Sloan says.

Christian laughs at the absurdity of her question, until he notices the look of childlike innocence on her face, as if this is the question she's been waiting to have answered her whole life.

"Well, the short answer is that it involves transcending your ego. Getting beyond your selfish desires, including the desire to have a purpose. You get rid of the boundaries between yourself and others so that questions about personal fulfillment don't even arise, because there's no person to fulfill. You transcend your own identity and work entirely on behalf of others, or for no one at all, because you no longer have an ego to feed."

"I want that," Sloan says with the same childish look on her face.

Christian snorts again and walks into the kitchen. "Give me a break."

Overcome with annoyance at the size of his apartment, where the kitchen and the living room are the same, where it's too small to retreat to a corner, Christian rushes to the front door and grabs the knob. "Honestly, I'm really tired and I need to go to bed." He opens the front door and stands stone-faced like a doorman.

Sloan rises and slowly walks toward the door. "I'm sorry I woke you up," she says.

"You didn't wake me up," Christian replies. "I was awake, wide awake."

"I really like what you said about transcending your identity."

"Right. I'm a regular font of wisdom," Christian scoffs.

Sloan gives him a quick smile and leaves.

"I moved here because of you."

CHAPTER TWENTY

Having slept poorly after her confrontation with Christian, Sloan awakens late. Her sleep has been uneven since Christian left, and she's needed more of it. As she enters the living room, she glances through an open curtain and spots the Prius owned by her new neighbors in their driveway across the street.

Through the sidelights of her front door, Sloan can see the thin man, Dee, lying recumbent on a ratty lawn recliner in the front yard. Lenny sits nearby on a torn living room chair, reading a book. A beach umbrella juts uselessly at an angle from the weed-strewn yard. For reasons she can't now (nor later) define, Sloan throws on a beach wrap, grabs a bottle of red wine from the kitchen, and heads out the door.

Lenny notices Sloan first as she enters their yard. He rises from his chair and extends a hand.

"Hello, my dear!" Lenny says. He doubles back and slaps Dee across the head. "Get up! Our new neighbor is here, and she brought wine!"

Dee doesn't move. Lenny takes the bottle of wine from Sloan's hands and bangs it against Dee's head. A smile forms. "That has the timbre of cheap wine," Dee says.

Sloan knows that the wine is by no means cheap and senses a game.

"Apologies," she says. "I have to save the good wine for my better neighbors."

Dee leaps up from his recliner. He rushes with great athleticism toward Sloan, cocking his head first to one side and then the other like a dog. Sloan's heart bangs inside her chest. She can smell wine on Dee's breath.

Dee smiles. "Tell me. Do you see us as dirty degenerates who are going to lower your property values?"

"Not at all," Sloan fires back, though her legs begin to quiver. "I see you as very clean degenerates, and I frankly don't care about my property values."

Dee jumps from foot to foot like a mad troll. "Oh, maybe it is her, Lenny!"

"Dee, please." Lenny glares at Dee like a schoolmarm. "Let's sit, shall we?"

Lenny pulls up a lawn chair behind Sloan, who feels lightheaded and is relieved to sit.

Dee sprints off after a black cat in the yard, meowing himself.

Lenny fishes two glasses out of a picnic basket beside his chair, opens the wine, and pours a glass for himself and for Sloan. "Is it awful to drink wine this early in the morning?" he says, raising his glass.

Sloan touches her glass to Lenny's. "Five o'clock somewhere," she replies.

"Just before you came," Lenny says, "Dee and I were discussing the events at the football game the other night. You heard the story of the cheerleaders running onto the field?"

"Yes," Sloan says, who got the entire story in a data dump from her daughter via text.

Lenny frowns in Dee's direction. "I was telling Dee that girls of this age have not yet developed the agency to choose their behavior, so they cannot be fully responsible for their actions. I told him furthermore that it's unfair, if not immoral, to encourage such actions. Wouldn't you agree?"

"Agreed. But who would encourage such actions?" Sloan says.

"Meow," Dee says from the corner of the yard, raising one paw of the cat he now holds. "Meow, meow, meow, meow!"

Lenny turns his head and snorts at Dee. "People should never be manipulated."

"People aren't manipulated," Dee says, gently setting down the cat. He sashays back toward Lenny and Sloan. "There is only manipulation if there is agency, and we both know that people have no agency. So, no manipulation! Besides, the teenage girls in this town are far superior in every way to their dried-up mothers."

"Speaking as a dried-up mother," Sloan says, "I have to wonder why someone like you would even want to live here."

"She asked, Lenny!" Dee says, pinching Lenny's midsection before kneeling on the ground before Sloan. As Lenny starts to interrupt, Dee turns and slaps Lenny's leg.

Dee bows his head, then raises it.

"I moved here because of you."

Sloan loses her breath momentarily.

"Zagreus!" Lenny grabs Dee and pulls him to his feet.

Incongruously, Dee cackles. He rushes toward the corner of the yard. "Here, kitty, kitty!"

"I'm sorry, my dear," Lenny says with a deep sigh, slumping back into his chair.

"Is he okay?" Sloan says. "What does he mean?"

"He's going through a difficult time right now. Personal and professional problems," Lenny says.

"What do you people do professionally, anyway?" Sloan says, relieved to take a large gulp of her wine. "If you don't mind me asking."

"We are in the process of retiring," Lenny replies, weighing his answer. "But Dee is having trouble with retirement, as many men do."

"And not to put too fine a point on it, but you both strike me as pretty gay," Sloan continues. "I'm just going off the speedos and the jean shorts and leather vest. Are you a couple?"

"We are definitely a couple," Lenny says. "But not the kind you're thinking of."

Dee shouts from the corner of the yard, holding the cat's paw. "Ask her about the other thing, Lenny!"

"What's the other thing?" Sloan says, finishing her wine.

"The other thing," Lenny says, stopping to fill Sloan's glass, "is really just idle speculation, given that we are semiretired and both have too much time on our hands. The question is, would you prefer to live forever or die of old age in your sleep?"

Sloan takes a sip of her wine and realizes that, despite everything, she is enjoying herself.

"Hmm. Okay. Well, I guess it depends. How old am I when I start living forever? If forever starts when I'm ninety-seven and decrepit, I'd rather die than keep living at ninety-seven."

"Current age!" Dee shouts from the yard. "Meow, meow!"

"Current age?" Sloan frowns. "Well, I suppose I'd rather stay this age forever than die in my sleep at ninety-seven. Who wouldn't?"

An expression that Sloan interprets as despair passes across Lenny's face.

Dee gently drops the cat and rushes again to Sloan, this time sitting cross-legged before her like a disciple before a guru.

"Do you mean that?" Dee says excitedly. "You would really rather live forever than die?"

Sloan is unable to smirk.

"Oh, Lenny!" Dee says, turning to Lenny with emotion.

"I'm sorry, but just to clarify," Sloan laughs angrily, "who the fuck are you? I came here to say hello, bring some wine. I didn't plan on sitting through an inquisition."

"You're a lawyer," Dee says, taking Sloan's hand. "You're used to inquisitions, aren't you."

Sloan is about to ask how Dee knows she's a lawyer when she feels a warm, powerful energy coursing from Dee's hand through her arm, into her belly, and down into her loins. There, Sloan begins to feel a sexual arousal so extreme that she fears she may orgasm on the spot.

"I have to go!"

Sloan shoves Dee's hand away and rises. Her vision goes white, and Lenny stands quickly to steady her.

"I have to work," Sloan says feebly.

She turns and takes one step toward her house, staggering at first until she finally gains her equilibrium.

Dee shouts after Sloan, "One more thing! Please tell your husband to stay away from my wife, if you don't mind!"

"What—?" Sloan turns and starts to say more but, unsure of her footing, turns once again toward her house.

As she crosses into her yard, her hands begin to tingle. She opens her palms and notices a faint white light appearing and disappearing in the center of each palm. She stops walking and shuts her eyes for a long while. When she opens them, the light is gone.

CHAPTER TWENTY-ONE

Ari stands with her hand raised six inches from the door of the Apple home. She has just decided to leave without knocking when the door opens.

"Hello!" says a woman with a kind smile. "You must be Ari. I'm Ellen Apple. Come on in!"

Ari enters the Apple home, a modest but welcoming rancher, and finds a living room full of middle-aged women seated at card tables. Some turn and wave, while others remain in conversation or shuffle cards. All have copper mugs in front of them.

Ari's host, Ellen, is an athletic-looking woman with graying hair. Ari whispers to Ellen, "Is it okay that I don't know how to play the game?"

"All you have to do is roll dice, drink, and talk about people who aren't here," Ellen whispers back.

"Everyone!" Ellen shouts to the crowd. "This is Ari. Ari, everyone. We'll put you at table four. Who knows, you may make it to the queen's table, especially if any of our current queens pass out!"

Ellen pours Ari a Moscow mule, a gin-based concoction served in a festive mug. Ari is glad to see that there are pitchers of the stuff on the tables. She drinks half of her first mug in one swallow.

"Easy, new girl!" shouts someone from the queen's table.

Minutes after sitting down, it becomes clear to Ari that no one cares who wins bunco, and there really isn't much strategy to the game. They're here to talk and drink and to be together, which is exactly what Ari wants.

As she pours herself another Moscow mule, Ari relaxes and basks in the chatter of the women and the warmth of their bodies. She hears their words without really knowing or caring what they're saying:

"So why did they buy a Tahoe house if he's losing his job?"

"Isn't Hope their daughter's name? That's a helluva burden!"

"I do barre with her doctor. I heard it was colitis, not colon cancer."

"Psychology major but I obviously didn't learn shit!"

After an hour, Ari has moved to the queen's table, and she is now unquestionably drunk. She is also vaguely aware of mumbling to herself in Greek, which has drawn stares but also sympathetic pats on the back.

At Ari's new table is Brittany May, an absurdly fit forty-year-old in a Lycra workout suit, as well as Jenny, a nurse who put on a blouse after work but left on her nursing pants. Brittany desperately tries to form complete sentences and is frustrated that due to her drunkenness, she can't.

"I frickin' told him what the frick. I mean . . . Right?" Brittany laughs as if her point has been made and all present understand it. She turns to Ari. "You know what I mean?"

Ari has been expecting her intuition to diminish lately, but it hasn't, so she knows exactly what Brittany means.

"Your husband wants to put the Ping-Pong table in the garage," Ari says. "But you are worried it will take up all the space and not leave any room for the storage shelves you've already purchased and can't return."

"Exactly!" Brittany shouts, jamming her index finger dangerously close to Ari's eye.

One of the players at the queen's table raises her mug. "To stupid husbands!"

"To stupid husbands!"

"I hate my husband!" Ari shouts.

Brittany responds: "To stupid hating husbands!" and raises her glass.

"I want a good man!" Ari says.

"Good men are boring!" another woman says. The women hoot and holler.

"Bad men are boring too," Ari says. "My husband is so bad I kicked him in the testicles," she says, raising her glass. "Maybe I'm bad too." The entire room explodes with laughter and applause.

"The new girl's a keeper, Ellen!" a woman shouts.

"Three thousand years is too long to be married!" Ari says as she slams her copper mug on the table.

Responses of "I hear ya!" and "I feel like I'm going on ten thousand years!" fill the room.

"I would actually prefer to be done with it all," Ari continues, suddenly visibly distraught. The mood of the room shifts to accommodate her. "I want to be a regular person." She stares into her mug. "My son wants to be a regular person. I took up the cello and I bought oil paints. And now I'm here, trying to make friends. But it's not easy."

"It's okay, honey," Jenny the nurse says, placing a consoling hand on Ari's shoulder. "Marriage is hard."

"Everything is hard," Ari says bitterly. "Too hard."

Ari groans, and all twelve light bulbs in the chandelier above her table explode. Shards of glass rain down. All the women except Ari scatter from the table.

A hush falls over the room, which is now only illuminated by lights from the adjacent kitchen.

"Sorry," Ari says, stumbling as she gets up. She brushes glass splinters from the table into her hands. Her feet crunch glass as she staggers away from the table. Ellen Apple rushes forward with a broom and dustpan. Ari deposits the glass shards from her hands into the dustpan and looks from one stunned woman to the next.

"You're bleeding," Jenny the nurse says.

"I have to leave," Ari says, looking at the cut on her hand as she makes her way to the front door.

"Call an Uber!" a woman shouts.

"I need to walk," Ari says. "I live close, and I need the air."

"School night," another woman says matter-of-factly. "Let's pack it in." The women tuck in their chairs and begin to clean up.

Outside a mist has descended over the quiet neighborhood. Ari staggers down a side street away from Ellen's house. After two blocks, she drops to her knees and looks at the cut on her hand. She squeezes her flesh and licks the blood. "When will it be over?" she cries.

An image of Christian appears in her mind. Ari lifts her head, then her body, and runs down the street.

"Your breath and mine will stop someday
-- isn't that amazing?"

CHAPTER TWENTY-TWO

After locking his front door, Christian sits on his bed and sighs. He opens his boxers, licks four stamps, and curls them around his penis. Tonight, as he lowers onto his pillow, the stamps stay in place. Christian feels a twinge of pride followed by a wave of despair that such an event could cause him to feel pride—when there is a knock at the door.

"Christian Orr!"

Christian rushes to answer, forgetting to reinsert his penis into his boxers. He peers through the peephole and sees Ari on the front porch. She is turned away, shaking her head and muttering to herself as she leans dangerously over the third-story railing.

Christian opens the door, and Ari shrieks with delight.

"Christian Orr!" Ari pulls him onto the balcony, and Christian's bathrobe falls open, revealing his stamp-covered penis poking out of his boxers. Ari covers her mouth, laughing.

Christian makes a whining noise, closes his robe, and runs back into his apartment, closing the door all but a crack.

"I'm sorry," he says, poking his head through the door. "It was inadvertent, but that's no excuse, and I apologize. I wasn't prepared for visitors. I'm glad to see you, but it's a school night."

"A what night?" Ari moves toward the door with her hands together as if to cup Christian's cheeks in them. "I was in the neighborhood, and I remembered that you lived in this apartment building."

"How do you know where I live?" Christian replies with alarm.

"I don't know," Ari says, and in this moment, it occurs to Christian that Ari doesn't know. "I wanted to hear you sing last night, but then you left," she continues. "Is your migraine better?"

"Yes, much better!" Christian pulls his robe tighter with one hand while maintaining a firm grip on the door with the other.

"Why are you hiding behind the door?" Ari laughs.

"I'm not hiding," Christian says. "It's just that it's a school night and I have some work to do."

"What work?"

All at once, the entire landing jerks, and Christian is tossed forward through the door. Ari nearly falls over the railing. With a dexterity that surprises him, Christian grabs Ari around the waist and pulls her toward him.

The shaking stops as quickly as it starts, and the two of them are nose to nose. Ari smiles.

Christian feels the world go quiet. "That was an earthquake," he says softly.

"It was," Ari whispers.

Christian inhales her breath, which smells like oranges. "You were about to fall," he continues. "So I had to catch you."

"So you did." Ari raises an eyebrow at him and moves her lips so close to Christian's that he involuntarily closes his eyes.

"Your breath," Ari says in a whisper so soft that Christian feels like he might be dreaming her words. "It will stop someday. Mine too. Isn't that amazing?"

Gradually, the noise from the nearby freeway rises and, with it, Christian's awareness. "There might be aftershocks," he says. "We should get off the balcony."

"May I come in?" Ari says.

"Yes, okay, yes," Christian says. As they enter the apartment, Ari pulls Christian toward her and begins kissing him. He kisses back. Ari reaches inside his robe, and Christian impulsively grabs her hand.

"I'm sorry, I can't!" he shrieks. "I mean, I would, but I'm currently seeing a urologist!"

Ari coughs, then gags. She staggers away from Christian and runs to the kitchen sink, where she vomits.

Christian rushes to catch her as she slumps toward the floor.

"I'm sorry. I feel sick," Ari says.

"It's okay. Sit down," Christian says, guiding her toward the sofa.

"I should leave," Ari says.

Christian very much wants her to stay. "You don't have to leave."

"No," Ari says. "I should leave."

"I'll drive you home then."

"I need to walk," Ari says. "I need to walk and get my head on straight. I'm sorry for attacking you. I don't understand myself right now," she says angrily. "I've never really been drunk before."

"You don't want me to drive you?" Christian says, following Ari to the door.

Ari turns and holds Christian's face in her hands. "Will you see me again if I promise not to throw up on you?"

"Yes," Christian says, "of course." He detects a feeling of awe toward this woman who would throw up, offer to leave, and then ask for another date, all within the space of a minute.

"Come to my house tomorrow," Ari says. "We won't call it a date; we'll just call it a meeting. Like we had in your office except at my house. Will you come?"

"Yes," Christian says.

"Good." She kisses him on the cheek and leaves.

"Would you...pet me?"

CHAPTER TWENTY-THREE

The basement of Ari's rented house hasn't been remodeled since the early seventies. Popcorn ceilings and wood paneling surround a hunter-green shag carpet. Paintings of big-eyed girls loom on the walls.

In the middle of the basement sits a cream-colored sofa covered in plastic. The distance from the sofa to the nearest wall, as well as the stark overhead lighting, gives the room the appearance of a black box theater.

Seated on the couch, Francesca clutches Maron's broad shoulders and slurps at his mouth like a baby bird receiving a worm from its mother. The plastic crinkles beneath her as she tries to maneuver her tongue inside his mouth, while Maron turns his head slightly, a gesture that would indicate to anyone but Francesca that he doesn't want this. But Francesca is certain Maron wants this, because this is what boys want. It may even be what she wants, but she is not sure of anything at the moment except that she wants to be with him. Only when Francesca senses Maron closing his mouth, and finds her tongue now licking his lips, does she stop.

"Am I that unpalatable?" Francesca says, looking into his eyes. "It's okay to say yes."

"No, no," Maron says.

"If you want to skip the foreplay, we could just go for it," Francesca replies. "I don't know if I'm ready, but every other girl I know has done it."

"No, no," Maron says again, touching her cheek. "Let's just be together. That's all I want, just to be here with you."

"What, just sitting here?"

"Yes."

"Isn't that what boys say to ugly girls?"

Maron stares at her with genuine alarm. "You're not ugly. You're beautiful."

"Okay, maybe not ugly," Francesca says. "But beautiful is a stretch. You, on the other hand, are ridiculously good-looking, and every single one of the popular girls would trample over my dead body to be here with you right now. But you're with me?"

"Francesca, I've seen a million girls," Maron says, looking deeply into her eyes. "You are truly special. Trust me."

Francesca feels like she must be dreaming to have such a boy looking at her with such eyes and saying such words. But somehow, she can't let the compliment be.

"Wait," she says. "Why don't you want to have sex with me?"

"Because I don't want to rush anything. We've got plenty of time." He pauses. "Actually, there is something I would like you to do. It's a little embarrassing," he says, blushing.

"Sounds kinky," Francesca says. "Try me."

"Would you . . . Would you maybe stroke my hair?"

"What?" Francesca laughs.

"Stroke my hair. Like, you know, pet me?"

"Pet you?" Francesca laughs once again loudly, then, embarrassed that she has embarrassed Maron, covers her mouth. Slowly, she reaches for his hair.

"Like, what?" Francesca says. "Like this?"

Her first stroke is awkward, more like a pat than a pet. But eventually her wrist relaxes, and she begins to enjoy the liquid smoothness of Maron's thick, curly locks. Within a minute, Francesca has closed her eyes and is completely absorbed in the act.

Maron's face gradually relaxes into an expression of serenity. Francesca opens her eyes after a moment and studies his perfect black eyebrows. Maron makes a sound that Francesca will describe later in her journal as a "purr." As the petting continues, Francesca wonders if she has stumbled upon the essence of lovemaking. Not the penetration or the excitement or the fluids or the regret. Just the silent enjoyment of another person's enjoyment.

The young couple's bliss is shattered by a loud knock upstairs. To Francesca, it sounds like the police knocking, but that thought is immediately replaced by another, surer thought that causes her to grab Maron's hair with one hand and her phone with the other.

"No!" she says, looking at her unread messages. "That's my mother; I know it is. Is your mom here?"

"She's out," Maron replies. "Can you let go of my hair?"

"I'm sorry," Francesca says, only now realizing that she is pulling his hair.

She bounds up the winding staircase, turning at the top. Maron jogs up the stairs after her.

"Hey, Mom!" Francesca says breezily as she opens the door. "Sorry, we were downstairs. I had my ringer off. How did you find me? This is Maron."

"Hi, ma'am," Maron says, extending his hand.

"It's a pleasure to meet you, Maron," Sloan says. "May I speak to Francesca outside if you don't mind?"

Francesca, her posture slipping from hopeful to guilty, slinks out the front door. She closes it behind her. She and her mother stand under the porch light.

"I tracked you. I'm sorry," Sloan says. "You never don't respond to texts, and I didn't recognize the location, so I was worried."

"Do I have to be on my phone every second?" Francesca says indignantly. "And since when have you been so concerned about my location?"

"I just got worried. On the other hand, I can see why you shut off your ringer for this one. Nice work."

"Stop talking now please," Francesca says quickly. "You're not going to ask me to leave, are you?"

Sloan pats her daughter on the shoulder. "No, of course not."

A woman's voice is heard in the distance. At first it sounds like shouting, but in a moment it's clear that the woman is singing.

Maron appears in the doorway and hustles onto the porch. "Sorry, I need to . . ." he says before rushing to the driveway.

Ari steps off the street in front of the house, humming a wordless tune. She caresses Maron's cheek when he approaches but then gently shoves away his attempts to support her. She is weaving and clearly intoxicated.

"Hello!" Ari says. As she nears the front porch, she sees Sloan and stops in her tracks. She steps forward and studies Sloan's face for a long time.

"It's you, isn't it?" Ari says, finally.

Sloan lets out a laugh that is half amused, half offended. "I'm sorry, do we know each other?"

Ari sighs and turns to Francesca. "Hello, my dear. Are you and Maron having fun?"

"Mom, it's late," Maron says, taking Ari by the elbow. "I'm going to take you inside."

"Excuse me," Sloan says, stepping forward with the easy aggression that has always amazed both her daughter and her husband. "You seem to know me, so I'm just wondering where we met."

Ari regards the other woman fondly. "We could have been friends," she says. "We should be friends."

"Mom, please, let's just go in," Maron says, guiding his mother toward the door.

Ari breaks free and staggers onto the grass. She drops to her knees on the lawn. As Maron arrives, she reaches back and touches his arm.

"Oh, Maron. We did the right thing, didn't we?"

A few of the neighboring porch lights come on. Maron lifts his mother, not entirely gently, from the lawn and hurries her to the porch.

"It was a pleasure to meet you, ma'am," Maron says to Sloan as he passes by. "Good night, Francesca. I'll talk to you soon."

The front door closes. There is a long silence on the porch.

"Okay, that was not the best thing," Francesca begins. "I think Maron's mom just had too much to drink. She's actually really nice. Whoa, look. I just got a text from Annie. Looks like she's having some kind of crisis with her boyfriend or something. I should go."

"Honey, he's a charming boy," Sloan says, "and I've seen drunk women before. Why do you think she thinks she knows me?"

"I don't know," Francesca says. "I'll be home later. Or I might stay at Annie's. You can track me if you want! I'll text you!" She kisses her mother on the cheek and runs off into the night.

Sloan stands alone in the driveway of Ari's house for a long time, watching the lights go off in the surrounding houses. Only one porch light remains lit. On that porch stands a man with a cane, in silhouette but clearly looking at Sloan.

"Show's over, Pops!" she shouts. The old man responds by shuffling inside his house and turning off the light.

As Sloan heads toward her car, she feels the tingling sensation in her hands she felt the day before. She opens her palms, and for a second time the white lights appear and disappear.

CHAPTER TWENTY-FOUR

Mark Apple paces excitedly in front of Christian's desk, his hair damp with sweat.

"That thing about the mass hysteria was great," Apple says. "What's it called? Conversion disorder? That's awesome. No idea what it means, but nobody else does either, which is perfect. Main thing is there's 'science' behind it, and it's not our fault."

"Conversion disorder and mass hysteria are actually two different things," Christian begins pedantically, quoting his daughter quoting the internet. "Conversion disorder is thought to originate in the amygdala. Whereas mass hysteria is a maladaptive version of the empathy response. Like when one person starts yawning, and other people yawn."

Apple yawns at the mention of yawning.

"Perfect," Apple says. "Main thing is we're done with covens and sex ed, right? Water supply? Cafeteria food? The school's off the hook now, am I right?"

"Not yet, but the blurb the administration sent out has been gaining traction, so that's good," Christian says as Apple continues pacing and sweating. "Mark, are you okay? You seem agitated. And kinda sweaty."

"Well, that's because I have leukemia," Apple says quickly, and then halts. He laughs out loud and stares at the ceiling. "Ha! Well, that wasn't hard!"

Christian sits motionless and open-mouthed in his chair.

"Yeah," Apple says, his head dropping. "I haven't told anyone except Ellen, and there I just said it. You're the first to know. Feel honored? Honestly it was getting old keeping it to myself. Fuck it, yes, I have leukemia."

"Leukemia," Christian repeats the word. "You?"

"Correct," Apple continues. "Aggressive and fast-moving too, apparently. You'd think somebody like you would be more likely to have cancer than me."

"I guess so," Christian says weakly.

"I go to the gym every fucking day for the last twenty years. I drink kale smoothies like Tom Brady. And you"—Apple gestures to Christian without looking at him, as if he can't bear the incongruity—"you don't exercise. It looks from your desk like your primary food source is gummy bears. You're pale as a ghost, you're not obese, but you obviously don't do anything to keep yourself in shape. And yet it's me." Apple's voice breaks. "It's me."

There is a long silence that Christian can't find words to fill. When he finally speaks, his voice wavers. "I've read there are good treatments now," he begins. "Leukemia is not the . . ." He stops before saying the words "death sentence." "It's not what it once was."

"Thirty-five percent," Apple says. "They told me I've got a thirty-five percent chance of beating this. Of course, that number drops if the cancer spreads further."

"My aunt's sister—I guess that makes her my second aunt—"

"Hey, Chris," Apple interrupts him. "I didn't mean to tell you any of this, or maybe I did, because you're a good listener or whatever and I like you. But keep this to yourself. I don't care about people knowing. I just can't deal with the fucking pity. I hate pity. I will say that you should learn not to be so fucking glum all the time. Appreciate what you've got while you have it. Every single minute of life is amazing, even if it's shitty."

"Okay," Christian says.

"But you gotta live that life." Apple clenches his fist as a tear rolls down his cheek. "Enjoy it. And I'll be rooting for you, from down here or up there. Go kick Stu Sherwater's ass and steal that full-time gig from Laura Hartwood."

"Laura is frankly a lot more qualified than me."

"Fuck her," Apple says. "That phony earth-goddess Wonder-Woman flowing-dresses bullshit, it's always bugged me. You deserve that job. And somebody needs to go up if I'm going to go down. Gotta keep the balance in the universe, right?"

"You're not going down," Christian protests. It occurs to him that he's never known anyone his age to die—that his perception of death is like that of a child, something that happens to stooped, gray-haired people, and no one really cries at their funerals.

Apple suddenly pulls Christian from his chair and hugs him. Christian smells the acrid sweat coming from the principal's shirt and wonders if this is what cancer smells like.

"Sherwater's a fucking fridge-head." Apple holds Christian tightly. "Kick his ass."

"Okay," Christian responds.

"Good," Apple says, disengaging. "You're my champion now. And remember, you're going home today loving life—loving it!—because you don't have fucking leukemia. Say it with me."

"I don't have leukemia," Christian says, together with Apple.

"Exactly," Apple says, patting Christian on both shoulders. "You're king of the world, a god among men!"

He then pats Christian once on the cheek and leaves his office.

CHAPTER TWENTY-FIVE

Heads turn as Lenny enters the Glenhaven Unitarian Universalist Church. He strides down the aisle wearing a leather vest, denim shorts, Doc Martens, and various necklaces, all of which terminate in the foot of some woodland animal or another. He smiles and extends his hand warmly to all who will take it.

Multicolored prayer flags hang from the rafters of the sanctuary, while the floor-to-ceiling windows behind the pulpit present a vista that looks like an ad for butter.

The minister, a trim, gray-haired septuagenarian with electric-blue eyes, catches himself gawking at the bizarre figure from the dais. Lenny seats himself with queenlike gentility in one of the pews.

The minister clears his throat. "Welcome to our special afternoon celebration of the life of Alan Vega."

The choir director taps his baton against a music stand.

"We'll begin with Hymn 455," the minister says. "'Never the Same River Twice.'"

The mostly elderly congregation pulls itself to its feet, struggling to page through the hymnals. Lenny rises and, with a hop from one foot to the other, rearranges his genitals beneath his snug denim shorts.

The minister begins to sing, followed by the choir director and, mumbling, most of the congregation:

"You never step into the same river twice.
There is nothing but flow,
As Heraclitus reminded us so long ago . . ."

At the mention of Heraclitus, Lenny nods approvingly. He sings along unmelodically.

"You never step into the same river twice.
There is only the doing, not the knowing.
There is only the being, only the flowing."

Though the hymn is dirgelike, Lenny steps into the aisle and dances. A few of the older ladies smile, but most of the congregation looks worried.

The hymn ends, and the minister bows his head. There is a long silence before he raises his eyes.

"There's a normal phase in child development," the minister begins, pausing for effect. "A period when children ask 'why' all the time. Some of you with children may remember this."

There's a twitter of laughter followed by coughing.

"Why does it rain, Daddy?" the minister continues, using a child's voice. "Well, the clouds get filled with water vapor," he responds in an adult voice. "And when they can't hold any more water, it falls as rain. 'But why is there rain, Daddy?' 'Well, it's part of the water cycle and—listen, how about I make you another blueberry waffle.'"

A louder rumble of laughter rises from the sanctuary. Lenny nudges an elderly man wearing a hearing aid next to him. "Blueberry waffle!" he laughs. "That's a good one!"

The minister avoids looking directly at Lenny, waits for the laughter to subside, then tilts his head pensively to one side. "I always felt that Alan Vega had a childlike spirit," he says, gesturing toward the large photo of the decedent that sits on an easel near the choir. "My questioning, like Alan's, went well past its developmentally appropriate period. It persisted through elementary and middle school, to high school and beyond. As a teenager, I personally felt like I never got good answers to the most basic questions, such as 'Why be good? Why should I care about my neighbor? Why is life valuable? And if the purpose of life is only to generate other humans who fail to get answers to the same questions, why should I bother? Why should there be endless generations of people who don't know why they're here?'"

Among the congregation, there is an impatient shifting of seats. A few of the parishioners smile wanly at their neighbors. Lenny, meanwhile, nods solemnly. "Good questions," he says. "Good questions, all."

"As an adult, can I now say that I've gotten answers that satisfy me?" The minister's voice rises high.

There is another pregnant pause, during which at least one of the congregants begins snoring.

"No," the minister says flatly. "But what I can say is, and Alan would have agreed with me on this, is that I've grown comfortable in the not knowing. I've accepted that while there may very well be an order and a reason for things, I may never find out that order or that reason. And I also have found myself willing to accept that there may be no order or reason at all."

More audible snoring is heard in the room. Lenny, tears streaming down his cheeks, shouts toward the pulpit. "Not true, sir! Don't give up, sir!"

─────────────

Lenny stuffs a donut into his mouth as he stands beneath a paper sign that reads WELCOME, VISITORS. The welcome table is covered with donuts, bagels, and coffee decanters. The minister appears.

"Come here, you!" Lenny says, hugging the minister forcefully. It crosses the minister's mind that the strange fellow might break his ribs.

"Welcome." The minister nods as his color slowly returns. "Is this your first time at a Unitarian church?"

"Naw," Lenny replies, waving his hand, "I've been to hundreds of them. My condolences to Alan and his family. Sounds like a good sort."

"Thank you," the minister says uncertainly.

Lenny steps forward again, close enough that the minister can smell wine on his breath. "I do feel badly though," Lenny says solemnly, "for that little boy who never got the answers to his questions."

"Well . . ." The minister blushes and takes a step back. "I do too, but as I said, those questions may be unanswerable."

"They're not," Lenny says, picking up another donut and offering it to the minister, who declines. Lenny takes a bite of his second donut and chews contemplatively. "The problem with your Unitarian church is that it's just like Christian church, only you've taken God out. You have a pulpit but no cross behind it; you sing hymns, but there's no God in them, just a 'swirling mystery.' And you have a minister who preaches a homily that sounds like it could have been written by Albert Camus."

The minister manages a slight chuckle. "This minister happens to be an unabashed fan of Camus. He was a great humanitarian."

"Perhaps, but where was his hope?" Lenny says indignantly. "He had no hope! No hope at all!"

"Well, I would argue that he encouraged us to find hope in one another and thereby to create a better world."

"That's cooperation," Lenny says, "not hope! People will still go to bed full of doubt and regret and fear every night if they feast on you and Camus."

"I disagree," the reverend says, blushing with some anger. "The Unitarian mission has always been to encourage people to define God on their own terms. There are plenty of churches, nearly all the churches nearby, in fact, where God has human attributes and the promise of a blissful afterlife is spoken of regularly. If that's what you're getting at when you talk about hope. Philosophically speaking, the

Unitarians—and I, certainly—believe that God is greater and more mysterious than we can ever conceive of."

"That's where you're wrong," Lenny says, gesturing with the remains of his powdered donut. "The gods are remarkably boring and predictable. Small-minded and petty even!" As he takes another bite, the powder falls into his beard. He chews for a while and shrugs. "Some gods anyway."

"Some?" the minister laughs.

"Yes, some," Lenny says. "There are stupid gods, jealous gods. Gods who are sick of their work. Gods who aren't half as curious as you were as a child."

"One can't help but wonder who would worship such gods," the minister says, smirking.

"Regular people," Lenny says, his expression firming. "*Regular* people who don't give a rat's ass about deep ontological questions. They just want to fall asleep at night feeling hopeful. That's where your Unitarian religion, and the swirling mystery you've replaced God with, fails. Somewhere along the way, smart people like you decided the *only* questions worth asking were the ones you knew you could never get answers to. This is impossible for the regular person, who only wants to have a good day and sleep well at night. But you moved today to someday and someday to never!"

The minister, whose face has been smoothed into an expression of deep thought, opens his mouth and is about to respond when one of the church elders, a sprightly octogenarian woman in a colorful skirt, shuffles toward Lenny with her hand extended.

"I *so* enjoyed your little dance in the aisles, young man," the woman says, shaking Lenny's hand vigorously. "We need more dancing in the aisles, don't you think, Reverend?"

"We do, Missus Fallon," the minister says, lowering his gaze.

"Are you from another church?" the woman asks Lenny. "We welcome all transplants," she says coquettishly. "Even apostates!"

"I assure you I am not an apostate," Lenny says, kissing the back of her hand. "I am as divine as they come!"

"You certainly are!" the woman says. "Toodle-loo!"

After the old lady leaves, the minister looks seriously at Lenny. "I can't help but think you came here for some other reason than to lecture me about Camus and God."

Lenny nods. "I did. And I don't wish to lecture you. You are obviously a kind and generous person. I came here today to ask if I might hire you to perform a funeral service, for a friend that has passed."

"I'm very sorry to hear that your friend has passed," the reverend says perfunctorily. "But I don't generally do funerals. We prefer celebrations of life, and I only do those for members of our congregation."

"In this case I ask you to make an exception. Even though the gentleman in question is not exactly a friend," Lenny says, "and he has not yet passed. But I do have a date for the funeral, and I will pay you handsomely for your time."

The minister looks at Lenny askance. "You have a date for the funeral of a man who hasn't passed?"

Lenny leans forward and whispers in the minister's ear: "And I can promise you answers for your little child," he says, with a twinkle in his eye. "Promise."

A new gaggle of congregants descends upon the minister. Lenny smiles, backs away, and raises a pretend phone to his ear, mouthing the words "I'll call you."

"This is all the blood I get!"

CHAPTER TWENTY-SIX

Francesca arrives at the Booster Club Crab Feed ostensibly to cover the event for the school's paper and social media, but she is really here to be close to Maron. She politely makes her way past stained cafeteria tables filled with football players and their parents until she sees Maron seated at the far end of a table by himself, peering up at a skylight as if wishing he could escape through it.

Francesca sits on a folding chair in a distant corner, away from Maron. She removes her camera from her bag to indicate her press credentials. She notices that there is surprisingly little conversation going on in the room. The fathers all seem guarded. This strikes her as odd, since the boys must have played football together for years. There's not even the usual chitchat about summer vacations and traffic. Francesca ponders the difference between these silent, burly men and her own father, who is helplessly chatty and who has avoided men like these his whole life. Christian would have died young in caveman times, Francesca thinks, whereas these sturdy men would have flourished.

Six plastic bowls filled with crab sit on a utility table at the head of the room. There are three loaves of bread on an adjacent table and beside them a serrated knife. A metal tub on the floor is filled with ice, canned sodas, and plastic water bottles. Tongs, presumably to serve crab, rest unhygienically atop the beverages.

Scanning the room, Francesca locates Hayden Findlay, who has a purple bruise under his left eye after his fight with Maron. To avoid Hayden's gaze, Francesca raises her camera and wheels it around until her viewfinder lands upon a strange, leathery-faced man with blue eyes who has just entered the room. The man sashays toward Francesca, mugging for the camera and pursing his lips.

"I'm ready for my close-up!"

The man blows a long kiss at the camera as he strikes a bombshell pose, one hand on the back of his head and the other on his hip.

Some of the thick-necked men turn uncomfortably toward the newcomer, who wears billowy pants and a concert T-shirt for someone named GG Allin (Francesca makes a mental note to Google the name). On the man's feet are dusty, surf-looking sandals. His arms are thin but muscular, his age somewhere between forty and fifty. A second, heavier man in jean shorts and a black leather vest follows him, shaking his phone. "It's black, Zagreus," the fat man says, holding the phone toward the thin man. "Does that mean it's dead?"

The thin man shouts, "Maron!" and with arms extended strides across the room. Francesca realizes that this must be Maron's estranged father, Dee.

Dee kisses his son on both cheeks and then, with an emphatic smack, once on the lips. He holds the boy's head in his hands, adoring him. Then, as if a timer set for intimacy just expired, he lets go of Maron and turns toward the assembled guests.

"What's for dinner?" Dee says, rubbing his hands together. He grabs a hunk of crab off the table, deftly cracks open the shell, and begins eating. He turns to a red-faced, wary father and whispers loudly to him, "Do you know if there's some kind of sauce, or are we supposed to eat this like savages?" The man shrugs. Dee chews noisily on his crab, looking from one football father to the next.

"Some party!" Dee continues. "Remember, meat puppets, you get a hundred summers, if you're lucky! It won't kill you to enjoy them.

This place is like a morgue!"

Francesca inadvertently laughs. Dee leaps toward her like Fred Astaire and lands on one knee at her feet. "Hello, my dear," Dee says. "Thank you for laughing at my joke. I was beginning to feel unwelcome."

"You are unwelcome, you piece of shit." Hayden Findlay's father, Mike, rises from his chair and takes two steps toward Dee. "Why don't you do us all a favor, get out of here, and take your prima donna son with you!"

"Prima donna?" Dee rises and approaches Findlay. "Prima donna . . ." Dee strokes his chin, musing. "A prima donna is the primary singer in an opera company if I'm not mistaken. My son is not a prima donna. He's a student and a football player. But perhaps"—Dee looks around the room, grinning—"perhaps *you* are a prima donna?"

"Father!" Maron yells from the far end of the room.

A series of strange expressions passes over Mike Findlay's face—constipation, nausea, fear. He steps forward and, in a fine tenor, begins to sing, to the tune of Verdi's "La Donna e mobile":

"My liver is gone,
But I keep drinking!
My wife doesn't stop me.
She thinks the kids'd be better off
if I were dead."

Mrs. Findlay covers her mouth as her husband's eyes go wide. Dee claps his hands. "Bravo!" he shouts.

"I'm cruel to everyone around me.
I steal from my company.
Cheat clients.
Beat Carla!
Beat my kids!
And I'm impotent!"

Dee slides toward Mrs. Findlay. "At least he's impotent. Silver linings, eh, missus?"

He shuffles toward Hayden Findlay, who is beet-red and fighting back tears.

"Remember you are not your father, darling," Dee says. "My son has made that abundantly clear to me."

"Agrios, let's go," Lenny sighs as he stares at his phone.

Maron appears and shoves his father to the floor. He grabs the serrated knife off the table and slices the back of his arm with it.

"See this, Father?" Maron says as blood drips onto the floor. "This is all the blood I get! When it's gone, I'm dead!" A woman faints in her chair. "I can't wait!"

Francesca rushes toward Maron, peels off her Spartans sweatshirt, and wraps it tightly around his wound.

Dee drops to his knees and begins shuffling on them toward his son. "Oh no, my son!" he cries. "Forgive me!"

"Fuck off!" Maron kicks at his father as Francesca's sweatshirt falls to the floor. "You don't mean it! You're not sorry at all!"

Lenny lifts Dee to his feet. "Let's go, Agrios," he says, exasperated.

"I've tried to be a good father," Dee cries as Lenny pulls him away. "I have. But there's my work!"

"You have no work!" Maron scoffs. "You're a joke!"

"But we share a destiny," Dee blubbers.

"We share nothing!" Maron shouts. "I'm done with your destiny! It's over!"

Lenny drags Dee toward the door.

Maron drops into a chair. There is a long silence. Francesca retrieves the fallen sweatshirt and is about to rewrap Maron's arm when she realizes that the bleeding has stopped.

Maron turns toward Hayden Findlay and sighs.

"Hayden, I came here tonight to apologize. To all of you. You're my teammates. I lost my temper, and I shouldn't have. More than anything, I really want to be a part of this team."

Francesca notices that the wound on Maron's arm has now closed. She also recognizes, with alarm, that she is falling in love with a boy whose problems are much worse than hers.

Netflix and the television explodes.

CHAPTER TWENTY-SEVEN

Christian arrives at Ari's house just before dusk. He stands on the front porch for several minutes, wiping his sweaty palms onto his pants. Finally, he knocks. The front door opens, and Ari appears, wearing blue jeans, a white blouse, and a red-and-white checkered apron. Christian wonders whether she is about to hit him with the wooden spoon she holds high in her right hand.

"Come in!" Ari says excitedly, nearly jumping into the air. "Thank you for coming to our meeting! I have pasta and popcorn and there are chips on the table," she says breathlessly. "Also, I am not drunk. There's baseball on the television. Do you like baseball?"

Christian mutters, "Sure" as he makes his way into the house. He notices the popcorn ceiling and the gaudy spherical tricolored chandelier suspended from it. A cheap replica of Botticelli's *Birth of Venus* sits on the wall above the fireplace. In front of the fireplace stands an easel with some oil paints in a tray, and beside that a ratty recliner with an old cello leaning against it.

"How about Netflix? Do you like Netflix?" Ari says excitedly. "There's a show about a woman who gets murdered, and it's fourteen shows. Can you imagine?"

The baseball game currently playing on the television is deafening.

"Can we turn this down a little?" Christian says, suddenly aware of his lifelong tendency to be grouchy in circumstances where he ought to be—and even is—excited.

Ari quickly shuts off the television, maintaining her perky demeanor. "I used to wonder how people could sit there and watch television all day and night. But now I want to do exactly that: sit and watch television and not move. Will you do that with me? We can watch all fourteen murder shows, and we won't leave until it's over!"

"Sure," Christian says, brightening at the thought of sitting on the couch with Ari.

"Wine?" She pours him a glass and takes a sip from her water glass.

"You're not having any?" Christian says.

"I really shouldn't be drinking right now," Ari replies, frowning. "My body is behaving strangely, and I'd rather be normal."

"Normalcy is something we all crave when we're in crisis," Christian says, immediately ashamed of his habit of producing pat psychological dictums.

"Normalcy," Ari gushes. "I like that! I want to live in a house with normalcy and have normal dinners with normal friends and talk about Netflix and normal things. Do you have a lot of friends?"

"Well, I wouldn't say a lot, but . . ." He looks at the floor, trying to recall a single friend. Mark Apple comes to mind.

"We can make friends together!" Ari looks warmly at Christian.

Meeting her gaze, he feels a twinge of both excitement and fear. She comes closer, and Christian recalls their moment on the landing when she breathed onto his lips and he felt as though time had stopped.

"I want to apologize for last night," Ari says. "I should not be getting drunk and throwing up in people's apartments."

"We've all been there," Christian responds, resigned now to becoming a cliché-generating machine.

"Or assaulting people." Ari laughs.

"That was not assault," Christian responds fervently. "Whatever happened between us, or didn't, it was certainly consenting. It's just that I have . . . certain issues going on that I mentioned. But it's only temporary."

"It's fine," Ari says. "We don't need to have sex."

"We don't?" Christian says as his heart starts to race.

A timer goes off, and Ari rushes into the kitchen. "The noodles are ready!"

Christian grits his teeth. He steps forward stiffly, his voice high.

"At the risk of oversharing," he begins, "I have, on many occasions, found myself being the guy who women tell their problems to but don't want to have sex with. It's a pattern in my life, always winding up in the friend zone." Christian struggles with whether to continue and then does. "I'm just saying that when you say, 'We don't need to have sex,' it triggers uncomfortable feelings in me, and so I just needed to share that."

"That's not what I meant at all." Ari moves toward Christian and grabs him by the shoulders. "I would have sex with you exactly when you're ready to have sex with me," she says. "I like sex. Do you understand? You and me." She makes the finger-in-the-hole gesture with her hands. "All night."

Christian blushes. As Ari moves happily back into the kitchen, he feels an urge to drop to his knees in gratitude.

"But I'm also talking about having dinner with someone you actually like," Ari continues blithely, stirring the sauce. "Someone you can talk to. Someone you know is not going to ruin an evening because he's a jerk."

"Jerks can be exciting though, can't they?" Christian asks, aware that he's fishing for reassurance that Ari could like an unexciting man like him.

"Exciting gets old."

"Exciting, by definition, should never get old," Christian opines. "I'm guessing that you think your ex-husband is a jerk. Or shouldn't we talk about him this early in the evening?"

"Let's talk about whatever comes up," Ari says brightly.

Christian pauses and then leans on the island counter. "So, was he always a jerk? Or did he used to be nice?"

Ari stops stirring the sauce. "That's a good question." She ponders. "Yes, I would say that he was always a jerk. But he used to be a useful jerk. He believed in what he did. He was proud of his work, and I was too. Now he's just a horrible and cynical old jerk. Okay, tell me something about your marriage now."

"What do you want to know?" Christian asks uncertainly.

"How long did it take for your marriage to grow . . . I don't know, old?"

"Hmm," Christian mutters. "I don't think my marriage was ever exactly young. Looking back, it all seemed more like a mature transaction, like a merger and acquisition."

"All marriages are deals," Ari says flatly.

"I guess so," Christian says. "But at the beginning, at least, it should feel like something other than a deal. I know marriages can't have endless passionate love, but maybe they can have endless regular love at least."

"Endless regular love," Ari says. "I like that."

The house groans, and the chandelier in the living room plummets to the floor with an immense thud.

Ari yells, curses in Greek, then steps forward and kicks at the chandelier.

"Fuck off!"

She grabs Christian and leads him past the broken glass to the couch. "C'mon. Let's sit down and watch our Netflix show."

"Why did that fall?" Christian shrieks. "What happened to that chandelier? That didn't feel like an earthquake. Is the ceiling collapsing? We're not going to clean that up?"

"No!" Ari snarls. "We're going to sit and watch our murder show and not worry about the chandelier! And I'm going to lean my head on your shoulder, and we're going to have a date, and we're not going to worry about anything."

Ari shoves Christian down onto the couch and slams her head upon his shoulder. For a long while Christian stares ahead at the muted baseball game. He can hear Ari breathing heavily and feel, through her temple, her pulse racing against his shoulder.

Gently, he lifts his arm, and she snuggles closer to him, tucking her knees into a fetal position. She sighs and relaxes. It occurs to Christian then that, for the first time in decades, he may possibly be taking the first few steps toward having something he might credibly call a girlfriend. A girlfriend who likes him not just despite his problems but perhaps because of them.

"Netflix murder, please?" Ari says from Christian's chest.

Christian picks up the remote, presses a button, and the television explodes. Christian feels tiny bits of glass land right above his shoes. All the lights in the house go out.

"Malaga pusti Asto diallo!" Ari jumps up and begins screaming in the dark. She lets out one loud, five-second howl. Christian hears her rush into the kitchen and grab what sounds like car keys.

"I have to go," Ari says in the dark, and then Christian feels a kiss on his cheek. "I'll call you."

Before he can respond, she is out the front door. He rises from the sofa and steps out onto the front porch, just in time to see Ari jerk her car into the reverse and screech away down the street.

Christian turns back into the house and, through the dark, surveys the damage. He pads into the kitchen, searching for a broom and dustpan, when suddenly he hears the tinny sound of music.

The song is Led Zeppelin's "Whole Lotta Love," and it seems to Christian to be coming from nowhere and everywhere at once. When his phone pings, Christian jumps.

He races out of the house and reads a text from his daughter.

I'M AT HUBCAPS. MEET ME THERE?

CHAPTER TWENTY-EIGHT

"His father is such an asshole!" Francesca says, gesturing with a french fry as she sits across from her father at HubCaps, an aging burger joint littered with fifties decor.

"Although I do admit," she continues, "I felt a little sorry for the guy at the end, when he got sad about Maron. But the mind-trick thing he did on Hayden Findlay's dad was insane! I asked Maron about it, but he didn't want to talk about it. I swear to God, his father is some kind of witch. What I don't understand is why Maron wants to be part of the football team anyway. I mean, yeah, he's great, but he'd be great at anything. And they're such jerks—Hayden Findlay, Tim Knight, all of them."

Christian nods with interest. He has always held the belief that when it comes to children, there is no such thing as allowing too much speech. As Francesca keeps talking, Christian recalls the days when he and Francesca and Sloan came to HubCaps as a family. Christian would listen to Francesca talk about her school day while Sloan read emails on her phone. The mini jukeboxes at the booths worked then. HubCaps' descent into disrepair has pained Christian. The torn banquettes and broken tiles represent to him the loss of the joy and innocence he imagines Francesca must have felt as a child and that he once felt as a father.

"But of course, when Maron cut himself, I realized how much

pain he's in and what it must be like having a father like that. But his family's not him. That's what I was telling him, just like I'm not yours and Mom's shitty marriage."

Christian starts to defend . . . which? Himself? His marriage? "Be careful," he says finally. "I know Maron's in pain, but a boy who's cutting himself needs professional help, and it's also a major red flag relationship-wise."

"He did it just to get back at his father," Francesca counters angrily, "not as an act of self-hatred, and besides, who cares about red flags? I mean, all anybody ever does around here is pretend they don't have red flags. Everyone is constantly bleaching their flags."

"Your mother and I haven't forced you to bleach your flags, have we?" Christian says, slurping on his malted milkshake.

"No. But I still feel like a red-flag person. That's how everybody sees me. Actually, I'm not even a red flag; that makes me sound exciting and dangerous. I'm just a shit-brown flag."

Christian is formulating a response to the shit-brown flag comment when he spots Ari walking on the other side of the street with women he recognizes as members of the bunco crowd. He starts to call her name but stops himself, wondering why Ari would have left him only to meet up with friends.

———————

Inside Residual Sugar, a narrow, dimly lit wine bar, Ari fishes through her purse, looking for a tampon. She is not sure if she is leaking, but then she is so unsure of most of her bodily functions lately that she wants to be prepared.

"It's auto-flashing, ugh!" says Brittany May, the fitness mom, as she looks at the cell phone fastened to an extension pole in front of her. "That light makes me look ancient. Here, let's get one with Man-bun the bartender in the background."

"Brittany, we just got here," Jenny Templeton says. "Shouldn't we have the fun first before we document it?"

"I only get out once a month. I have to prove it!" Brittany says, laughing. "Hey, Man-bun!" she yells to the twenty-something bartender. "Can you get behind us and raise a couple of bottles? New girl, get in here!" Brittany shouts to Ari. "Pix or it didn't happen!"

"Coming!" Ari says, stowing her purse under the bar. She ducks under the selfie stick, and Brittany takes the picture, flashing a smile so broad and clenched that it draws giggles from some of the younger patrons.

"Done!" Brittany says with relief. "Now we can have the fun." She turns toward Ari and looks her up and down. "God, you just look flat-out ageless," Brittany says. "Isn't she beautiful?" She appeals to the other women for confirmation. "How old are you, anyway?"

"Oh, I'm about your age," says Ari, smiling.

"Good one," Brittany says, turning to Jenny. "She's a good one."

───────────

One of HubCaps' few working jukeboxes grinds to life at a nearby table, playing "Earth Angel," as Christian watches Francesca thread her way back from the restroom. Her movements have always brought a smile to his face, and even her increasingly adult features haven't robbed her of her childish gait. Christian loves his daughter more than ever now, though he discerns a new neediness to his love. He recalls Ari's question about friends and wonders whether his daughter might be his only real friend.

"Shall we get ice cream?" Francesca says. "Two doors down. You're buying?"

───────────

"Daughter of Minos!"

A commotion at the front door of Residual Sugar causes the bunco women to turn their heads.

Brittany whispers in Ari's ear, "Honey, there's a hot dude at the door looking right at you."

Dee saunters in, grinning broadly as he raises a large ceramic vase. "I brought wine!" He jiggles the chipped, ancient-looking vase with paintings of goddesses and bulls on it. "Look, ladies," he says, approaching Ari and her friends. He points at a female figure on the vase. "This is your friend, right here, riding the bull. She hasn't changed a bit. Bacchantes, let me pour you a glass."

Ari steps forward. "Leave now."

"C'mon, one drink!" Dee says.

Ari grabs the vase from Dee's hands and smashes it to the ground.

The entire bar falls silent. Dee scratches his forehead, then turns and faces the gawking patrons.

"That was a very old jug," Dee says. "But then she"—he gestures toward Ari with a smile—"is a very old woman."

Brittany spits out her drink. "Whoa! Is this your ex?"

Ari shoves Dee and heads for the door, but Dee grabs her firmly by the arm.

"Introduce me to your new friends," he says, wheeling her around. He walks past each of Ari's friends, looking them up and down, acting like a judge in the Westminster Dog Show.

With surprising force for a woman her size, Ari wrests her arm from Dee's grasp and throws him against the bar. The bunco women gasp. Dee rights himself, then hops up into a seated position on the bar and downs the nearest glass of wine.

"Twenty dollars a glass for this urine?" he says. Then Dee snaps his fingers, and the bulbs in all the light fixtures explode. The patrons gasp as the bar goes dark.

―――――――――――

At the ice cream shop next door to HubCaps, Christian yawns and starts to nod off, still holding his milkshake. Francesca now sits with a female classmate at an adjacent table. Her spontaneous social engagements are painfully rare, and Christian can tell from her body language that she is in a high state of excitement.

Christian's eyes have drifted closed when he hears shouts coming from the street.

"Thunderer! VoHe!"

Christian turns and sees Heather Templeton's mother, Jenny, running down the opposite sidewalk, shirtless in her bra. She laughs and pumps her fist before swatting a passing UPS man in the ass.

"Thunderer! Thunderer!"

Ten yards behind Jenny are Shelley Beane, Tina Lowry, Grace Murphy, and Brittany May, all in their bras and all laughing and shouting. Grace Murphy begins ululating, and the others join in, their heads raised like wolves howling at the moon.

Francesca rushes to her father's side. "Dad," she says, gazing open-mouthed. "That's the sound the cheerleaders were making at Lime Ridge."

Christian stands and spots Ari and Dee arguing at an adjacent street corner. Hopping down the steps of the ice cream shop, he runs into the street, vaguely aware with each step that it may be not in his best interest to take another.

"Dad!" Francesca shouts after her father.

———

Christian arrives breathless at the street corner. "I realize she's your wife, or your ex-wife," he begins. "But I think the lady wants to be left alone!"

Dee turns to Christian and smiles like a proud father. "There he is! What a specimen! Here, let me look at you!" He grabs Christian by the shoulders, spins him to one side, and looks him up and down. "He is definitely human, *all too* human," he says, turning to Ari, "as our friend Nietzsche used to say."

"Just leave her alone, please!" Christian yells.

"First of all, don't say please," Dee sighs with exasperation. "Try 'Let her go or I'll pluck your eyeballs out, you loathsome pig-fucker.' No?"

Ari steps forward, kicks Dee in the groin, and then storms off down the sidewalk, cursing in her native language. At that moment, all five of the bunco women appear and join hands in a circle around Dee and Christian. They begin to dance and chant:

"Thunderer! Thunderer! VoHe! VoHe!"

Purple clouds roll in from the east as thunder rumbles overhead. Christian tries to exit the circle, but the women hold him in with their arms. Dee pulls Christian into a ballroom dance pose and sashays him back and forth, muttering the same Led Zeppelin tune: "You need cooling. Baby, I ain't fooling."

Raindrops fall. The women continue to chant. The cacophony created by the two songs renders Christian dizzy.

"VoHe! VoHe! VoHe! VoHe!"

Dee leans close and whispers into Christian's ear: "Don't worry, rock star. I'm going to give you everything you want."

"What?" Christian says.

"The Hammer of the Gods. Everything you've always wanted. And more."

"Hammer of the Gods?" Christian shrieks.

"You just need to give me one thing in return," Dee continues as they dance. "One little thing." He places his cheek on Christian's shoulder. "Do you want to know what that one thing is?"

"What?" Christian says mindlessly. "What do you want?"

"Stay away from my wife."

"But I like your wife," Christian hears himself saying.

"Of course you do," Dee says, raising his head. "That's why it's a deal. You give up something to get something." He pulls Christian close again. "Don't worry, there will be plenty of other women for you. Starting with these women." Dee twirls Christian toward the bunco women.

The women cover Christian like a blanket. Brittany May rubs her breasts along his forearm as Tina Lowry and Jenny Templeton draw their fingertips up and down his back. Grace Murphy gently kisses the lobe of Christian's ear. For the first time in months, he feels warmth in his genital area.

"How does that feel?" Dee says.

Christian can no longer see him, and Christian wonders if Dee's voice might be only in his head.

"Do we have a deal?"

As his penis grows firmer, Christian feels a response to Dee's question rising from his loins. He clenches his teeth and opens his mouth.

"Yes!" Christian shouts.

"Yes, what?" Dee appears inside the circle.

"Yes!"

"You agree to stay away from Ari?"

"Yes!" Christian shouts again.

Dee kisses Christian with a smack on the lips and then ducks out of the circle. The bunco women once again descend upon Christian, stroking and kissing him.

A whole lotta love.

CHAPTER TWENTY-NINE

Christian struggles to open his eyes, which are sticky. He perceives daylight pushing through the curtain of his bedroom window.

Christian first senses and then sees a body beside him and turned away under the covers. Holding his breath, he scans the room. There is a blouse flung over a standing lamp, a pair of panties on the dresser. A second pair of panties is draped over the neck of his guitar.

"Two pairs of panties?" Christian mutters aloud. The body stirs beside him. He studies the back of the woman's head. From the hair color and shape, he can tell that it is neither Sloan nor Ari, the only two women he could imagine being in bed with him.

Christian lets out his breath quietly as he turns to face the ceiling. He tries to recall who this person might be. He tries to recall anything from the previous night. He finds he has no memories after the exchange with Dee on the street.

The woman next to him stirs, rolls over, and blinks at him.

It's Brittany May, Tessa's mother. Her eyeliner is streaked. Her nose seems larger than Christian remembers it from the few encounters he's had with her over the years. Brittany stares at him for a long time. Christian braces for expressions of regret or disgust, but none appear. Instead, Brittany laughs and pulls the sheet over her head. "Oh my god!" she says.

"Hi," Christian begins, extending his right hand like a flipper from his rib cage. "You're Tessa's mom, right?"

Brittany answers through the sheet. "Yep, I'm Tessa's mom!"

"Tessa went to the jazz competition in Irvine if I recall," Christian begins. "And . . . she plays field hockey."

Brittany removes the sheet from her face. "Correct!"

"I'm Tessa's guidance counselor," Christian continues, fighting the impulse to once again extend his hand. "I have L through Z, and Ms. Hartwood has A through K, and Tessa is M, so . . ."

Brittany looks at Christian directly. "Do you not remember what happened last night?"

"I remember," Christian says faintly, not remembering at all. "Something . . ."

"I just want to know what kind of man comes three times and stays hard?" Brittany says. "Seriously, how is that possible? Do you just have a constant hard-on?" She pulls back the covers.

Christian's throat seizes as he beholds his erect penis. It looks huge and alien. For a moment, he feels that he must be looking at someone else's penis, or that perhaps he's become another person and he's looking at that person's penis. Christian pulls the sheet back over himself.

"You should register that thing as a lethal weapon." Brittany laughs at the ceiling.

"God. Does that mean we . . . ?"

"Are you kidding? Yes, we definitely! At least four times!"

"Four times!" Christian feels a rush of energy from his heart to his pelvis. He feels his penis grow even harder.

"You don't remember?" Brittany says. "We walked from downtown. Danced, more like." She turns to Christian, with sudden emotion in her eyes. "It was actually a lot of fun. It was like being a teenager again. The moon was out. We were singing stupid eighties songs. You knew all the lyrics."

"I like eighties songs," Christian says mechanically.

"And then we came here." Brittany looks at Christian. "We were chasing each other around the apartment."

"Chasing?" Christian says.

"Yeah," Brittany says. "Jenny and you and Tina and me. We were playing tag. And then somehow that just morphed into having sex. I don't even remember how."

"Savannah's mom was here?"

"You don't remember?" Brittany repeats, looking at Christian incredulously. "You had sex with her for at least twenty minutes. It got so steamy in here I had to open a window. Tina got sick and left. I mean, I felt strange too. We all did. The whole night, I felt like I was dreaming or on an amusement ride, which was fun, but I also felt like I might throw up."

Christian squints at her. "Do you feel sick now?"

"No." Brittany looks at him for confirmation. "Do you?"

He stares at the ceiling. "No."

"It's crazy that you don't remember any of it. Last night, it was just like I always wanted sex to be. No bullshit, no ego, just . . . fun. Honestly, I'm getting wet just thinking about it." Brittany reaches for Christian's erection. "Can we . . . ?"

Christian's eyes go wide. "No! You're married!"

"I know, but we already did it," Brittany says, pulling back the sheet. "What does one more time matter? Come on, this is never going to happen again. My life is so boring!"

Christian feels another surge of energy in his pelvis as Brittany climbs on top of him. He raises his hands politely in front of Brittany's breasts, without touching them, as if to protect her in case she should fall.

As Brittany begins to ride him, Christian feels his entire body relax. The muscles in his neck, jaw, and forehead soften. A wave of pleasure rises from his belly and crests in his mind, spraying stray images and sounds from the previous night: laughter, hair, skin, sweat. Without thinking, he grabs Brittany's thighs and then her ass. He thrusts his pelvis upward in rhythm with Brittany's movements.

Suddenly, Led Zeppelin's "Whole Lotta Love" rises from within the room. Christian lifts his head from the pillow and strains to discern the source of the music, a move which causes his penis to plunge deeper inside Brittany, who moans in response.

The song grows in volume until it reaches the portion where Robert Plant shrieks acapella:

"Waaaaay down inside . . .
Honey, you need it . . ."

The guitar chords follow, and Plant now wails wordlessly.

"Ahhhhhhhhhhhhhhhhh . . ."

Brittany's moans synchronize with the voice of Robert Plant. In a moment, Brittany, Christian, and the song all climax at once.

Brittany lifts herself off Christian and flops onto her back. The music has stopped, and the room falls silent.

"Did you hear that music?" Christian says.

"What music?" Brittany says, rolling toward him. She laughs as her body shudders beneath the sheets. "God, I feel like I'm still coming. This has to be the last time. Otherwise, we have to keep doing it. Look at you; you're still hard. You're like a sex god."

"A what?" Christian says.

Brittany rolls off the bed. She grabs her panties from the neck of the guitar, slips them on, and then puts on her black dress. "Jenny just texted to see if I'm still here," she says, looking at her phone. "Not answering that."

"Jenny's Kaden's mom, right?" Christian says. "Kaden plays lacrosse?"

"Yes. Kaden plays lacrosse. And my daughter plays field hockey and went to the jazz competition. And Jenny Templeton is Savannah's mom."

Brittany grabs her purse and moves toward the door.

"You definitely know your students, Christian," she says, smiling and cocking her head. "And now you know their moms."

After Brittany leaves, Christian grabs his phone from his nightstand. He writes and then deletes the following text to Ari: ARI, ARE YOU OKAY?

Christian hops out of bed, moves into his living room, and stands naked in front of his floor mirror, looking at his erection. On the floor lies the tennis ball he has been using to improve his throwing motion. He raises the ball and throws it as hard as he can against the wall. The ball hits the wall with a loud smack and bounces back to him at high speed. Christian checks his throwing motion in the mirror, steps forward again, and throws. The ball carroms off three walls before knocking over a beer bottle on his kitchen table.

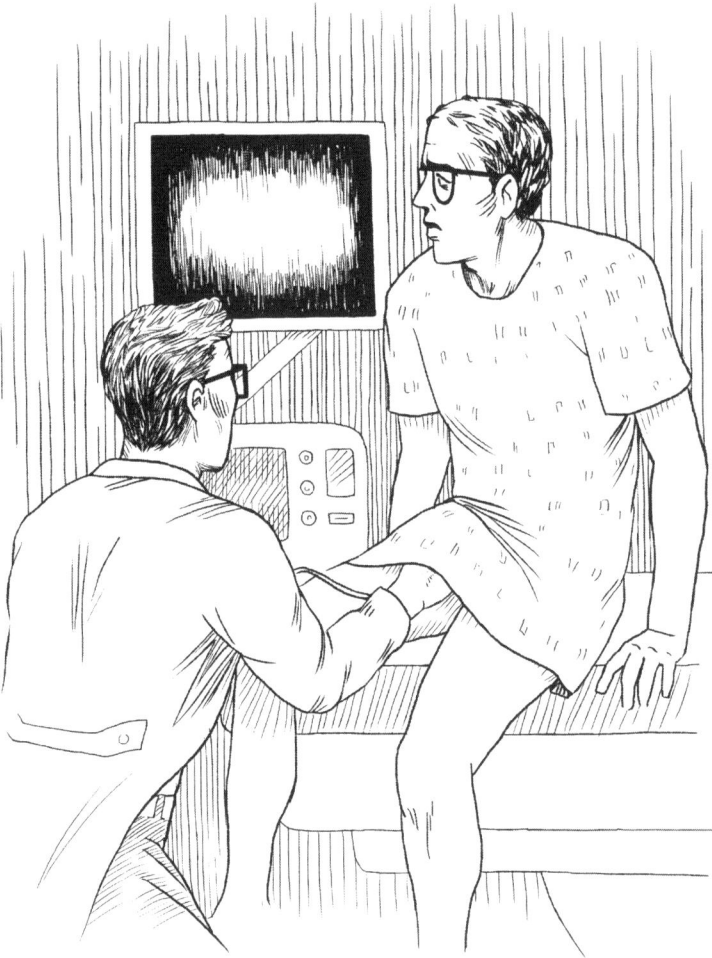

"Forgive me for stroking your penis.
It's an occupational hazard."

CHAPTER THIRTY

"Forgive me for stroking your penis. It's an occupational hazard."
Urologist Kevin Fuchs slathers Christian's penis with gel.
"I'm sure the irony is not lost on either of us," Fuchs continues, "that the last time you came in you couldn't get an erection, and now you can't get rid of one."

"Nope," Christian sighs. "Irony not lost. Irony pretty clear."

"I don't mean to make light of it. Priapism can be a serious and painful condition," Fuchs says, looking at a nearby monitor.

"The internet says priapism is supposed to hurt," Christian says. "But this doesn't hurt. In fact, overall I feel really good physically. Look." He raises himself off the exam table like a gymnast on a pommel horse.

"Very nice," Fuchs replies, moving the sonogram wand across Christian's penis. "Once we find out whether you have nonischemic priapism or ischemic priapism, we'll know a lot more. How long have you been erect for now?"

Christian looks at his watch. "Twelve . . . sixteen hours?"

"And how many orgasms during that time?"

"Five? Maybe six?"

"Busy man!" Fuchs chuckles. He flips another switch on a monitor. Christian looks slack-jawed at the sonogram, which shows a warbling blob of whiteness that he guesses must be the inside of his penis.

"What this little wand is doing," Fuchs begins pedantically, "is bouncing high-frequency sound waves off the red blood cells in your penis. What we're trying to determine"—he slides the device deep underneath Christian's penis, causing him to grunt—"is whether these little buggers are moving in there or whether they're trapped in an ischemic dam. Picture beavers building a log jam."

"Yes," Christian interjects. "I know what a dam is. You want to know if there's blockage or not."

"Correct," Fuchs says. He peers intently at the screen. "And it looks to me, as I suspected, that there is no blockage, meaning . . ."

The doctor rises to his feet and stuffs the ultrasound wand into its holster. He takes off his exam gloves and tosses them into the waste bin.

"Meaning?" Christian says finally.

"Meaning you aren't ischemic," Fuchs replies. "So there is no risk, at least currently, of tissue damage, which is good news."

"So, what's wrong with me?"

"I don't know."

"When will it go away?"

"Eventually."

"When?"

"Well, we're not clear on the etiology, so it's hard to know what course it will take." Fuchs sits on the edge of his desk. "You mentioned that you were out on the street last night when it started, and there was some kind of argument."

"Not an argument." Christian searches for the right term. "Just a bizarre . . . exchange."

"And was this exchange traumatic or exciting somehow in a sexual way?"

"Well, a man kissed me on the lips. It was inappropriate, but it certainly wasn't exciting, and I don't think it was traumatic."

Fuchs replies gently, "Is it possible that this kiss aroused a . . . latent desire that perhaps you had been blocking?"

"No," Christian snorts. "There was no latent desire. Nothing was aroused."

"Yet you said your erection began around the time of this kiss." Fuchs narrows his eyes.

Christian sighs. "It actually began when these women were stroking me."

"Women were stroking you on the street?"

"I think the guy who kissed me gave these women some kind of roofie. And then he gave me some drug, somehow. I don't know—like a Viagra roofie if there is such a thing." Christian sighs again at the absurdity. "Then he said he was going to give me the Hammer, and then I had an erection."

"The Hammer?" Fuchs squints over his red glasses.

"The terrible part of it," Christian continues, now lost in recollection, "is that I don't remember anything after that, and then I learn this morning that I had sex with two women. Or three."

Fuchs blushes. "You're not sure how many women you had sex with?"

"And I have all this weird energy today. I threw a tennis ball really well, and I usually can't throw."

"And with these three women, you had orgasms each time?"

"I think so," Christian says. "But my penis never went soft. It just stayed hard after, like it is now. Doctor, I can't go out in public like this."

Fuchs nods for a long while and says finally, "I think the first thing we need to do is to give this thing time. If it doesn't resolve soon, we'll consider alternative treatments—if it continues beyond, say, two or three weeks."

"Three weeks!"

"There is a gel we can inject," Fuchs says. "And there are surgeries."

"No surgeries!"

"That's why we watch and wait."

Christian hops off the table and presses down on his erection. "I work at a high school. I can't go to work every day with a permanent erection!"

"Not permanent," Fuchs raises a finger.

"I can't go to work with any erection!"

Fuchs nods. "Do you have any PTO you can take for a couple of weeks?"

"I get paid by the hour, Doctor," Christian says. "There is no PTO. The only way for me to get time off is to quit. And I am this close to getting a full-time job so I can have real benefits and stop taking my ex-wife's money."

"I can give you some medication that may help a little with the erection and will definitely help with your anxiety."

"I don't have anxiety," Christian says. "I just need this to go away."

"Well, I'll write you the prescription and you can decide. I almost forgot. Look what I got!" He picks up a box of animal crackers from his desk and tosses it to Christian. "There's plenty more where that came from." He winks. "My secretary, Mrs. Wentworth, just arrived, and there's a big box under her desk. Ask her for some on your way out." Fuchs looks at his watch. "I have a lunch appointment."

At the door, Fuchs turns and squints. "I was in a threesome once, but everyone was too polite, and no one could relax. We had to give up on it. Oh well. Youth."

After Fuchs leaves the room, Christian stuffs a fistful of animal crackers into his mouth, removes his exam gown, and, with difficulty, pulls his pants up over his erection. Standing in front of the mirror shirtless, he flexes his muscles. He notes that even though he doesn't *look* stronger, he feels stronger.

Slipping on the trench coat he wore to cover his erection, Christian fishes in his pocket, pulls out his phone, and texts Ari.

CAN WE FINISH THAT DINNER WE STARTED? CRAZY NIGHT, SORRY I MISSED YOU.

As he sends his text, a new text arrives from Brittany May: SORRY, I LIED ABOUT IT BEING THE LAST TIME! I WANT MORE! (EGGPLANT EMOJI, LOOPY FACE)

There's a knock at the door, and a buxom woman with bleached-blond hair enters the room. She wears a nurse's uniform.

"I'm sorry," Christian says. "I'll be out in a moment."

"Don't leave," the woman says in a sultry voice. "The doctor asked me to take care of you."

"You're not Mrs. Wentworth," Christian replies.

"You need cooling.
Baby, I'm not fooling."

"Do you hear that music?" Christian leaps upon a nearby chair to inspect the HVAC vent in the ceiling. " Is it coming from the vent?" he says, looking down at the nurse.

"You need cooling," the woman says flatly as she takes off her lab coat.

"Where's Mrs. Wentworth?"

Christian hops down from the chair and feverishly searches the room for the source of the music.

"Way down inside," the nurse continues, in sync with Robert Plant. She removes her blouse and grabs Christian by the lapel of his trench coat. "Honey, you need it."

"What I need is Mrs. Wentworth to schedule my next urology appointment. What are you doing?" He grabs the woman's hand.

"I'm going to give you my love," the nurse says. "I'm going to give you every inch of my love."

"No, you're not," Christian says.

"You're sexy and a Wilhelm Reich scholar," the woman says, grabbing onto him. "You help teenagers in crisis. You got twelve hundred the first time you took the SAT and nearly a fourteen hundred the second time."

"How do you know this?" Christian cries.

The woman presses herself against him and kisses him. His penis gets harder as his mind goes soft. Delirious, he pulls the woman close. The nurse moans with pleasure.

"Wait a minute!" Christian jumps back. "We can't do this. I don't know you. I have to go."

He rushes out the door.

"I need a man who can explain
Reich's theory of armoring!"

CHAPTER THIRTY-ONE

Christian hobbles along the sidewalk, pressing down on his erection. A car zooms past as he wanders blindly through an intersection. Rounding the corner onto the street where his car is parked, he runs headlong into a woman in a bridal gown, knocking her to the curb.

"Oh my gosh, miss," Christian says, extending his hand. "Are you okay?"

The bride pulls Christian down onto the curb beside her. "No," she says tearfully. "I'm supposed to get married today."

Once again, "Whole Lotta Love" starts to play. Christian jumps to his feet and rushes back and forth along the sidewalk, determined to discover where the music is coming from.

"But my fiancé," the woman continues, grabbing Christian's arm and pulling him back down to the curb, "he can't satisfy me the way I need to be satisfied. Even Father O'Rourke can't satisfy me."

"O'Rourke?" Christian says with alarm, recognizing the name of the preacher in his favorite porn video.

"No man can satisfy me," the bride continues tearfully. "The pizza man can't satisfy me. The plumber can't satisfy me. The pool boy can't satisfy me. I need a man who can explain Reich's theory of armoring, who helps teenagers in crisis, who scored over twelve hundred the first time he took the SAT and nearly fourteen hundred the second. A man who is the best singer at Tuesday-night karaoke."

The woman slides her hand under Christian's trench coat, and he leaps up.

"No! Who are you? How do you know about me? Who sent you here?"

As Christian races away, he turns to see the woman extending her arms toward him like a distraught heroine from a nineteenth-century novel.

═══════════════

Christian reaches his apartment and opens the front door to find another woman leaning seductively against his kitchen counter. She wears a tool belt, hot pants, high-heeled boots, and a yellow construction helmet.

"Who are you?" Christian says. "How did you get in here?"

"I'm the plumber," the woman says flatly. "I'm here to drain your pipe."

As Robert Plant begins his wailing, Christian rushes toward his kitchen, picks up a Bluetooth speaker, shakes it, and then throws it at the floor. He turns to the woman. "How did you get in here? Who let you in?"

"You need cooling," the woman says in sync with the music as she approaches Christian. "Baby, I ain't fooling."

"Did a man called Dee let you in—a long-haired man?" Christian cries. "Did he pay you to come here?"

"Explain Reich's theories of the function of the orgasm to me," the plumber says, reaching for Christian's crotch. "Tell me about orgone accumulators and cloudbusters."

"Listen to me!" Christian grabs the woman's hand. "I don't know who you are, but you're under the influence of some kind of drug right now! Do you even know what you're saying?"

"I want to give you my love," the woman says. "I want to give you every inch of my love."

"The guy has long hair," Christian continues. "Dresses like a hippie-surfer freak, flip-flops, tank top. He paid you to come here, right?"

The woman places her index finger to her lips and gently shoves Christian toward the sofa. "Shh. You need to relax."

"What's happening?" Christian says as his legs go weak. He falls back onto the sofa. "Why do I feel dizzy? Did you give me something?"

"Relax," the woman whispers. "Pleasure is the point. Grab the Hammer, Christian."

The Hammer of the Gods.

CHAPTER THIRTY-TWO

Christian feels a hand strike his cheek. He awakens to find himself in the back seat of his own car, speeding down the freeway. Beside him, Dee fumbles with the penis pump Christian purchased and which until recently was sitting unopened on his kitchen table.

"How does this thing work?" Dee says, turning the penis pump over in his hands. "Is it like a bicycle pump?" He leans toward the gray-bearded man driving Christian's car. "You can't pump a penis, can you, Lenny? It's not a balloon."

Christian clutches the driver's seat headrest. "Who are you? Why are you driving my car?"

"I'm Lenny," Lenny says, giving Christian a friendly finger wave in the rearview mirror. "And I'm driving because you were sleeping."

"How did I get here?" Christian says to Dee.

"Tell me about our deal," Dee says. "How is it progressing?"

"What deal?"

"What deal?" Dee laughs toward Lenny. "The deal you just made with me to stay away from my wife."

"I never made a deal with you," Christian says.

"I told you, Agrios," Lenny says. "Get it in writing. That's what the lawyers say."

Dee opens Christian's window and throws the penis pump onto the freeway. He frowns at Christian. "I knew I should have consulted your lawyer wife on this."

"My wife?" Christian says.

"Walk me through your wedding night with Sloan," Dee says brightly. "You say the vows? She takes the ring? Throws the bouquet? And then, after the cake has been cut and presents opened, the two of you go back to your room in Cancún. And she actually . . . with you?" Dee shivers and looks at Lenny. "It's unimaginable."

"How do you know we were in Cancún?" Christian says angrily. "What happened last night? What did you do to me? Who are all these women you're sending to my house?"

Dee replies, "Just remember that you chose to sleep with Ari's best friends *the same night* after your first date with her. That level of betrayal is frankly shocking. At this point it may hardly matter whether you keep our deal. Ari is kind of an old-world girl, and sleeping around is not the way to win her; trust me."

"What did you do to me?" Christian says. "Why do I have this erection I can't get rid of?"

"Silenus," Dee says, leaning toward Lenny, "have you ever heard an impotent man complain about getting an erection?" Dee turns to Christian. "What would Wilhelm Reich say?"

Christian feels dizzy at the mention of his hero. "How do you know about Reich?"

"He's an old friend. *Was*, until they killed him. Lenny, isn't it awful that humans always kill their saviors?"

"They don't kill all of them," Lenny says, grinning. "*You're* still alive."

Christian looks down and sees that he's dressed in his fancy, gold-sequin glam-rock costume, including his extra-special, once-a-year-only karaoke platform shoes.

"Why am I wearing this? I don't remember putting this on. Where are we going?" Christian cries.

The car screeches into the parking lot of Retro Junkie and comes to a halt.

Lenny turns around and hands Christian a leather flask.

"Drink this," Lenny says.

"I'm not drinking that!" Christian shouts.

Dee grabs the flask with one hand, squeezes Christian's mouth open with the other, and pours the drink down his throat. Christian sputters and gags on the strange brew that tastes like alcoholic milk. Lenny opens the door and ushers Christian out of the back seat.

Christian totters on his platform shoes in the parking lot. "Why are we at Retro Junkie?" he says. "What's happening?"

Lenny smiles and pats Christian on the shoulder. "You are."

Inside Retro Junkie, the rhythmic thump of a large crowd stamping its feet in unison shakes Christian's testicles. Lenny guides him through the backstage area, where he hears Morris's voice.

"The moment you've been waiting for. Next up, Christian Orr, singing 'Whole Lotta Love.'"

As the signature guitar riff begins, Christian notices that it's not the distant, airy version he's been hearing lately, nor the thin karaoke soundtrack he would typically hear at Retro Junkie. This is the heavy, crunching sound of a real metal band.

Christian approaches the stage from the rear and sees no less than 200 people jammed into the club. Gone are the potbellied middle-aged parents and their embarrassing eighties concert T-shirts. The crowd is mostly twenty-something girls with long hair. They look like attendees of the original Woodstock.

Onstage, a guitar player who looks remarkably like a young Jimmy Page bangs out the chugging intro to "Whole Lotta Love." He turns and gestures to Christian to take the microphone.

As Christian steps forward, the crowd roars. The floor shakes even harder. A pair of women's panties strikes him in the face. Roses land at his feet. Looking down into the audience, he sees girls blowing him kisses.

The Jimmy Page character smiles and nods again toward the microphone. Christian grabs the microphone and, without thinking, sings in his best falsetto:

> *"You need cooling*
> *Baby, I'm not fooling"*

The crowd roars. Christian's voice is firm and tight, like Robert Plant's.

> *"Way down inside*
> *Honey, you need it*
> *I'm gonna give you every inch of my love*
> *I'm gonna give you every inch of my love"*

Jimmy Page slides up next to Christian for the chorus.

> *"Want a whole lotta love*
> *Want a whole lotta love"*

Jimmy Page steps back, plucks a Fender Stratocaster from a stand, and tosses it to Christian. Christian throws the guitar over his shoulder and begins to play. He covers the rhythm for a few bars and then steps forward to play a lead solo that drives the crowd wild. He lifts his guitar and raises it over his head. To wild cheers, he smashes the Stratocaster against the stage over and over.

The crowd surges, and a dozen hippie girls ascend the stage. They slither forward like snakes and begin caressing Christian's legs. Suddenly, he is lifted into the air and passed on to the crowd. Borne aloft by a sea of hands, Christian stretches his arms wide. Onstage, Jimmy Page continues to bang out the monotonous rhythm of "Whole Lotta Love."

When the human conveyor finally deposits Christian back on the stage, Jimmy Page steps forward and kicks open the door to a large four-sided box that has appeared.

Christian steps into the box, which is a foot taller than his head, and runs his fingers across the walls, which are made of a layer of wood covered by a layer of metal and another layer of wood.

"An orgone box," Christian whispers. "Reich . . . It's an orgone accumulator."

"You have always been a god."

At these words, Christian turns to see the figure of a woman in the doorway of the box. He squints and perceives that the woman is more a being of light than an actual woman. The contours of her body are not fixed but flicker like a flame.

"You will never be sad again."

Christian hears the woman's voice as she approaches him.

"You will never be lonely again. You will never feel small again."

The door to the orgone box closes. A bright-blue light like an aurora borealis swirls above his head and then parts, revealing an infinite field of stars and nebulae. The woman embraces him.

CHAPTER THIRTY-THREE

Christian awakens with his right cheek stuck to a table. He raises his head to discover that he is in his own apartment, at his own kitchen table.

In front of him sits his laptop, open and humming. There are three guitar picks next to an empty beer bottle, as well as a capo. Christian feels for his penis, which is still erect. He rushes to the front door and sees his Fiesta parked below in the lot, askew but unharmed. He enters his bedroom and finds it empty. Finally, Christian notices that he's still wearing his gold lamé top and platform shoes.

Open on his laptop appears to be his dissertation on Reich, a document he has come to fear and loathe, a document he hasn't touched in months. He quickly scrolls. What was once forty-three pages of stray ideas and inspirational writing memes now appears to be three hundred pages of fully formed text.

Christian reads the current page:

Reich called this life force orgone, deliberately using a word similar to the word "orgasm," since he believed that the capacity for healthy orgasm was the foundation of a healthy life.

Reich claims that "the pleasure of living and the pleasure of the orgasm are identical. Extreme orgasm anxiety forms the basis of the general fear of life," and complete release in orgasm is the fullest expression of human existence. Millennia of sexual and political suppression has corrupted the average person's ability to achieve a proper orgasm and left the modern world with a sexually disabled population.

According to Reich, "life is like nature. It does not care who carries it. It is being carried. There are good and bad carriers of Life." And so each person's job is to undo the knots created by this maladaptive response, become a good carrier of life, and not remain a sick, diseased carrier.

Reich felt that orgone energy could be trapped and used. He invented what he called an orgone accumulator, a device designed to bathe a person in positive universal energy. The first orgone accumulator was a box similar in size to an armoire. It was made with alternating organic and metallic materials and was designed to draw universal energy from the universe and trap it inside the box.

The earliest versions of these boxes were destroyed in a fire in 1954 when Reich's home in Maine was raided by agents of the FDA.

Writers such as William Burroughs referred to the orgone box in their work, and musician Kurt Cobain was famously photographed inside one such box at Burroughs's home in Lawrence, Kansas.

Christian sits back in his chair and for the first time recalls a few images from the previous night: the car ride with Dee, the sea of hands at Retro Junkie, the Jimmy Page character who played an electric guitar through an actual amplifier. The ethereal woman who spoke kind words to him. He texts Morris: Was I there last night?

Christian watches the bubbles form in his message app until Morris responds.

Didn't see you. We had Flock of Seagulls cover band called Flock of Sea-girls. Awesome.

Christian sits back in his chair. His phone pings with a new text from Mark Apple.

COMING IN TODAY OR SEIZING THE DAY? OKAY IF YOU WANT TO PLAY HOOKY.

Christian arrives at Glenhaven High wearing a dashiki, which he purchased on the way to avoid wearing the trench coat. Beyond the extra length provided by the overlong shirt, he feels that the dizzying geometric patterns might provide extra camouflage for his bulge.

As he skulks through the hallways, he nearly runs into Diane Sharp and her daughter. Christian raises his phone but not quickly enough.

"Hello, Diane," Christian says, blushing.

"What kind of shirt is that?"

"A dashiki," Christian replies. "How are you feeling, Caitlin? Better?" He studies Caitlin's face, waiting for the blazing eyes and cryptic insults he received from her at their last meeting. Caitlin smiles back placidly.

"The girls have gotten better, thank God," Diane says with a sigh. "The last two days, the cursing, the tics, the drawings, it's all died down." She strokes her daughter's hair. "She's sort of back to her old self. Not perfect, but good enough for me."

Caitlin rolls her eyes at her mother.

"That's great news," Christian says weakly. "You know, Caitlin, I was thinking about what you said to me the last time we spoke. I was wondering why you said those things and if anyone told you to say them?"

Caitlin looks at her mother and then back at Christian. "What did I say?"

"You mentioned a girlfriend," Christian begins. "And then you sang a Led Zeppelin song called 'Whole Lotta Love.'"

Caitlin looks at her mother. "Led who?"

"The girls are fine now," Diane says, "and they don't need to be reminded of it. So please leave her alone. I'm still filing my complaint with the school board about the sex-ed class."

"Health class," Christian says.

"'Forum for perversion' is a better name for it," Diane replies, pulling her daughter toward her. "All I know is, your sex-ed class had something to do with all this shit. Let's go, Caitlin."

———————————

Christian enters his office to find Mark Apple seated in his chair with his feet on Christian's desk.

"Glad you could make it," Apple says, lowering his feet. "You look a little hungover. Are you out partying for me now?"

"Sorry I'm late," Christian says.

"Nothing more important than punctuality," Apple says, wagging his finger. "On my deathbed, I'm definitely going to say why, why, oh why wasn't I on time for more staff meetings?'"

"How are you feeling today?" Christian says.

"I'm feeling good," Apple says. "Really good. You wanna arm wrestle?"

Christian sets his backpack on his desk. "Uh. I don't—"

"C'mon!" Apple says, quickly arranging two chairs at the corner of Christian's desk. "Two seconds. Real quick."

Christian reluctantly sits across from Apple. The two men lock right hands. "Are you ready?" Apple says cheerfully. "Go!"

Before either man can exhale, Christian has pinned Apple's hand to the desk. The two of them look at each other in shock, still holding hands.

"Mark, I—"

Apple quickly hops up from his chair. "Hey, no worries. You must be stronger than you look." He squeezes Christian's bicep. "Bro, you lifting now? Anyway, good news. Apparently, the cheerleaders have returned to their normal stupid selves. No more crazy witch shit. Nobody knows why, but who cares? There are rumors flying about some moms going wild around town, but that's not my problem."

Christian stands. "Moms? What moms?"

"What names did I hear?" Apple tries to remember. "Jenny Tempelton, Brittany May, Tina Lowry, a few others. Same shit as the teenagers, basically. Witchy stuff at Lime Ridge, and they say there's security footage of them spray-painting dicks all over downtown."

"Dicks?" Christian says.

"Seems like good clean mom fun to me," Apple says. "Important thing is they're not students, so who cares. Nice shirt. Actually, what kind of shirt is that?"

"It's a dashiki. West African."

"Is today some kind of Black day? Kwanzaa or something?"

"Nope." Christian shrugs. "Just a regular day to, you know, celebrate cultural diversity."

"Cultural diversity!" Apple laughs. "Nice try, pal. But you're not going to out-PC Laura Hartwood. That woman has a corner on the market, cultural diversity, all of it. Your angle on getting this job is that you're already here, the school board likes you, and your PhD beats her master's. If you should ever finish it."

"I'm actually almost done," Christian says, stunned.

"Really?" Apple says, blushing with what Christian immediately registers to be envy. "You told me the other day you hadn't worked on it in months."

"I know."

"Well," Apple says. "Getting shit done; I like it. And strong as an ox." He squeezes Christian's bicep again. "Crazy."

"I'm glad to hear you're feeling better today," Christian says tentatively. "How have things been?"

"Great. Working on legal stuff, estate stuff. Not that I'm loaded, but there's some property my grandfather left and family land that no one's had the heart to sell. So, I've been doing that, plus a good deal of drinking."

"You probably shouldn't be drinking, Mark," Christian says, looking down. "You want to give your body every chance to recover."

Apple laughs. "Recover, I like that! Like I've got a cold! I like you, Chris. One thing on my bucket list is to see you get back on your feet and get this full-time job."

"Thank you. But if you don't mind me asking," Christian says, "why do you care so much about what happens to me?"

Apple shrugs. "I guess it's because I was a jerk to guys like you in high school, and maybe I want to make amends. Do you wonder what happens to those jocks, like Findlay or Knight, when they grow up?" He taps his chest. "They become me."

"You're way better than those guys," Christian says with conviction.

"I don't know," Apple says. "People assume that dicks are dicks because they had an evil dad or because they're compensating for low self-esteem. But I acted like a dick in high school because I could. Because people let me. And I kind of enjoyed it."

"I understand what you're saying, but I can't relate to any of those things," Christian says plainly.

"Of course you can't. You weren't a dick. That's why I like you."

"Maybe I wanted to be a dick," Christian says with sudden conviction. "And if I could have, I would have. Maybe every guy wants to be a dick and dominate everything."

"Right, does every man want to be a dick?" Apple strokes his chin as Christian notes his friend's growing interest in philosophical inquiry. "And if he's not a dick, is it because society won't let him, or because other dicks are more powerful than him, or because he doesn't have real dick-ishness in him to begin with?"

"That relates to what Nietzsche called the will to power," Christian says.

"Nietzsche? The Nazi?" Apple turns and paces. "I mean, look at me. Did I deserve to become principal? I don't know shit about education. It's just that some people get things handed to them and get to go on being dicks, while other people just suffer the actions of dicks. How is that fair?"

"It's not," Christian says.

"Right," Apple says. "And what I'm saying is that I'm the guy who shat on you in high school. Just like Laura fucking Hartwood shat on the nice girls around her. She's like the female version of a dick—a cunt, I guess. She went to St. Agatha, but I knew her brother. She was cruel as shit to other girls. She played girls against each other, backstabbed, the whole nine. And now she's some kind of earth goddess? Give me a fucking break."

"People can change," Christian says, pulling down his dashiki.

"No, they can't." Apple steps forward. "You want to think they can, but they can't." He raises his hand in Scout's honor. "I'm telling you as a man with one foot in the grave. People never change. They put on different clothes, like Laura Hartwood puts on her hippie dress and you put on whatever the fuck it is you're wearing."

"A dashiki."

"But no one changes. Laura Hartwood was a bitch then, and now she's a new-age bitch. You were a sweet, nerdy guy who never believed he deserved good things, and now you're an adult version of that. Except now you are going all Nelson Mandela, and why is that again?"

Christian smiles uncertainly. "Maybe I want to shake things up."

Apple laughs, then paces some more. "Shake things up, shake things up," he mutters. "I want to shake things up too. I want to shake the Magic 8 Ball again and not have it come back with 'looks like leukemia.'"

Christian fails to keep from checking the wall clock.

"What I wish," Apple says as he turns toward the window tearfully, "is for just a little more time to be a better version of me. It's hard to get it all done with a gun to my head. Best case now is I start chemo and my hair falls out and I'm weak as shit. Worst case I take a quick nosedive and I'm out."

"I thought you were feeling better today," Christian says sadly.

"I am." Apple nods. "I'm feeling good today."

Christian considers suggesting that Apple's good day might be the start of many good days but decides against it.

"They were talking about a bone marrow transplant," Apple says to the window. "If I make it that far. Brand-new white blood cells—ha! And here I am saying people can't change."

Tears roll down the principal's cheek as he laughs. It occurs to Christian that Apple is getting good at crying, an indication of the very change he desires. Apple's phone buzzes.

"Oh, shit." Apple blinks back his tears as he looks at his phone. "Right, school day! Gotta go. Listen, if I were you, I'd take that shirt off, because it looks like your mom just took you to *The Lion King* matinee."

Apple hugs Christian, holding the embrace for a long time. Then he quickly leaves.

Christian studies the patterns on his shirt. He tries to recall *The Lion King* and wonders whether dashikis might be sold as souvenirs at the theater. He imagines Mark Apple as the old lion king who dies.

Just then, Laura Hartwood enters the doorway and stops. Her face is wooden as she stares at the floor, and she speaks in a monotone.

"When a teenager is in crisis, you are the one who helps them. You are the man who got twelve hundred the first time he took the SAT and nearly a fourteen hundred the second."

"Laura," Christian says, extending his hand. "Are you okay? Please, sit down."

"You are a brilliant man," Laura says mechanically as she raises her right hand to ward off Christian. "Women love you and men admire you."

"Laura, are you sure you don't want to sit down?" Christian says.

"Your daughter will win her race today," Laura says. "If you will it."

"My daughter?"

As Laura disappears from the doorway, Christian's phone pings. There's a text from Francesca.

ABOUT TO DO HUNDRED FREE. NO WORRIES IF YOU CAN'T MAKE IT SINCE I SUCK ANYWAY.

CHAPTER THIRTY-FOUR

Arriving at the pool deck, Christian first spots Stu Sherwater, who sits on a diving block, holding a clipboard. Christian approaches Stu and places a firm hand on his shoulder.

"I want you to put Francesca in the first heat today."

Stu looks at Christian's hand on his shoulder and then grins slowly. "The first heat is where you put the fast swimmers," he says. "The slower swimmers go in the later heats. That's what's fair."

"Is that what's fair, Stu?" Christian says, keeping his hand on Stu's shoulder. "I asked Francesca once, and she said that you only pay attention to the top swimmers and that she and the other girls just splash around in the water like two-year-olds. Does that sound fair?"

Stu tries to rise, but Christian presses down on the other man's shoulder. Stu, with an acumen unique to athletes, realizes that he will not currently be able to rise against the force being applied to him. He puzzles over how this much strength could be coming from a man as slight and flabby as Christian, a man who couldn't hoist his own body out of the water.

"Can you take your hand off my shoulder?" Stu says.

"Put her in the first heat," Christian says. "Please."

"Fine," Stu says. He stands and looks Christian in the eye. "Are we even now?"

"Even?"

Christian is distracted by the sound of his daughter's voice. Francesca stands at the near end of the pool, chatting with some of her teammates and looking out of place in her ill-fitting, flowery one-piece grandma swimsuit. Most of the other girls wear sleek, black, all-body tech suits.

Christian jogs toward a tent where a twenty-something vendor of the high-end suits displays her wares.

"I'll take this one," Christian says as he pulls a black bodysuit off the rack.

"We're just displaying today," the woman begins, "but you can order online, and we'll ship to you within—"

Christian pulls out his credit card. "I need it today." He hands the woman the card.

"I don't have a machine," the woman says.

"I'll owe you." Christian takes the suit and walks off.

Francesca meets him on the pool deck.

"Dad? What?" Francesca says.

Christian hands her the suit. "You can't swim in that. Put this on."

Francesca takes the suit. "This is like a four-hundred-dollar suit," she says. "And Mr. Sherwater just put me in the first heat of hundred free! Why?"

"Because you're a great swimmer," Christian says firmly.

"No, I'm not!" Francesca abruptly notices Christian's dashiki. "What are you wearing?"

"It's a dashiki."

"You understand I'm going to be humiliated," Francesca says. "Those girls are going to lap me."

"Please, just put on the suit."

As Christian settles in the bleachers, he grows dizzy. Images from the previous night at Retro Junkie flood his mind at a rapid rate. He wonders about the strange brew he drank; he thinks of Laura

Hartwood and whether she encountered Dee this morning and is this very moment reporting back to him or whether she is still wandering the school, muttering to herself. Christian makes a pained noise, which draws stares. His phone pings, and he looks at it reflexively. There's another text from Brittany May.

HOW BOUT I JUST PAY YOU FOR SEX. JK (NOT!)

The starter's voice is heard over the loudspeaker: *"Lane eight. Would the swimmer in lane eight please report to the block."*

Francesca hurriedly emerges from the locker room, looking sleek in her all-black tech suit but covering her chest with her arms like the cold five-year-old Christian remembers from her early swim lessons.

As the starter gun sounds, Christian feels himself falling into a trance, during which more images from the previous night fill his mind. When he opens his eyes, the race is over and Francesca's teammates are congratulating her. Francesca is laughing and crying and shaking her head all at once.

Christian checks the scoreboard, sees his daughter's name in the top slot, and chooses to let his daughter enjoy her victory without his interference.

———————

As he reaches the parking lot, Christian finds Maron sitting on the hood of his Fiesta.

"Hi, Mr. Orr," Maron says, sliding off the car. "Can we talk for a minute?"

Christian sets his backpack on the hood. "Of course, Maron. What's up?"

"I know it's none of my business, but I need to ask you to stop seeing my mother."

Christian laughs. "You're right. That's none of your business."

"I can't explain everything right now," Maron continues. "My mother is sick with the flu."

"I'm sorry to hear that," Christian says. "I've been trying to reach her. I'll bring her some hot soup."

"No!" Maron shouts. "You need to leave her alone."

"I'm not going to leave her alone. Your mother and I are friends, and I'll see her again if she wants to see me," Christian says firmly.

"If you and my mother are such good friends, then why did you sleep with her friends right after your first date?" Maron demands.

Christian looks at Maron for a long time. "Who told you that?"

Maron steps forward. "What did my father promise you? Whatever it is, don't believe him. Did you make some kind of deal with him?"

"No," Christian says, blushing. "Not at all."

Maron does not look convinced. "Mr. Orr, you've been kind to me. I know you're a good person, and I know my mother likes you. Maybe someday you can be friends with her. It's the same with Francesca. I really like her, but because of the way things are, we can't be friends right now. Someday! But please, just stay away from my family right now. Otherwise, things will get worse, for everyone! I have to go!"

Maron grabs his backpack and dashes across the parking lot.

Phallic mounds?

CHAPTER THIRTY-FIVE

Sloan left work early after Francesca promised to have high tea with her. Since the coffeehouse incident, Francesca has refused to meet her mother in public places, but she agreed to meet for iced tea on Sloan's back patio.

Sloan brushes away her hair as an afternoon breeze pushes the Tibetan bamboo wind chimes into one another. Francesca sits in a wicker chair and scrolls through her phone.

"So, can I ask if you are having sex with your boyfriend yet?" Sloan says, stirring her tea.

"Um, no, you can't!" Francesca laughs.

"It's alright if you are," Sloan continues placidly. "Just use spermicide with a condom if you can. Don't rely on him to pull out. I'm sure he's sweet, but boys are like dogs when it comes to sex."

"Thanks," Francesca says, putting down her phone. "He's actually the furthest thing from a dog. I had to literally beg him to kiss me the other night. He wanted me to pat him on the head."

Sloan frowns. "Weird. You don't want to start being anybody's mother. I can tell he and his mother are going through a hard time."

"Who isn't?" Francesca says defiantly. "She's separating from her husband, and he's caught in the middle. Sound familiar? And so what if Maron's mom was drunk? Dad knows all about their issues, and he likes her."

"What does Dad know about it?"

"I believe that's confidential."

Sloan laughs. "I always told your father you'd make a great lawyer."

"You never told me that." Francesca frowns.

Sloan feels a pang of guilt. She thinks of the years she stayed late in the city after work when she could have been home with her daughter. The thousands of nights spent sweating at the gym, out at bars with clients, and more that she kept secret, when she could have been listening to her daughter like she is now, asking her what she might like to be when she grows up.

"I think you'd make a great lawyer," Sloan says finally, with emotion.

"And be a jerk for a living?" Francesca replies. "No thanks."

"What do you want to be then?"

Francesca laughs. "Wow, twenty questions! Uh, no clue! I like journalism, but I think I'm probably best off being some kind of psychologist or social worker, like Dad."

"You want to be like your father?"

"I'm not saying that," Francesca replies. "I just think human psychology is what I know best. Definitely getting a crash course in abnormal psych this year! It's amazing how screwed up adults are. They have all these psychological knots they don't even know about. Even their knots have knots."

"You have to make compromises when you're an adult," Sloan starts. "A compromise can feel like a knot."

"You can make compromises without making knots," Francesca says. "I've made lots of compromises lately, but I don't feel like I'm making any knots. The knots are the lies you tell yourself to justify making compromises. If you compromise without trying to justify it, there's no knot."

"Who needs a therapist when I have you?" Sloan says.

"You don't. I'm brilliant and I don't charge." Francesca raises her glass. "Except iced tea and movie night."

"Movie night!" Sloan says, perking up. "What shall we watch?"

"*March of the Penguins*."

"March of the what?" Sloan says.

"Ugh. Have you ever even sat through an entire movie, like once, ever?" Francesca laughs.

The faint sound of cursing rises from across the street.

Sloan jumps up and rushes through the house. Francesca follows her, noting that for all of Sloan's seriousness, she's never lost the ability to enjoy a good scandal.

Across the street in Dee's front yard, Craig Entwerp raises his shovel and beats down a large earthen mound. "Frickin' mortar?" Craig shouts. "Really?"

Sloan emerges onto the lawn. "What's going on, Craig?"

"What's going on," Craig replies, pointing at the mound with his shovel, "is that some of the neighborhood 'ladies' were building a phallic mound here last night."

"Phallic mound?" Sloan takes a few steps forward. "Isn't that just a pile of dirt?"

"Only since I've been beating it," Craig says.

"How long have you been beating your phallic mound, Craig?" Sloan says as Francesca slaps her on the shoulder.

"And then, about three a.m.," Craig continues, oblivious to the unfolding mockery, "according to my Ring cam, five teenage boys came. They squirted mayonnaise on the top of this thing to make it look like you-know-what."

"What?" Sloan says, giggling while Francesca continues to nudge various parts of Sloan's body with her elbow.

"C'mon, Sloan," Craig mumbles. "You know what! Like a dick jisming!"

Francesca falls onto the grass below the hedge line, laughing.

"I'm sorry," Sloan says, with lawyerly precision. "Did you say 'dick jism-ing'?"

"It's Craig's Twitter handle!" Francesca says from the ground.

A thought enters Sloan's mind, as Francesca playfully tugs on her pant leg, that she and her daughter might currently be experiencing the best moment they've ever had together. Instantly forgetting the conversation with Craig, Sloan drops down beside Francesca and looks her in the eye.

"Why don't you stay here with me tonight after movie night and not sleep at Annie's?"

Francesca is taken aback by her mother's sincerity. "Okay, yeah!" she says excitedly.

"We can sleep in the living room," Sloan whispers. "Like camping."

From across the street, a deep voice is heard.

"Hello, neighbor!"

Sloan and Francesca crawl on their bellies and peer through an opening in the hedge. Lenny approaches Craig, holding a large glass of water. "You look like you could use a cool drink!"

Craig waves the water away. "I knocked on your door before, but you didn't answer. I just felt that for the good of the neighborhood, somebody had to get rid of this thing."

"What thing?" Lenny says, looking at the mound.

"You didn't hear the women here last night?" Craig begins breathlessly. "Tina Lowry, Jenny Templeton, two other women I didn't recognize. I have it on my Ring cam. They were drinking wine and dancing outside your windows, and then they started digging in the dirt and building this thing with their hands."

"And what is this?" Lenny says, studying the mound.

Craig sighs "Well, it's dirt now, but it used to be a phallus."

"A phallus?" Lenny replies. He walks carefully around the dirt pile. "It looks a bit flaccid for a phallus. Was it erect when you got here?"

Behind the bush, Francesca nudges Sloan. "Wow. He's fucking with Craig."

Sloan nods. "And he's the nice one."

Lenny places his hand on Craig's shoulder. "It's been my experience that people tend to get excited about problems that don't directly concern them when they're at loose ends," Lenny says avuncularly.

Craig's face turns red. "Loose ends?"

"For example, this mound. You've put a great deal of hard work into defeating it. But perhaps you're simply lonely."

"Lonely?" Craig shouts.

Lenny steps closer to Craig. "I'm aware that your wife left you and your daughter hasn't spoken to you in years. But I also know that you're a person with great potential for love and kindness. I can't help but wonder whether all this phallic pounding is a way to keep from feeling pain in here." Lenny places his hand over Craig's heart.

Craig, whose face has grown purple over the course of Lenny's speech, swats the hand away. "How dare you?" he says. Like an angry baseball manager, Craig kicks dirt at Lenny's feet. "You know nothing about me. Nothing."

"I know everything," Lenny says, stepping forward and touching Craig's shoulder again. "All you need to know is that joy and liberation from anxiety are possible."

"I don't need your goddamned advice!" Craig kicks more dirt at Lenny.

Francesca notices that her mother has lost interest in the mound drama. She follows Sloan's gaze toward the front door of the house, where a shadowy figure has appeared in the doorway. Francesca shudders as she recognizes Dee.

"I'll be back in a few minutes," Sloan says, rising and scooting sideways through an opening in the hedge.

"Mom, where are you going?" Francesca shouts. "Our movie!"

"Craig, Lenny, as you were," Sloan says, giving a thumbs-up as she crosses the street. She turns toward Francesca and taps an imaginary wristwatch. "Five minutes."

"But *March of the Penguins!*" Francesca yells.

Dee holds open his front door for Sloan as she approaches. When Sloan enters, Dee smiles at Francesca and then turns and closes the door behind him.

CHAPTER THIRTY-SIX

Francesca felt guilty for tiptoeing over to Dee's house and eavesdropping on her mother. Crouched below the kitchen window, she heard laughter, wineglasses clinking, and her mother haltingly speaking a language that, with the help of a phone app, she confirmed to be Greek.

However, upon arriving back at her mother's house, what Francesca mostly feels as she sits in front of the dormant television set is fear. Fear that her mother is now in the early stages of leaving her in a new way. Fear that she has never been loved enough to be prioritized, and that even now, in the midst of her parents' separation, when everyone agrees she should be foremost in everyone's mind, she remains an afterthought.

When Sloan finally arrives home two hours past her five-minute estimate, Francesca lets her anger and indignation guide her. "Everything good over there?" she says crisply.

"Hi, 'Cesca," Sloan replies, moving away from her daughter and into the kitchen for reasons that Francesca suspects involve the smell of alcohol, drugs, or sex on her body.

Francesca follows her mother. "What have you been doing over there for two hours?"

"It's not really any of your business," Sloan says, opening a jar of peanut butter and eating it with a spoon.

"Your eyes look glassy."

Sloan seems genuinely surprised by this assertion and studies her reflection in the kitchen window. "I was learning Greek," Sloan says. "Dee and Lenny were teaching me."

"Were they?" Francesca says.

"Were you spying on me?" Sloan says.

"I wanted to know why you were bailing on our movie night," Francesca says, "which you *just* planned with me. It's always fun when you realize that your mother would rather spend time with strangers than her own daughter."

"That's not true," Sloan says.

"That guy," Francesca says, shaking her head as she follows her mother into the living room, "he is seriously bad news, and if you don't see it, I don't know how to help you."

"I don't need your help," Sloan says, sitting.

"Maybe you don't," Francesca says. She sits across from her mother. "But you should know that he's mean and crazy. And I guarantee you are nothing but a joke to him. Guarantee it."

"Would you prefer I visit Craig Entwerp?" Sloan shrugs. "What am I supposed to do with your father gone and you at Annie's every night."

"I'm not at Annie's tonight, am I? We had plans," Francesa replies.

"I'm sorry," Sloan says. "I lost track of time. They're the new neighbors, they just moved in, and I want to make sure they feel welcome."

"Bullshit, you've got the hots for that asshole," Francesca says.

"The hots!" Sloan laughs.

"I'm the teenager, Mom," Francesca says. "I'm the one who's supposed to be making bad choices."

"You have plenty of time to make bad choices. Trust me," Sloan says.

"Don't patronize me!" Francesca yells.

Sloan sighs and looks fondly at her daughter. "I don't think it's technically possible for me to patronize you. Without question, you're the smartest person in this family."

"Bullshit!" Francesca cries.

"And it's good that you get angry," Sloan continues. "You're not a polite idealist like your father."

"Don't beat up on Dad," Francesca says.

"I'm not beating up on him. I'm just saying that he's willing to sacrifice everything to maintain politeness. He really believes that if you're nice enough, you eventually get rewarded for it. It never happens, but he never loses faith."

"At least he has faith in something," Francesca says.

"But he lives in a fantasy. That's why he stayed in academia so long, because that world is the closest thing to a fantasy world. He'd still be there if I hadn't dragged him out."

"Maybe you shouldn't have dragged him out," Francesca says with emotion. "Maybe you should have let him stay in a place that wasn't full of nihilistic people like you spouting nihilistic platitudes."

Sloan opens her hands and looks at them. The white light appears in each palm.

"Why are you looking at your hands?" Francesca demands.

Sloan groans, clenches her fists, and stands.

"What's wrong with your hands?" Francesca says.

"Nothing," Sloan says tersely.

"Whatever. I know you're bored and restless," Francesca says. "It's boring in Glenhaven. The problem is, every time you act on your boredom, I end up paying the price. You're like: I'm so bored! Maybe I should screw Stu Sherwater. But, oops! Dad finds out and leaves the house. And now my daughter has the whole school snickering behind her back. But you're *still* bored. So then you're like: Gee, maybe I'll pursue the craziest asshole I can find, 'learn Greek,' and blow off my daughter, because basically anything is more important than her!"

Francesca loses her breath and struggles to get her words out.

"I am so tired of getting the short end of the stick!"

She dissolves into sobs. Sloan slides next to her on the couch and hugs her. As she buries her head in her mother's shoulder, Francesca tries to remember being held by this woman when she was an infant, but can't, which makes her cry more deeply.

"You're right," Sloan says, clutching her daughter. "Our whole life together—my life—I put my career over everything, including you."

Francesca breaks free. "Not just your career, everything. You put everything over me. Anything! And look, you're still doing it!"

"I'm sorry, Francesca," Sloan says. She pulls Francesca into another tight hug. "I know I'm selfish, and I know you don't feel it, but I love you more than anything. You're the best thing that ever happened to me."

Francesca lets herself sob for a while, half aware that she may now be settling for whatever scraps exist of her mother's love.

"You're wonderful," Sloan continues. "This world is so lucky to have you."

"I don't want to be wonderful, and I don't give a shit about this world," Francesca blubbers, letting her tears fall. "I just want to be happy."

"Why haven't you been honest with me?"

CHAPTER THIRTY-SEVEN

Christian leans against Ari's old Audi in her driveway as he pecks out another text to her. After five minutes, he goes to her front door and knocks. He waits a moment, then shuffles alongside the house until he reaches Ari's bedroom window, where he immediately hears her voice.

"Stop stalking me."

Christian places his hand against the curtained window and speaks through the glass. "I'm not stalking you," he says. "Maron told me you have the flu, and so I brought you some NyQuil."

"What's NyQuil?"

"It's medicine. It'll make you feel better."

There's a long silence.

"I had a great time on our date," Christian continues. "I'm sorry it got cut short. I miss you and I want to finish our dinner. Why aren't you responding to my texts and calls?"

There is another long silence. Christian steps closer to the window. "Ari, are you still there?"

"Bring me the NyQuil."

Christian tries the front door, finds it open, and pads down the hallway toward Ari's bedroom.

"I got the purple kind. I hope that works!" Christian calls out.

Gently pushing open the bedroom door, Christian finds Ari lying under the covers with a water bottle on her forehead, a thermometer sticking out of her mouth, and her feet on a pillow. She looks like a cartoon of a sick person.

"What does my temperature say?" Ari pulls the thermometer out of her mouth and hands it to Christian without looking at him.

"Let's see," Christian says, raising the thermometer to the light. "One hundred and one point five."

"It was a hundred and two before," Ari says with frustration. "Why is it going down?"

"Down is good," Christian says, sitting on the bed.

"Where's the medicine?" Ari grabs the plastic bag out of Christian's hand and rips open the packaging. She unscrews a NyQuil bottle and guzzles a third of it.

"Whoa, whoa," Christian says. "You don't need that much."

Ari takes another swig and sets it on the nightstand. She rolls over, facing away from Christian. "I don't want to be in pain," Ari says into her pillow. "I thought I would like pain, but I don't."

Christian screws the cap onto the bottle. "I'm sorry you're sick," he says.

"You can go now," Ari replies.

"Why haven't you responded to me?"

"Because you haven't been honest with me."

"What do you mean?" Christian blushes.

Ari rolls over and looks at him. "When's the last time you saw my husband?"

"Your husband?" Christian stammers. "That night I saw you, downtown."

"And what happened after I left?" Ari regards Christian severely.

The color of his face changes from pink to red. "Well, your husband was acting crazy. Everybody was acting crazy. I remember you kicked him in the balls, which was crazy. And then you left. So, I went home."

"Alone?" Ari says.

"I think what happened was your husband gave me some kind of drug, because I've had a hard time remembering exactly what happened that night."

"How hard?" Ari nods toward Christian's pants.

He looks down and realizes that his dashiki has somehow folded in such a way that it no longer covers his bulge.

"That's quite a stiffy you've got there," she says flatly.

"That was another thing I wanted to tell you about," Christian begins. "I went to my urologist, and I think he may have over-fixed my ED problem."

"Over-fixed!" Ari says. "What an amazing urologist."

With a vigor unusual for a feverish person, Ari reaches for Christian's dashiki and pulls it off over his head.

"What are you doing?" Christian cries.

"You said you wanted to have sex with me once your condition improved," Ari says. "Remember how important it was for you not to wind up in the friend zone? Because what kind of man would want to be friends with a woman?" She pulls Christian onto the bed. "So now your problem is fixed, let's go."

"Ari, I—"

"Priapism is such an unusual disorder," Ari says as she unbuckles Christian's pants. "Priapus isn't even a major god. In fact, he's an actual prick."

"My doctor said it's not technically priapism because it's nonischemic!" Christian shouts. "Ari, maybe we should wait."

"Wait? Don't you want to be a big man who fucks a lot of women?"

Christian looks at her. "No," he says gently. "I just think we should, you know, finish our date first."

"This *is* finishing our date," Ari says, raising her nightgown and mounting Christian. She reaches for the NyQuil bottle on the nightstand, drains the rest of the bottle, and cracks open another as she begins to ride him.

"I really care about you, Ari!" Christian cries. "I mean it. You're unlike anyone I've ever met! You're special!"

"Why lie to me then?" Ari replies, taking another swig.

Christian's mind blurs as Ari moves back and forth across him. Pleasure fills every space in his body where anxiety normally resides. He struggles to summon any enthusiasm for continuing the argument.

"Mom, do you need this?"

Maron enters the room just as Christian comes inside Ari. There's a long silence as Maron stands, mouth agape, holding a manila envelope.

"What are you doing here?" Maron finally shouts at Christian.

Ari dismounts Christian and crawls under her covers.

"Maron, get out of here." Ari rolls to one side and covers her head with the bed sheet. "Both of you."

"Hi, Maron," Christian says as he covers his still-erect penis with a pillow.

Maron steps forward. "We just talked, Mr. Orr!" he says, angrily. "We just talked!"

"We did, we did," Christian says. With difficulty, he manages to slide on pants over his erection. "And it was a good talk."

"It obviously wasn't! Why would you do this?" Maron shouts.

"Well, as I told you," Christian begins, "during our talk. What happens between your mother and me is between your mother and me."

From underneath the covers, Ari screams, "Get out! Both of you!"

Christian grabs his shoes with one hand, presses down on his dashiki with the other, and hurries past Maron into the hallway.

CHAPTER THIRTY-EIGHT

Christian ascends the last flight of stairs to his apartment and beholds Brittany May leaning against his front door.

"Hi," she says, her face drained of color. "Can we talk inside for a moment?"

Upon entering his apartment, Brittany throws herself into a kitchen chair and sighs. She holds her head in her hands.

"Something bad happened," she says.

Christian pulls up the other kitchen chair and sits across from her. "What?"

Brittany shakes her head for a long time. "The bunco group. Jenny, Tina, Rachel, Cindy. They had a party, and . . ." Brittany frowns and looks up at Christian. "Some of the boys from the football team were there."

"What?" A knot forms in his stomach. "The high school football team?"

"Yes," Brittany says. "Tina called me at about seven. She said that she and Glenn Hammond were in the hot tub."

"Glenn Hammond?!" Christian says. "Junior Glen Hammond?"

"And then Glenn called his friends." Brittany looks at Christian. "Seven or eight boys from the football team came over. I went too."

"Why? Why did you go?" Christian cries.

"I don't know." Brittany shakes her head. "I felt like it."

Christian starts to respond but instead slouches in despair.

"When we got there," Brittany says softly, "Tina and Grace and Jenny and a bunch of the boys were in the hot tub and in the bedroom."

"Was Maron there?" Christian says, clenching his fists.

"Who?" Brittany says.

"Maron," Christian replies. "The running back. New kid. Dark curly hair."

"No," Brittany says. "He wasn't there. Why?"

Christian sighs. "What happened?"

Brittany shrugs. "What do you think happened?"

Christian begins rubbing his temples.

"Most of them were into it," Brittany continues. "The boys, I mean. But there were a couple who got scared and left."

"No kidding?" Christian yells angrily. "Statutory rape and child abuse bothers some kids. Go figure!"

His sudden anger somehow calms Brittany. There is a period of silence, during which Christian recovers his composure.

"So, how long did it go on?" Christian says. "When did it end?"

"I woke up before dawn," Brittany says. "And by then it was mostly empty. But the hot tub was still going. There were wine bottles everywhere. It was like a dream."

Christian recalls similar descriptions of orgies in the *Hammer of the Gods* book. Hot tubs, wine bottles, overflowing ashtrays, coke mirrors, guitars and tambourines strewn across hotel suites. He wonders at his teenage self, and his adult self, for consuming such scenes as though they represented a heaven on earth.

"Tina asked me to meet her and the others tonight on Lime Ridge," Brittany says. "I don't think I'm going to go."

"Was the guy from downtown at the party?" Christian asks urgently. "The long-haired guy we saw on the street the night you came to my apartment? Was he at the party? Or at Lime Ridge?"

Brittany looks uncertain. "He wasn't at the party. But we did go by his house the other night. I haven't been to Lime Ridge yet."

Christian says, "Don't go to his house and don't go to Lime Ridge. Don't do anything with him, and don't do anything more with these women. He's the one who's responsible for all of this. He did something to all of us, drugged us. I don't understand exactly how, but I know it's him."

"When did he drug us?" Brittany says. "Maybe the first night. But how could a drug stay in my system this many days?"

"All I know"—Christian gestures toward the bulge in his pants— "is that I did not do *this*. I'm not on Viagra, and this is not normal."

"Does it hurt?" Brittany leans forward, inspecting Christian's erection like a dentist looking at a cavity. "Maybe he just gave you a huge dose of Viagra?"

"It's more than Viagra," Christian says. "There's a mind-altering element. Weird, hallucinogenic shit has been happening. It's like I'm having waking dreams."

Brittany nods. "I know what you mean. My mind feels different too. When Tina called me to come over, I tried to think about it, but I couldn't. I just went. And I'm sorry, but it felt good, and I didn't think about it."

"Try not to tell the police that." Christian gets up and paces. Brittany follows Christian with her gaze.

"You think the police are going to find out?"

"No, no," Christian says with a wave of his hand. "I doubt that any of the boys will . . . I don't see them talking."

In frustration, he forgets himself and pushes down on his erection. Brittany notices.

"So, with your erection," Brittany says. "When you have it, do you always feel horny?"

"Always," Christian says, finding himself somewhat relieved to talk about it. "And when I have sex, it feels really good. Like amazingly good. Like I've never felt so good in my life. I get completely lost in it. It's like all my problems go away, like I never had any."

"That's how I felt with you the first night. That's why I've been wanting to do it again."

"I've seen the eggplant texts," Christian says.

"Don't worry," Brittany laughs. "I'm just telling you that it was like a huge liberation for me too. Like being at a rave, where everything feels alive, you're lost in the music, and you just feel nothing but . . . good."

Christian feels his penis growing harder. He covers it with both hands. "I get it," he says. "But life isn't about acting on every impulse."

Brittany snorts "Really? Life is about *not* acting on impulses? What a stupid thing for life to be about."

"Grown women can't sleep with high school boys, Brittany," Christian says resolutely. "Beyond the criminal liability, those boys don't know what they're doing. Their sexuality isn't developed. Who knows how something like that could affect their relationships going forward?"

Brittany looks past Christian out the window. The two of them sit in silence for a long while. Christian wonders whether, as a teenage boy, he would have leaped at the chance to sleep with the sexy moms from his neighborhood. Teenage Mark Apple probably would have gone.

"I have to go," Brittany says, looking at her phone. "You don't think the boys will tell the police?"

Christian shakes his head. "No, I don't."

Brittany moves toward the door. "My husband is cooking tonight. Jerk chicken. His specialty." She laughs. "Jeff is frankly a jerk chicken himself. But he's a good guy. He loves our kids, and he works hard." She stares at her hand on the doorknob. "I love my life, I guess. Even if it's not fun or exciting." She turns and looks at Christian sadly. "It's just hard when you realize that it can be different."

Christian smiles sympathetically.

"I probably won't see you again," Brittany says. "Except at school things. I'll stop texting you pictures of my tits, I promise. Good luck with everything. You're one of the good guys, Christian. Don't forget that."

Brittany closes the door, then opens it again. She grabs up a small cardboard box from the landing and tosses it to Christian. "Amazon—catch."

Christian catches the box and opens it as Brittany leaves. The label reads GYM ATHLETIC SUPPORTER WITH HARD CUP. Christian removes the device and dangles it in front of him. It looks like an elaborate G-string with a baseball cup. Christian drops his pants and, with difficulty, manages to shove his penis inside the cup.

After covering the device with his underwear and his underwear with pants, Christian stands before a mirror and analyzes his crotch. He may now look like a pudgy male ballet dancer or a plastic Ken doll, but at least he no longer looks like a man with an erection.

"Too late, it's already done."

CHAPTER THIRTY-NINE

Sloan dreams she is listening to Ari by a waterfall. The waterfall is so loud that Sloan can't discern any of Ari's words. At times, Ari's voice seems out of sync with her mouth, and Sloan wonders whether perhaps the waterfall itself might be speaking, with Ari only opening and closing her mouth.

Then Ari raises her arms, which transform into wings. Her face morphs into that of a large black bird, and Ari the bird rises thirty feet into the air.

In the dream, Sloan shouts after Ari, "What am I supposed to do!"

The bird dives down and stops an inch from Sloan's face. It opens its beak, caws, and then speaks: "Too late. It's already done."

Sloan awakens with a start in her bed. She reaches for her forehead, which hurts. Padding into the kitchen, she presses a button on her coffee maker and wanders toward the front door.

Through the windows Sloan sees Craig Entwerp cross the street toward Dee's house. Craig appears merry in his hiking boots and khaki shorts and is whistling. Sloan steps through her front door and hides behind the pillar of her pergola to get a better view.

A small white goat wanders out the front door onto the flagstone walkway. The goat baas and brays and nuzzles at Craig's leg.

"Hey, little fella!" Craig kneels and pats the goat. He shouts toward the house, "Hey, Lenny, should I bring him in?"

Lenny emerges from the house. The two embrace in a long hug, like old friends.

"What the fuck?" Sloan mutters to herself.

Craig and Lenny enter the house, leaving the white goat on the porch.

Sloan stares at the white goat, who cocks his head and looks directly at her.

Her throat seizes and her heart begins to race. She feels a powerful urge to rush back into the house. The goat first quivers, then stretches and grows. It rises on its hind legs and opens its jaw. White fur pops off its body like popcorn, and beneath it, pink flesh appears. Human hands and feet push through the goat's cloven hooves. Sloan squeezes her eyes shut and then covers her ears at the sound of cartilage being stretched. When she finally opens her eyes, a fully naked Dee stands in his yard across from her, glistening. He grins broadly at Sloan.

She feels a tremendous heat in her palms and opens them.

She awakens again in her bed and looks at her palms, from which the white light shines brightly.

CHAPTER FORTY

Christian once again stands at Ari's window, pleading. "I understand that you want me to go away. And I will, if you really want me to. But I have to tell you everything first, and I want to apologize. Please, it's important!"

"Go away!"

Christian walks toward the front door and hollers back toward Ari's window, "I'm coming inside now!"

As he enters the bedroom, Ari rolls over in her bed and looks at him briefly. "What do you want?" she says.

"Are you feeling better?" Christian says.

"No."

"Is your temperature down?" He feels her forehead before Ari brushes his hand away. "You feel cooler."

On Ari's nightstand are five bottles of NyQuil, and another ten on the floor.

"Where did you get all this NyQuil?" Christian says.

"Leave me alone."

"I want to tell you everything," Christian says, sitting on the bed. "Everything I know at least. Or think I know."

"I don't care," Ari says.

"Your husband did something to me. You have to know that. He's responsible for all of this."

"You'd like to believe that, wouldn't you?" Ari throws back her covers, rises naked from her bed, puts on her robe, and heads for the hallway. "You're pathetic."

"Pathetic?" Christian follows her. "Pathetic how?"

"What do they call it?" Ari says as she turns into the kitchen. "Bait and switch? You bait me with decent person, then switch to asshole. And then you blame someone else for it."

"Asshole? Me?" Christian rushes after her.

She places a teapot on the stove and turns. "I saw you as somebody who was sincere and clumsy and real." She lights a cigarette. "You reacted like a baby to everything."

"That's patronizing," Christian snaps back, "and definitely wrong. I may be clumsy, but I've never been like a baby. Babies trust. Babies are happy. I've been suspicious and anxious my entire life."

"You're not the victim here," Ari says, taking a drag from her cigarette.

"Okay, okay. I admit I have not behaved entirely honestly lately, and that's on me."

"How gallant," Ari says. She pulls the teapot off the stove.

Hands shaking, Christian begins, "I think it's basically impossible for women to appreciate how much the erectile dysfunction thing hurts. It's the ultimate insult. Any man would do anything to fix it. And so when your husband said he could . . . I don't know why I believed him. He gave me a drug, I guess, or maybe he tricked me into believing I was better."

"It wasn't the erection you wanted," Ari says, stubbing out her cigarette. "It was power." She grabs her mug and walks past him down the hallway.

"Okay!" Christian yells in the hallway. "You want to talk about power? Of course I wanted power. I've never felt powerful, not for one second, *ever*, in my entire life. I've had to watch powerful assholes always get everything they want: the job, the car, the girl, the money, everything. They don't care about other people's feelings. I *do* care about other people's feelings, I'm a good person, and what do I get for it? Cheated on by my wife, laughed at by teenagers, a part-time job with no benefits. And erectile dysfunction! So yes, I fucking wanted power! Who wouldn't? Who wouldn't want the Hammer of the Gods!"

As Christian reaches Ari's bedroom door, she suddenly rushes back out.

"Move," Ari says, shoving Christian aside with one hand as she covers her mouth with the other.

He starts to follow her toward the bathroom when he hears her vomit into the toilet.

"What—" Christian opens the door. "Are you okay?"

Ari looks up at him from the floor by the toilet. "Go away."

"Kiklêskô Dionyson Eribromon, Euastêra!

CHAPTER FORTY-ONE

"I don't understand what's happening right now." Parker Fanning wipes his brow as he receives another banker's box from Sloan.

"It's simple, Parker," Sloan says, her large frame silhouetted against the window of her thirty-fifth-floor corner office. "I'm quitting, and you're taking my cases. It's good for you. Be excited."

"The partners are going to freak," Parker says.

"Let them."

"You're Sloan Green," Parker says with awe. "You're the fucking bomb."

"I don't want to be the bomb anymore," Sloan says, handing him another box.

Parker peers at the label on one of the boxes. "I know literally nothing about this case. When are you going to bring me up to speed?"

"You'll be fine," Sloan says, blowing hair out of her eyes. "Remember, you and I were about to have sex last time you were in my office, Parker. There was flirty talk; I could see you had a little erection. What happened to that?"

Parker blushes. "Well, I think we decided not to. Which I respect. Since there were HR issues, obviously."

"I'm leaving now," Sloan says. "So, no HR issues."

"Right." Parker nods.

"Why did you want to have sex with me, Parker?" Sloan says. "Is it because I'm so good-looking, or because you'd fuck any woman, or because you think it'd help you get ahead somehow?"

"I don't know," Parker says with an uncertain chuckle. "All of the above?"

Sloan shoves Parker down onto a chair. She sits on his lap, straddling his legs.

"Do you want me to get off of you?"

Parker shakes his head and mutters, "No."

"I have your consent to sit on your lap?"

"Yes."

"Look at me." Parker looks at Sloan, whose pupils, he notices, are severely dilated. She opens her palms and then faces them toward Parker, who shields his eyes against the brightness emanating from them.

"What is that?" Parker yells. "What's wrong with your hands?

"Kiklêskô Dionyson Eribromon, Euastêra!" Sloan chants.

"Ms. Green," Parker says stridently. "I think you're in a crisis!"

"Kiklêskô Dionyson Eribromon, Euastêra!" Sloan continues chanting.

The giant bay window behind Sloan's desk begins to warp and undulate.

"Dionysus is the reality of nature hidden deep within the body," Sloan says now in English, her eyes shining past Parker. "He loosens chains and breaks down walls."

The bay window continues to billow.

"There's something happening to the window!" Parker shouts.

"Singing again the ancient songs of dying trees and withered stems." Sloan raises her arms. "Of new beginnings and lightning crashing. Such are the lovers of Dionysus!"

With one percussive boom, the window shatters, and the salty bay air rushes in a violent wave through the office. Sloan rises and walks toward the window, her arms raised, her hair blown back by the wind.

"Hey!" Parker shouts. "Who are you?"

"Feel the breeze, Parker," Sloan says. "That's all there is."

Parker staggers through the wind and flying papers toward the door and shuts it behind him.

CHAPTER FORTY-TWO

Francesca peers down from the top of the bleachers toward her father, who leans against the fence bordering the football field, watching the second Glenhaven game of the season.

Francesca has always been able to feel her father's pain, the way people feel rain in their joints, and she can feel it now. She recalls her mother's words about Christian's idealism, how it perpetuates his misery, how it amounts to a flaw in his character. She feels resentment toward her mother and toward a world that punishes idealists so mercilessly.

There's a commotion near the entrance to the stadium. Francesca spots Dee on the track that surrounds the field, shouting, striding quickly, and being followed by Ari. The two are evidently arguing. Dee leaps the fence and rushes onto the football field.

The kickoff is currently sailing toward Maron, who stands on the ten-yard line. Maron catches the ball, and Francesca feels a thrill as he springs into motion. A wave of blockers moves right to create a wall for Maron, who makes his way upfield, alternately probing, shoving, and sprinting.

Francesca starts down the steps, noticing that Dee is now jogging after the players. She marvels at how Dee doesn't seem the slightest bit concerned about entering the fray.

Head Coach Mike Carlson, mouth agape on the sidelines, takes two steps forward. "Hey, asshole, get the fuck off the field!" he yells.

A confused referee throws a flag in the general direction of Dee, who picks it up and tosses it back politely. With no apparent effort, Dee begins yanking players from both teams off his son. He extricates Maron from the pile, pulls him to his feet, and begins guiding him off the field.

Francesca stops at the bottom of the bleachers and watches Maron shove his father back. Dee clasps his hands together and pleads. Maron spits on the ground near Dee and keeps walking.

The crowd boos loudly. Coach Carlson rips off his headset and runs toward Dee. As he approaches with some other coaches, Dee raises his finger. "Turn around, sunshine."

Assistant Coach Tork Shanley rushes at Dee. A moment before he can tackle him, Stanley doubles over as if suffering a sudden belly cramp.

Mike Carlson and the other coaches double over as well, reaching for their crotches.

"You'll be fine in the morning," Dee says. "Or maybe not." Then he turns and runs after Maron, who has just now leaped over the fence. The boos continue. Ari chases after her son and husband.

The coaches hobble back toward the safety of the sidelines. It occurs to Francesca that they all have erections. A word rises from the depths of her memory. "Priapism," she says out loud. "Priapus. A Greek god."

Francesca fears she peed herself.

CHAPTER FORTY-THREE

The parking lot at Glenhaven High funnels onto a bridge that crosses a creek and leads to a busy intersection. To the right of the bridge, on the street side, is a grassy area where students congregate in the morning and after school.

Tonight, because of the sold-out football game, this area is deserted. Francesca, having discreetly followed Maron's family, crouches behind the last rail at the end of the bridge. She is witnessing what is clearly a family argument, or perhaps more accurately a family brawl. Maron, Dee, and Ari all move restlessly around the grassy area, speaking at top volume and simultaneously in Greek.

"Prosehi pos milas!"

"Arketa!"

Maron, still in his football gear, breaks free from his mother's grip and rushes at his father. Dee raises his right hand, and Maron *lifts into the air* until he is about twenty feet high. Ari screams. Francesca covers her mouth.

Limbs flailing, Maron drifts slowly toward the busy street below. Francesca hears herself whimper and covers her mouth. She squeezes her legs together, fearing she has peed herself.

Ten feet from the road, Dee pulls Maron back over the grass. He opens his hand, and Maron drops to the ground.

Ari pounds on Dee's chest with her fists.

"Darling, please," Dee says, weathering Ari's blows. He staggers toward Maron, who is still on the ground, and falls to his knees. "I'm only thinking of you, son. All I can think about is you dying."

"So you drop me into traffic instead?" Maron says, standing. "Just remember that I chose death over everlasting life as your son. We both did! How bad would it have to be for me to do that?"

"I can change," Dee says.

"Really? How much more time do you need? Will another thousand years do it?"

Dee turns toward Ari and crawls to her on his knees.

"Darling, you knew who I was when I rescued you from Naxos," Dee begins. "I've never been father material. I don't understand children. What do they want? And I'm not really husband material either."

"What material are you then?" Ari stalks forward.

Dee jumps to his feet and roars, "I'm god material!" He turns his palms toward a nearby pine tree, which bursts into flame. He pulls the burning tree out of the ground by its roots and raises it high.

"You're a joke!" Ari shouts.

Dee chucks the burning tree into the creek below.

"You don't even do your job anymore," Ari yells.

"I can't do it without you," Dee says. "You're my partner, Ari!"

"Partner?!" Ari gets in Dee's face. "Don't lie. You already have a new partner, and you know it! Go to her already and let us live our own lives!"

A spasm of fear runs down Francesca's spine. She recalls the night on Ari's lawn when Ari claimed to know Sloan and said the words "It's you, isn't it?"

"No, no," Francesca mutters to herself. She rises and runs as fast as her legs will carry her back to the school.

Francesca finally arrives, breathless, at the empty tennis courts and drops onto a bench. Her heart races. She wants to cry, feels that she ought to cry, but finds that she can't cry.

When she hears Maron's voice behind her a few minutes later, she wonders if it's coming from within her own mind.

"I'm sorry."

Maron stands behind her, holding his helmet in his hand.

"Why did you have to follow me?" Maron says in a plaintive tone.

Francesca fidgets, realizing she has no good answer. "I was . . . concerned about you. I thought you might be—"

"Might be what?" Maron says with anger. Francesca notices that he is shaking. "Having a fight with my family? Who hasn't had a fight with their family?"

"Of course," Francesca says softly. "But—"

"I know I'm just a freak to you," Maron says. "Your life is so boring, you need to spice it up. So you spy on me and my family! Spy on the freaks!" His voice rises with each word.

"That's not true!" Francesca yells back at equal volume. "You're just angry because you feel exposed. I followed you because I was worried about you. Your father was being a jerk, and you sliced yourself up at the crab feed like a crazy person, and I was worried! You're only upset because I saw what happened and I wasn't supposed to. You feel violated and I get that, but that's not my fault!"

"You were spying on us!" Maron shouts.

"Why don't you just tell me what the fuck is going on?" Francesca says. "Your father picked you up and almost threw you into the road. He lit a tree on fire. What the fuck!"

"I'm not going to explain it," Maron mutters, lowering his head.

She rises from the bench and stands in front of him. "If you're here to break up with me, at least do it like a man! Tell me you don't want to see me. Tell me you're done with me." Tears begin rolling down Francesca's cheeks. "Or not, I don't care. Whatever."

Maron suddenly hugs her desperately.

"I can't be a regular person, Francesca," Maron cries. "I've tried. It's never going to happen. And they're going to kick me out of school if I stop playing football."

"No, they won't," Francesca says without conviction.

"I'm just tired of it! My mother, too. She's so tired," Maron says, tears rolling down his cheeks. "We started too late."

"Started what too late?" Francesca says.

Maron turns to her. "Please, Francesca, promise me you won't give up on families. I know my family is bad, but there are wonderful families out there. I've seen thousands of them. You have to believe in families and have one of your own someday. Because families keep everything together. Do you hear me?"

Francesca recalls their first meeting when Maron studied her eyes the way he is now. It felt to her then that he was learning everything about her. Now it feels like he's trying to remember her forever.

"I'm not going to let my family hurt you anymore," Maron says, smiling through his tears as he cups Francesca's cheeks in his hands. "I like you too much! In fact, I love you!"

Maron kisses Francesca deeply and runs off.

CHAPTER FORTY-FOUR

Christian sits in his cheap office chair as Mark Apple strides back and forth in front of him, alternately crying and laughing. Christian checks the clock on the wall. He realizes that he has now become Mark Apple's confessor—and that short of telling a sick man, who is also his superior, that he no longer wants this role, there is nothing to do but listen.

"I think maybe I wanted this," Apple says, shrugging. "I think I wanted to get cancer. Maybe I wanted to die?"

Christian frowns. "That's ridiculous. Why?"

"Why would I want to die?" Apple says. "I agree it doesn't make sense. I've never been suicidal. I've never even been depressed. And yet, I can't shake the feeling that I brought this on. Have you ever wanted to die?"

"Not exactly," Christian begins. "Sometimes when I'm standing on the train platform, I feel a really strong urge to jump."

"Meh, that's the call of the void. That's impulse control. I'm talking about thinking about dying, wishing you could die, and then thinking about how it might happen."

Christian shakes his head.

"No, because you're not actually depressed," Apple points at Christian. "You seem like you should be depressed, but you aren't."

Fired up by this contradiction and apparently uninterested in the passing school day, Apple stares out the window.

He continues, "I think you're one of those people who, when things don't work out, just pushes the goalposts back. You don't get embarrassed that you keep moving your goalposts. In fact, you forget about it right after you do it, which is really the key." He turns to Christian. "It's a blessing to forget!"

"But isn't everyone like that?" Christian replies. "The only reason you're not moving the goalposts now is because you're trying to protect yourself in case you don't get better. But you will get better, and you will move the goalposts again. Cancer happens to some people, it's happened to you, and you had nothing to do with it."

"That's a solid angle, and I appreciate that," Apple says, now looking more like the jock than the anguished philosopher. "But I think people don't recognize how responsible they are for their own fate until it grabs them by the balls. When it first happens, you feel like a victim. But then, when you start thinking about it"—Apple gets closer and whispers conspiratorially—"you start to wonder if you were somehow . . . in on it."

"What does that mean?" Christian responds, surprised at his own vehemence. "That's bullshit. You're just trying to make sense out of something that makes no sense. Does someone who gets hit by a bus want to get hit by a bus?"

"Three months ago, I would have said no, but now I say yes."

"Somebody wants to get hit by a meteor?"

"What I say is that somebody wanted to get hit by that meteor more than somebody else," Apple says. "There's a reason why I get hit by that meteor and not you."

"So, everyone in the buildings on 9/11?" Christian says, his voice rising. "Each one had a death wish? C'mon, Mark, it doesn't make sense. You're just scrambling to find an answer because there isn't one. And all you're really doing is beating yourself up right now, when you need to preserve your strength."

"I don't think my strength is going to save me." Apple shakes his head. "What I need now is to accept. I need to accept . . . something. Anything, really. I just don't know what to accept, other than the obvious. Maybe I just wish I understood something basic about why we're here, something elemental, before I get turned off like a light."

"You're talking about a religious feeling," Christian says, surprised at how absorbed he is in this conversation. "I'm not personally a religious person, but have you ever had some kind of religious or spiritual practice?"

Apple laughs. "Are you fucking kidding me? I'm a jock from the California suburbs. My spirituality is, I don't know, sunshine."

"It seems to me that you have a deep spiritual side," Christian says earnestly. "I'm hearing it right now."

"That's, well, that's . . ." Apple replies, choking up. "That's because I'm up against the wall with the rifles pointed at me."

"I don't think so," Christian replies. "It feels authentic to me. It's like humanistic wisdom. Victor Frankl, Bertrand Russell. Buddhism, in a way. This is the kind of questioning you're doing right now."

Just then, Francesca bursts into the room and throws her backpack on the floor like a gauntlet. "Did one of you kick Maron out of school?"

"Francesca!" Christian yells with a sternness that surprises him.

Apple wipes his eyes, moves toward the door. "Hey, gotta go. Got a meeting!" He turns to Francesca. "Hi, Francesca! If you're talking about the football player, I did not kick him out. As far as I know, he's still enrolled."

"Well, he's gone!" Francesca steps toward Christian with her fists clenched as Apple leaves.

Christian is appalled by his daughter's insouciance. "Honey, you can't talk to your principal like that."

"Maron didn't come to school," Francesca says, "and he's not answering his phone, and his math teacher said she couldn't tell me anything because of 'privacy.' What the fuck does that even mean?"

"Honey, no one has kicked Maron out," Christian says. "Maybe his family . . . you know, they're sort of itinerant. They don't have a history of staying anywhere for long."

Joyce Wilcox, Christian's aged and legally blind secretary, enters the room and shouts, "Leaving now, Christian!" before turning and leaving.

"God," Francesca says. "That woman. She's your secretary? She should be in a home. But they can't fire her, so they give her to you. Jesus!" She picks up her backpack. "All adults are insane failures. Every single one of them. You know that Mom just quit her job, don't you?"

"What?" Christian says, stunned.

"I don't even care!" Francesca yells. "I'm done dealing with everyone's problems!" She throws her backpack over her shoulder and runs out the door.

"Ichos! VoHe!"

CHAPTER FORTY-FIVE

Francesca hops a city bus toward her mother's house, having quickly forgotten her resolution to be done dealing with other people's problems. Along the way, she puzzles over a story about her mother she heard from Annie earlier in the day.

"Phoebe said she saw your mom at Whole Foods," Annie told her. "Apparently, your mom started buying everyone's groceries in line, and people were cheering. But then she got weird and knocked over a banana stand, grabbed a bunch of bananas, and made monkey noises in people's faces, and then ran out the door."

Francesca arrives at her mother's house and sees Sloan's car in the driveway. As she heads toward the front door, Francesca hears laughter and shouts coming from the backyard of Craig Entwerp's house across the street.

Carefully opening the gate into Craig's side yard, Francesca has the sudden intuition that she is about to find her mother splashing around in the neighbor's pool.

She peers through the gate leading to the pool and sees her mother, completely naked, on the diving board. Craig, meanwhile, treads water in the middle of the pool. Mercifully, he appears to be wearing a bathing suit. Craig hoots and claps.

"VoHe! VoHe!" he shouts. "Do a double!"

Sloan wags her finger mischievously at Craig and then bounces once in preparation for her dive. Francesca notes that her mother's final jump takes her perilously high, ten feet or more into the air. Francesca imagines the scene as the EMTs arrive: Sloan naked and unconscious, Francesca explaining how Craig wasn't her husband, lover, or even friend.

High over the water, Sloan tucks and curls and does not one, not two, but three flips, plunging straight as an arrow into the water. Francesca's mouth opens.

Worried that her mother is about to swim to Craig and engage in some kind of B-movie pornographic love scene, Francesca covers her eyes. Instead, Craig eagerly climbs the ladder and begins running like a child, arms flailing, toward the diving board.

"Ichos! Ichos!" Craig shouts. Francesca recognizes this word, as well as the word *VoHe*, as words she heard the cheerleaders shouting around the fire at Lime Ridge.

As Craig steps onto the board, he affects a Charlie Chaplin walk, twirling an imaginary cane and whistling. Sloan squeals with laughter when Craig drops into the water. Then she climbs out of the pool and runs again toward the diving board.

Francesca winces at the prospect of having once again to watch her mother's bare breasts bounce in the air. However, this time her mother lies face forward on the board and presses up into a full handstand. Bouncing upside down on the board briefly, she leaps from her hands and lands feetfirst into the water, another perfect entry.

Francesca slumps down against the inside of the gate. She ponders whether her mother received severance, how much mortgage might be left on the house, how much savings Sloan has, and generally what sort of suburban family collapse she should be anticipating for herself right now.

"Hold on, 'Cesca! I'm coming!"

Francesca shrinks in place, sure that she hasn't been seen. Her mother's voice grows nearer.

"See ya, Craig. My daughter's here."

"Stay! Tell her to come swim with us!"

"Gotta go, bye!"

Francesca rushes out through the gate and toward Craig's driveway, ahead of her mother. Sloan emerges, casually wrapping a towel around her naked body.

"Hi, baby!" She rushes to her daughter and kisses her on the cheek.

"Mom!" Francesca says, her hands shaking. "Why are you swimming naked in Craig Entwerp's backyard? You hate that guy."

"Oh, I don't know. He's different now. He's better," Sloan says.

"Why are you naked, though?"

"Let's go inside," Sloan says. "I'm hungry. Are you hungry?"

"Please tell me you didn't quit your job?" Francesca pleads in the kitchen while Sloan lingers at her fridge in a robe, eating peanut butter from the jar with a spoon.

Sloan enunciates through her sticky mouth: "I did."

"I know you're in a midlife crisis, but you're supposed to act on some of your crazy impulses, not all of them."

Sloan closes the refrigerator and takes another lick from her spoon. "Protecting big corporations from lawsuits by poor people is not an impulse I want to act on ever again."

"You don't have to convince me. I always thought your job was evil. But what are you going to do now? Swim naked with Craig Entwerp every day?"

"No," Sloan replies.

"Then what?"

"Can we sit?" Sloan settles at the kitchen table with her peanut butter jar, and Francesca sits opposite her.

"Let's see," Sloan begins. Her eyes shine upward, and it occurs to Francesca that her mother is about to begin philosophizing.

"I feel like there was a train I was supposed to get on a long time ago, you know?" Sloan says. "And I didn't get on it. I got on a different train, and then I transferred to another train—and kept on transferring trains and getting farther away from the place I intended to go in the first place."

"Right," Francesca says. "That's called life. Lots of detours, wrong turns, and unplanned stops. I'm assuming that being my mother was a train you never wanted to get on?"

"Not at all." Sloan sets down her peanut butter jar and reaches for Francesca's hand. "You're without a doubt the best train I've ever been on."

"I feel like there's a big 'but' coming," Francesca says.

"But lately," Sloan says, taking another spoonful of peanut butter, "I find myself veering toward a place that maybe I was supposed to be in the first place."

"Veering or being pushed?" Francesca says.

"What do you mean?" Sloan says.

"I think you're placing a lot of trust in a freak you just met."

"I'm not," Sloan says. "This is not about him."

"I think it's a lot about him." Francesca takes her mother's hand now. "Listen to me. Last night I saw him lift—I mean *levitate*—his son, Maron, twenty feet into the air and wave him around like a kite. And then he set a tree on fire and lifted *that* out of the ground. Mom, this guy is—I know it sounds crazy—but he is some kind of witch. He literally has supernatural powers."

"Not a witch," Sloan says.

"What do you mean?" Francesca says. "What is he if he's not a witch?"

Sloan seems suddenly flustered. She frowns and rises. "You're right. I do need to find out some things. Can you wait for me here?" She sets the peanut butter on the counter. "I need to clarify a few things."

"Clarify what?" Francesca follows her mother into the living room. As it becomes clear that her mother is headed for the door, Francesca shouts, "Listen! I heard Maron's mother say that Dee is trying to replace her with you!"

Sloan stops at the threshold. "She said that?"

"What does that mean?"

"It doesn't mean anything," Sloan says. "No. No. I'm not replacing anyone."

"Then stay here with me and be my frickin' mother," Francesca begs.

Sloan rushes to her daughter, hugs her, and kisses her on the cheek. "I love you. I'll be right back."

"No, you won't!" Francesca follows Sloan into the front yard.

Francesca watches her thirty-eight-year-old mother, until recently a high-powered attorney at Strauss & Fell, run barefoot in a robe on a Tuesday afternoon toward the door of a witch's house.

Francesca pulls out her phone, dials, and waits for her father to pick up.

"Dad, I need you to come here right now."

"Take him away."

CHAPTER FORTY-SIX

Christian pulls into the driveway of Sloan's house and nearly hits his daughter as she rushes toward him like a NASCAR pit crew member.

"Never run toward a moving car, please!" Christian says peevishly as he gets out. He stuffs his keys into Francesca's hands. "Please go to my apartment. I'll handle this."

"I only have my permit," Francesca says. "What are you going to do?"

"Just take my car." Christian places his hands on his hips, facing Dee's house.

"Don't mess with him, Dad," Francesca says plaintively. "He's a witch—literally a witch. He's incredibly dangerous."

"If he wanted to hurt me, I think he would have done it already," Christian says with a steely tone.

"Not necessarily," Francesca says. "Today could be the day he hurts you."

"Take surface streets." Christian turns toward Francesca. "Not the freeway. Go to my apartment and wait there. I'll be fine."

"I'm calling you in twenty minutes, and if you don't answer, I'm calling the police." Francesca hugs her father. "Don't do anything stupid."

Moments later, Christian circles Dee's house. He overhears snippets of a conversation among Dee, Sloan, and Lenny coming from within the house.

"What does she mean, fuck doll?"

"She has cold feet, Agrios."

"Fuck you!"

"Such language is beneath a woman of your station."

"Fuck you and your station."

"My dear . . ."

"I want to know everything. How it all works. What we do. Or I'm out of here."

"I was starting to tell you about Kierkegaard's leap of faith?"

"Fuck off."

Christian hears chairs moving, followed by the sounds of objects falling on the ground and hitting the walls. He circles around the house just in time to see Dee tossed out the front door.

Dee lands on the walkway. Sloan appears in the doorway in her robe. She rushes at Dee, picks him up like a WWE wrestler, raises him over her head, and throws him into a bush.

Christian covers his mouth. "Oh my god!"

"Sloan, please!" Lenny emerges from the house, holding a champagne flute.

Dee extricates himself from the bush, brushes himself off, and walks toward Sloan.

"You have quite the arm there, little lady. Where did you get such strength, I wonder?"

Sloan rushes at Dee and shoves him to the ground. As she leaps on him, Dee places the soles of his feet against Sloan's chest and launches her into the air. Sloan lands with a thud on the hood of Dee's Prius.

"Oh my god!" Christian cries again.

Sloan hops off the car, opens the driver's door, and shoves the Prius forward toward Dee.

"Is this how lawyers negotiate?" Dee says. "They run each other over?"

He gestures toward the neighbors' houses, where a few porch lights have come on in the dusk light. "The neighbors are trying to sleep!" he shouts. He looks at his mostly naked body. "And I haven't dressed for dinner. Silenus!"

Lenny steps toward Dee. "She just wants clear answers, Zagreus," Lenny says. "It's understandable."

Both men duck as a brick flies past their heads.

"She needs more details on her role, your role, the entire thing, really," Lenny says calmly as two more bricks fly.

Sirens blip, and moments later two police cars pull into the driveway.

"Hands where I can see them!" shouts an unseen officer.

"He attacked me," Sloan says. "He's an animal. Take him away."

Sloan crosses the driveway toward Christian and raises her right elbow. Christian dutifully steps forward and takes her arm.

The officer follows Sloan as she and Christian cross the street.

"Ma'am, we'll need you to make a statement if you intend to press charges."

"I'm a lawyer. I'll call the station tomorrow," Sloan responds over her shoulder. "Rough him up a little for me while he's in jail, would you?"

Christian and Sloan walk in silence until they reach the front porch.

"What's happening?" Christian says finally. "What did Lenny mean by 'cold feet'? How did you push that car forward? What's happening to you?"

Sloan turns and smiles. "A lot."

"I can see that," Christian says. "But—"

"That's it," Sloan interrupts. "A lot is happening. I'm making changes."

"Sloan, that man is evil," Christian says carefully.

"No," Sloan says. "He's not. Lost. Wild. Desperate, yes. But not evil. I can help him, if he'll let me."

"I never took you for the rescuer type."

"I told you, this isn't about him," Sloan says. "This is about me." She looks skyward. "It's not even really about me, which is what's so mind-blowing!"

"What do you mean?"

Sloan kisses Christian on the cheek. "You're a good man, Christian. You're good and I ruined our marriage because I was missing something. I just had no idea it was this."

"But what is this?"

"Things are going to get better for both of us now," Sloan says. "I know it. Go see Ari. She needs you."

"Ari?"

Sloan walks toward her house.

"Hey, Mr. Human-All-Too-Human!" From across the street, Dee sticks his head out of the back of the police car and shouts at Christian. "New terms for our deal. Both wives are off limits now, you hear? Your wife *and* my wife; that's two wives! But things will work out. How's your sex life these days? Better?"

As the police car rolls away Dee sticks his head further out the window to be heard.

"It's funny that you're named Christian," he hollers, "since Christ was really the beginning of the end for me. Maybe you've come to finish me off. Wouldn't that be ironic?"

Dee blows Christian a kiss as the police car rounds the corner and disappears.

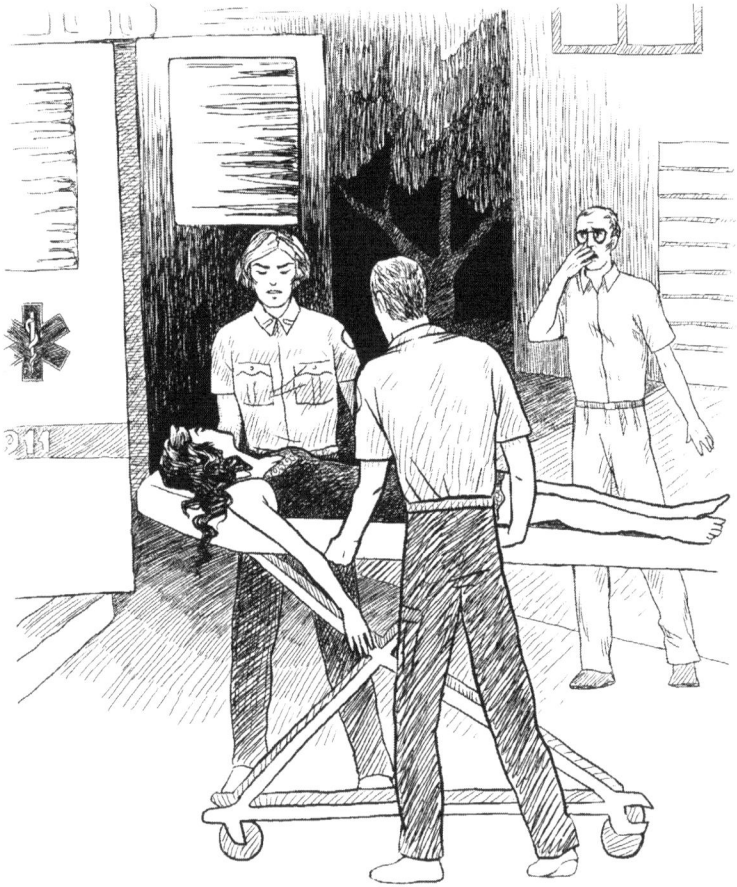

"That's gotta be a lot of NyQuil."

CHAPTER FORTY-SEVEN

Christian texts Francesca as he trudges up the street leading away from Sloan's house.

ARE U AT THE APARTMENT? I NEED CAR.

Francesca texts back immediately.

HE DIDN'T KILL YOU? WALKED TO ANNIE'S. YR CAR AROUND CORNER ON LILAC.

As Christian opens the door to his Fiesta, his phone pings again with a text from Ari.

SORRY WE COULDN'T FINISH THAT DINNER. GOODBYE.

―――――――――――

Christian screeches to a halt in Ari's driveway. The house is dark except for a dim light coming from her bedroom. Christian races to the door and turns the handle. For the first time in his experience, the door is locked. He runs along the front side of the house and knocks on Ari's bedroom window.

"Ari? Hello? Hello?"

A faint light illuminates Ari's room. Christian strains to see through a slight opening in the curtains. It appears as though Ari is asleep in the bed, turned away. Christian shouts Ari's name again and desperately bangs on the window. Then his gaze falls on a pile of NyQuil bottles on the floor, perhaps thirty of them. Christian dials 911.

"There's an overdose!" Christian shouts into his phone. "My friend just overdosed. My girlfriend. On NyQuil. Yes, NyQuil. Please come!"

Porch lights blink on in the neighboring houses. Christian runs to the back of the house and tries the slider, which is locked. The garage door is also locked.

In a few minutes, an EMT truck pulls into the driveway. Christian meets the EMTs as they get out of the truck.

"She's in the back bedroom. It's NyQuil!" he shrieks. "She took an overdose of NyQuil! Help her!"

As the EMTs grab their backpacks, Christian hears one of them mutter, "That's gotta be a lot of NyQuil."

"Get the battering ram thing!" Christian yells. "You have to break down the door. It's locked! She's not moving! Hurry!"

The two EMTs lunge with their shoulders at the door but fail to break it down. Christian backs up and with a scream rushes toward the door at top speed. He smashes it down. The paramedics glance at one another before entering.

In Ari's bedroom, the paramedics flip over Ari's limp body. "Ma'am, ma'am," they say, pinching and slapping her cheeks. One begins administering CPR. "Jesus," the EMT says, looking at the bottles on the floor, "that *is* a lot of NyQuil."

"Get the gurney!" the one administering CPR yells. As they wheel Ari away on the gurney, the EMT continues to administer CPR. "Call ahead to Sutter!" he shouts.

Christian's voice rises as it becomes clear that Ari is not waking up. "Do CPR! Keep doing it!" he yells. "You have to keep doing it!"

The EMTs load Ari into the back of the ambulance. Christian follows, shouting, "She's my girlfriend!" and attempts to hop in. But they shut the doors ahead of him. Christian turns and nearly bowls over an old man in a robe who has just arrived from across the street.

He scrambles to the end of the driveway, hops in his Fiesta, and drives it as fast as he can, attempting to stay on the heels of the van.

———————————

Arriving at the emergency room reception desk, Christian sees the tail end of the gurney carrying what he assumes to be Ari slipping through the doors into the ICU.

"I'm with that woman who just came in! She's my girlfriend!" Christian shouts to the triage nurse. He rushes to the ICU door, but it shuts in front of him. Christian uselessly paws the scan card sensor.

Later, as Christian paces in the lobby, a doctor finally emerges from the locked doors and tilts his head toward Christian.

"Are you with Ms. Woods?" he says.

"Yes!" Christian clenches his fists. "I'm her boyfriend."

"Not her husband?"

"No!" Christian shouts. "But we're together. Please!"

"I'm sorry," the doctor sighs. "We did everything we could. Her heart was stopped for too long."

"I'm not good for her anymore."

CHAPTER FORTY-EIGHT

An hour earlier at the Glenhaven police station, a clerk used a broom to shoo a small white goat out the front door. It didn't occur to the clerk to question how a goat came to be in their station. Another hour passed before anyone realized that the half-naked man brought in earlier was gone from the holding cell and that the cell door was still locked.

In the emergency room, Christian sits in a chair, sobbing. A nurse passes by and rests her hand on his shoulder. Suddenly there's a commotion at the front desk. Christian turns to see Dee storming past the triage nurse.

"Where is she?" Dee shouts. "Down there?" Dee doesn't wait for an answer but charges toward the locked ICU doors.

"I'm sorry, you can't go in there!" the nurse yells, chasing after Dee. Dee tries the doors, finds them locked, and then simply shoves them open. Alarms go off.

"Sir!" the nurse shouts. Large orderlies appear in the hallway and chase after Dee. He shoves one away, then another. As more orderlies arrive, Christian peers down the hall to see their bodies cast against the wall.

Now a policeman races past Christian with a gun drawn. As the policeman raises his gun, Dee waves his right hand, and all the lights go out.

After a few moments, the deep rumble of a generator is heard, and a few lights come back on.

Christian wanders down the hallway past the groaning bodies. The policeman with the gun stands motionless, frozen in time. As Christian reaches the threshold to the brightly lit operating room, he sees Dee bent over Ari's gurney with his head on her chest. Dee mutters a stream of words in Greek.

Christian enters. "What are you doing?"

Dee doesn't answer Christian but resumes intoning Greek words.

"You ruined her life!" Christian cries desperately. "And your son's. You're responsible for this!"

"Shut up!" Dee waves his hand again and sends two nearby gurneys rolling at top speed toward Christian, who manages to dodge them.

The room goes dark, and Christian can hear Dee occasionally sobbing as he continues to speak into Ari's ear. His words sound like a chant or a prayer.

The lights rise again. Dee is standing tall now, facing Christian and holding Ari's hand. Christian jumps when he notices the body beneath the sheet stirring.

Ari rolls her head slightly to one side and moans.

"My god! Ari!" Christian cries.

"Come," Dee says firmly.

Christian approaches. "How did she . . . how did you . . . ?"

"Don't talk," Dee says. "Your voice . . ." He shakes his head and winces. When he speaks, it is with difficulty, as if someone were forcing him to utter the following words: "I'm not good for her anymore. I don't why, but she thinks you are."

He takes Christian's hand and clasps it with Ari's. He leans so close to Christian that their lips are almost touching.

"I've known many men," Dee says. "You are the most pathetic man I have ever met. If the world depended upon men like you, there would be no humans left."

Christian, paying little attention to Dee's words, is unable to take his eyes off Ari, who begins to make small noises.

"Okay. Thank you," Christian says absently.

"You will be kind to her," Dee continues. "Look at me! You will be nothing but kind to her, or I will kill you. Do you understand?" He raises Christian's chin with his fingers. "I may kill you anyway. You understand?"

"You may kill me; got it," Christian says, still staring at Ari.

Dee takes one last mournful look at Ari, sighs, and walks out the door. Soon, Christian hears raised voices and the sounds of more bodies slamming against walls.

Ari blinks and finally opens her eyes weakly. She squints at Christian like a cat.

"Christian," Ari says softly.

"I'm here," Christian says.

"What happened?" Ari says. "The NyQuil didn't work?"

"No," Christian replies. "You're in a hospital. You're going to be okay."

Ari looks around the room until her gaze rests on the window overlooking the east side of Glenhaven. "It's all still there," she sighs.

"Yes, everything is still there," Christian says. "It's not going anywhere, and neither are you. You have a long life yet to live."

Ari laughs, then winces and touches her forehead.

"I'm sorry, Ari." Christian kneels beside the gurney. "I let you down."

Ari blinks a few times and manages to snort. "You think I did this because of you?"

"Well, no. I . . ." Christian fumbles.

Ari closes her eyes and rolls away from him.

Doctors, nurses, and police enter the room and pull Christian to the hall. A doctor gently places a stethoscope over Ari's heart while a nurse readies an IV. Three nursing assistants retreat into a huddle and whisper excitedly to one another.

CHAPTER FORTY-NINE

Seated on her living room sofa just before midnight, Sloan refills her glass of red wine. Strewn across the coffee table are photos of Francesca as a child as well as projects from her elementary school days. Sloan picks up a baby picture of Francesca. Tears well in her eyes. There's a knock at the door.

"May I come in?"

"No!" Sloan shouts.

There's another knock, followed by sounds of the door opening. Lenny appears in Sloan's living room.

"Five minutes, my dear," he says, smiling.

Sloan opens her hands. The lights appear dazzlingly and powerfully now, as they have for the last twelve hours. She raises both palms toward Lenny, who rises six inches off the ground and rotates ninety degrees until his body is parallel to the floor.

"This is really unnecessary," Lenny says calmly, his long gray hair dangling. "We need to talk." He raises his own right hand and gently moves himself upright until he stands on the floor.

He seats himself on the sectional across from Sloan and looks at the pictures of Francesca.

"What a darling girl," he says, picking up a photo. "You know that

Maron is quite smitten with her."

"What do you want?" Sloan says.

Lenny clears his throat. "I want to finish our conversation about Soren Kierkegaard, the atheist who in the end became something of a believer."

"Is this Bible study? I thought you guys were heathens," Sloan says flatly.

"I'm talking about faith," Lenny continues, "which transcends religion, and why it's important for you, and for us, going forward."

"I don't know if there is an us going forward," Sloan says.

"That's because you have questions about what is actually happening," Lenny responds. "I'm here to answer those questions."

He strokes his chin. "Let me ask you about a summer's day a long time ago. You were a little girl, seven or eight. You were in the woods behind your aunt's house. You had lost the trail and found yourself in a meadow that led to an unbroken forest."

Sloan sets down her wineglass.

"At the edge of the forest," Lenny continues softly, "you saw a woman in a white dress. She was tall and wore a necklace around her neck."

"A wreath," Sloan says quickly, and then looks with surprise at Lenny.

"You do remember." He moves to sit beside Sloan and smiles. "And there was some kind of animal with her."

Sloan leans forward. "A bull. Who's the woman?"

"Who do you think it is?" Lenny asks, frowning.

Sloan opens her palms. The white light is hot and blinding. She groans. "I feel sick."

"You have to take the leap of faith in order not to feel sick," Lenny says.

"I need you to get out of here."

"You can't blame that little girl for not recognizing her adult self," Lenny says gently. "How could she possibly know?"

"Get out!" Sloan shouts. Lenny is lifted into the air and thrown against the wall of her living room. He grunts, then slowly rises and rubs his buttocks as he shuffles toward the door.

"You're more like him than I thought," Lenny mumbles. "All ego."

Sloan opens the patio slider and rushes into the backyard. With incredible ease, she leaps the ten-foot fence into her neighbor's yard. From there, she quickly bounds across three more yards, leaping three more fences, until she emerges onto a deserted street, misty and lit with streetlamps.

Sloan opens her hands and slaps them together as if to crush the white light. She cries out, then aims her palms toward a streetlamp and bends it to the ground. She raises a parked car into the air and turns it over. The car's alarm blares.

Sloan leaps into a tree and huddles there. She lets herself imagine that she is a lemur or a possum, a creature with no responsibilities and no needs beyond food and shelter—a blessed recipient of a stupid and simple life.

"Don't scream!"

CHAPTER FIFTY

Francesca arrives at the school parking lot in day-old clothes, having spent the night at Annie's. She catches her bedraggled reflection in a car window, tilts her head back toward the sky, and then abruptly leaves campus. Eventually, she ends up back at her mother's empty house.

After clearing the wineglasses and bottles from the coffee table, Francesca sits in front of the old photos and school projects her mother has left there. She realizes that she was not particularly good-looking as a child either, noting that she has always displayed a disproportionate share of her father's genes. She wonders why her mother would be looking through memorabilia and vaguely recalls an argument between her parents in which Christian begged Sloan not to throw the old school projects away.

Francesca picks up one of her sixth-grade masterpieces and sees a handwritten title: GREEK GODS. Flipping through her trenchant and sarcastic analysis, she laughs. "Well, I am a good writer at least."

In the chapter dedicated to Dionysus, her eyes fall on the word *Maron*.

DIONYSUS AND ARIADNE HAD A SON NAMED MARON.

Francesca freezes. "Maron!" she says out loud. "Ari. Ariadne!" She drops the paper as if it were burning hot. "No! No! It can't be! It's ridiculous!"

Leaping off the couch, Francesca grabs her Dionysus paper and snags her mother's car keys out of a drawer.

As she buckles the front seat belt of her mother's BMW, she hears a voice from the back seat.

"Don't scream."

Francesca screams, hurting her own ears. Maron leans forward from the back.

"It's okay what you're doing right now," Maron says. "It just won't help."

"What am I doing?" Francesca says, trembling.

"It's complicated. Please trust me."

Francesca's whole body seizes as it occurs to her that Maron knows exactly what she's doing. And what she's thinking. And probably also what she's holding in her hand. She turns toward the back seat.

"You need to tell me who you are," Francesca says. "You need to tell me everything."

———————

"Back up," Francesca says, as she paces back and forth in the living room of her mother's house. "You *are* immortal or you're not immortal?"

"Not immortal," Maron says. "Not anymore."

"Because your mother made a deal with Zeus?"

"Yes."

"This would be Zeus from the Greek myths?"

"They're not myths."

"Apparently."

Francesca halts and glares at Maron. "Look, I saw you hover above the street, so I accept that supernatural stuff is going on here. Three-thousand-year-old people? It's ludicrous, but whatever. But Zeus? The old white guy in a beard? Sorry, that's just a hard no. Too obvious. Too patriarchal. Too . . . everything. Arthur Clarke said that if we ever meet aliens, they would be even stranger than we can imagine. That's what I think about God. If he or she exists, she's beyond our conception. So, when you start talking to me about old white guys with beards? It sounds very fairy tale, very Snow White. I'm sorry."

Maron sighs and looks out the window.

Francesca stares at him. "Well, aren't you going to say something? Defend yourself?"

He laughs. "No, definitely not."

After a long silence, she sits beside him on the couch. The two of them look at each other for a long while.

Touching her hand, Maron says, "Right now, I have only one goal, and that's to protect you and make sure that things don't get worse."

"That's two goals," Francesca replies. "And right now, my mother is swimming naked with Craig Entwerp and deeply involved with your father, so I think things are already worse. My father, meanwhile, is in some kind of existential love crisis with your mother and is also involved with your father in some bizarro way. And I . . . I'm just—"

Maron squeezes her hand. "You're what?"

Francesca throws up her hands. "I'm screwed! As always!"

"I won't screw you," Maron says.

"I know you won't!" she laughs. "No need to rub it in!"

Maron blushes. "I didn't mean it that way."

She places her hand on top of Maron's. "Okay, so let's just play the god-mortal thing out. Your father pulls you off the football field because he thinks you're going to get hurt, because now you're mortal. But then he practically throws you into traffic because . . ."

"Because he's an asshole," Maron says. Francesca laughs.

"He didn't hurt me," he continues, "because he doesn't really want to hurt me. He's an asshole. But he's not crazy. I mean he is crazy. But he's not insane. Well, he didn't used to be insane. The main thing is, I'm trying to make sure no one gets hurt."

Francesca rolls her eyes. "Too late for that. I, personally, am all kinds of hurt. And knowing only bits and pieces of what's going on only makes it worse."

"I'll tell you anything you want to know," Maron declares.

She grabs him by the hand and realizes, despite everything, that there's no place she'd rather be.

Francesca begins, "Okay, let's start here. If it's true that you, Maron, son of Dionysus, have been alive for whatever thousand years, why are you seventeen now? Why did you stop aging now, at this age?"

"Well, I'm not really this age," Maron says. "It's like what the Clarke guy said about things being stranger than you can imagine. The age part is like that."

"Okay, I have no idea what that means." Francesca shakes her head. "Moving on, because of the deal that you and your mother made with Zeus, you are from now on an actual mortal person who's going to get older and die one day?"

"Yes. I'm seventeen and next year I'll be eighteen. And the year after that I'll be nineteen. And, if I'm lucky, I'll get old and die."

"Why would you make that deal?"

Maron laughs. "Why? Because I don't want to be immortal anymore. I'm tired of it. My mother is tired of it. I've had plenty of years. Plenty, believe me! And my father is exhausting. Worse than that, being with him is punishing. Honestly, living with him wore us out."

"I get that. But does all that still make mortality a good deal?"

"I think so," Maron says, looking off to one side. Francesca recognizes Maron may not be entirely certain of his position.

She rises and resumes pacing. "For sure, death is the weirdest thing about life. It's like this huge open secret that no one talks about. I feel like if we did talk about it, we'd just kill ourselves or take to our beds and never do anything."

"But people don't do that, do they?" Maron says. "For the most part, they don't kill themselves and they don't take to their beds. Why do you think that is?"

Francesca imagines her mother arguing in court. "Well, because everyone always wants one more day," she responds. "One more day to get more fame or more money or more sex or more of whatever it is they want. We're like the cockroach that sees a little crumb on the other side of the kitchen, and even though the floor is crowded with people who are going to crush us, we go for it anyway, because who wants to hide under the refrigerator their whole life?"

"Right," Maron replies. "But that assumes the cockroach dies when it gets stepped on."

Francesca peers over her glasses. "Okay. Tell me what part of the dead cockroach is alive after it gets crushed."

Maron sighs. "Well, it's hard to explain. In words."

"Gotcha," Francesca replies. "No offense, but isn't that what gods always say, right before they ask you to kill your firstborn son or rape you as a swan? 'Hey, I'd love to show you how it all really is, eternal life and all, but it's hard to explain. Just trust me, and let me rape you, kill your firstborn child and get your eternal buy-in, and then I'll keep stringing you along until you forget what your question was.'" Francesca sighs, before adding: "I'm sorry, I have a lot of anger toward religion."

Maron laughs. "Don't apologize. I love that about you. I'll try to explain it a little better."

Francesca sits next to Maron. He scoots closer and takes a moment to gather his thoughts.

"So, the one good thing about my father—I know it's hard to believe there are good things, but there are—is that he and Lenny, for a long time now, thousands of years actually, have helped people answer the question about why death isn't something to be afraid of."

"How do they do that?"

"Well, what they do is create a setting in which people *experience* the answer as to why death shouldn't be feared. There aren't any words to explain it; it has to be felt. So my father and Lenny host a ceremony, a rite of initiation. Many things happen during this ceremony, and people are sworn to secrecy about it because if they tell other people, no one will understand or believe them. The main thing is that everyone emerges happier and more relaxed, and less afraid of death. Which results in a better life and a better community. The feeling stays with them because it happened *to* them; they didn't just hear about it from a book or a sermon."

Maron seems to be fighting back tears.

"You still love him," Francesca says.

"I love what he can do, or at least what he *has* done." Maron laughs again. "Right now, Lenny is the only thing keeping their work alive."

"Can you take me to one of these ceremonies?" Francesca asks. "Show me how I can feel like I'm not the dead cockroach?"

Maron frowns. "Remember, my goal is to not bring you any deeper into this."

"Don't you think it's a little late for that?"

Maron stands slowly. "Let me think about this. There is a funeral. I mean, there will be a funeral; it hasn't happened yet. Of a man who's dead. Or dying, I mean."

Francesca detects the temporal confusion in Maron's words but chooses not to probe. Instead, she stands on tiptoes and kisses Maron on the lips.

"You know what I feel really strongly about right now? You. *You*."

Ari is pregnant.

CHAPTER FIFTY-ONE

Christian told the police as little as he could about his interaction with the long-haired man who wrecked the emergency ward. Before Christian left the hospital, he was able to spend an hour at Ari's bedside while she slept. The doctors told Christian that Ari had suffered a major neurological event and needed silence and stillness. They warned Christian that brain activity of any kind could be dangerous for her, and that she would need uninterrupted bedrest for at least a week.

This is why, two hours later, at home, Christian is shocked to hear Ari's voice outside the door to his apartment.

"Christian Orr! Open up!"

Christian opens the door and Ari rushes in. "We need to talk," she says.

"Why aren't you in the hospital!" Christian shrieks. "You should be in the hospital!"

Ari says, "Listen, I'm going to tell you everything, and you can't talk while I'm talking. Do you understand?"

"No," Christian replies, searching for his keys. "I'm driving you back to the hospital now."

Ari sits in a chair. "The first thing is that I am not like other people. Neither is my son."

"How did you get out?" Christian sits on the sofa. "Did you get a doctor to sign you out?"

"You need to know that my husband . . ." Ari pauses. "He did things to you; you're right. He does things that other people can't do, because he's not really a person. A person does normal things and then dies. My husband is not normal. He was born but will never fucking die!"

Christian reaches for his phone. "I'm listening. I'm just looking up the number to the hospital while we're talking, okay?"

Ari grabs Christian's phone out of his hand and tucks it under her thigh. "He's like an idea in the shape of a person," she continues. "He used to be a good idea. Now he's a bad idea. In any case, he's really only an idea. Does that make sense?"

Christian shrugs. "We can definitely keep talking *while* we drive to the hospital." He leans forward and reaches for his car keys on the end table.

"Listen to me!" Ari says, shoving Christian back onto the couch. "My husband brought me back to life last night. You saw this happen. Look at me, Christian! Are you listening?"

Christian folds his hands on his lap and looks directly at Ari. "I'm listening."

She sighs. "My husband is Dionysus."

Christian snorts. "Dionysus?"

"Dionysus."

"You mean—"

"Yes."

"The Greek god of wine and song?"

"Song is generous. He has no pitch." Ari says. "But yes, Dionysus."

Christian stares, for a long time, with his mouth open. Then he lunges for Ari's lap. "May I please have my phone?"

Ari shoves Christian's phone further under her butt. "You saw what he did to you, to the cheerleaders!"

"Yes!" Christian shouts. "I know, he's bizarre and frightening and has unusual powers. I get that! But what are you talking about? Dionysus?"

"My name is Ariadne," Ari continues. "I was rescued by Dionysus from the island of Naxos three thousand years ago. Theseus left me there after I helped him escape the Minotaur. I married Dionysus mostly because he saved my life but also because he was kind to me. But he hasn't been kind for some time. The last two hundred years of our marriage have been unbearable. However, I'm mortal now because I asked Zeus for mortality and he agreed to it."

"Zeus?" Christian stands up, bug-eyed. "You mean the big guy, the top dog, the big cheese? Zeus?"

"Maron has the same arrangement," Ari continues. "We're both mortal now, meaning we will age and eventually die. Apparently, we both still have some powers, which doesn't make sense, since I certainly didn't ask to keep any of it. Of course, I had reservations about sentencing my son to death; who wouldn't? But that's what Maron wanted too, and I felt like he was old enough to make his own decision. It's definitely what I wanted. As you can see, I can barely deal with life as it is!"

Christian kneels before Ari. "There's so much going on right now. You've just been through a terrible trauma. In my work, when things get crazy, I try to pick one thing to focus on. And right now, my one focus is on keeping you safe. Protecting your body and brain. Because what you're doing right now is not safe for you."

She begins to laugh.

"Why are you laughing?" Christian says. "The doctors said you need to sleep for a week or else you could suffer brain damage. *Brain damage.*"

Ari laughs harder.

"Right now, by laughing, you're putting intracranial pressure on your cranium! Stop laughing!"

Ari's laughter spirals out of control.

Christian continues, "What you're saying right now about Dionysus and Zeus? It could be true, but it could also be the words of a person who's suffered a traumatic brain event."

She doubles over in her chair. "You're right!"

"Of course I'm right." Christian reaches for his keys on the end table. "Which is why I have to stick with my primary focus, which is getting you to the hospital. We can talk on the way there, but primary focus says we go to hospital, so we're going to the hospital!"

As Christian reaches for Ari's hand to pull her out of her chair, she lifts both palms and sends him flying back at high speed onto the sofa.

A hush falls over the room. For a long time, Christian stays crumpled on the cushions, his eyes wide. His expression is so absurd that Ari can't help but resume laughing.

"What . . ." Christian begins. "What did you . . . ?"

Christian sits up and stares with amazement at Ari, who stops laughing.

"I'm sorry," Ari says tenderly.

Christian takes a deep breath and exhales. "Let's say all of this is true. You're still mortal now, right? You just said it. So, if you're mortal, you're at risk and you need to take care of your body by taking it to the hospital."

"No hospital!" Ari roars. She raises her right hand, and the light fixture in the kitchen explodes. She raises her left hand, and the television screen shatters. Then she raises Christian's favorite electric guitar from its stand.

"Not my guitar!" he cries.

Gently, Ari brings the guitar through the air until it lands quietly on Christian's lap. Christian clutches it tightly.

"No hospital," Ari says evenly.

"Okay, no hospital."

"There's one more thing I have to tell you," Ari sighs. "It's actually a very common thing, a very natural thing, but not necessarily a simple thing right now."

Christian feels excitement spread throughout his belly. The image of Ari throwing up in the toilet fills his mind.

"You're pregnant!"

"Yes," Ari says.

"But how did it happen so quickly?"

"Things happen differently for me," Ari says. "My husband was born from Zeus's testicle. Time isn't the same for us."

Christian stands up, sits down, stands, then sits. He lurches forward and hugs Ari. He kisses one cheek, then the other.

"You're pregnant!" Christian says. "Wow! We can—I can—we can—! Is it mine?" He stops.

Ari smiles. "It's yours."

Christian nods vigorously. "Yes, yes, of course! I'm not god material, clearly. There's that. I'm not special. But I'm not the worst guy, right?"

Suddenly, the entire apartment is shaking.

"Earthquake!" Christian screams.

"Only here," Ari says morosely.

Christian is launched, guitar in hand, at high speed across the room into his karaoke mirror, which smashes into large pieces. He looks with desperation toward Ari and is about to speak when he is jettisoned across the room in the other direction toward his stove.

The oven door opens, and Christian enters headfirst. The door slams repeatedly against his shoulders and neck.

"What's happening?!" Christian shouts from inside the oven.

Ari stands up and with her hands raised draws Christian back toward the living room and plops him down on the sofa.

"My husband is not happy," Ari says. "This can't surprise you."

The front door flies open, and Christian is sucked across the threshold. At the last moment, he grabs the railing of his third-story balcony and hangs on.

"Heeeeelllllp!" Christian hollers.

Ari walks to the door. "Just let go," she says.

"I'll fall!" Christian shouts.

"He gave you some power, remember. Not much. But use it. You'll land."

"I will?"

Christian lets go and falls toward the parking lot thirty feet below, landing on his feet.

Ari arrives at the railing and shouts down to Christian, "He will calm down. But it may take a while. I'm a little concerned that he'd rather have me dead than pregnant with your child."

"He would never hurt you, would he?" Christian shouts.

Ari shrugs. "Hard to say. We've never been here before."

"I'll talk to him!"

"Don't," Ari says.

"No, I need to fix this. I'm going to go talk to him!" Christian shouts. "He obviously knows where I am, anyway."

"Come upstairs."

"He's gonna find me wherever I am!" Christian calls. "I've got to meet this head-on. For once in my life! Go and rest! Do you want pickles and ice cream?" He races around in circles, looking for his car, which is within ten feet of him. "Where's my car?"

Ari gestures with her palm, and the driver's door of Christian's car opens.

"Okay!" Christian shouts. "Go rest! I'll talk to him! Text me if you want pickles and ice cream!"

Flying over Glenhaven.

CHAPTER FIFTY-TWO

As Christian pulls out of the parking lot of the Divorced Dads Apartment Complex, a single black cloud in an otherwise blue sky appears over his Fiesta. The cloud roils and spews tiny lightning bolts.

"Wow!" Christian sticks his chin out the window and is nearly zapped.

Hail pelts down from the cloud as Christian makes his way toward Dee's house. The car's worn wiper blades shred themselves as they move back and forth. Christian takes a hard right, followed by two more left turns in an attempt to lose the cloud. As he approaches a stop sign, all four of the Fiesta's tires deflate, and the car sinks to the pavement.

Christian jumps out of his car right before it is hit by a sedan behind him.

The driver of the sedan stops and rolls down his window. "I'm sorry! I hit the brakes, but it just kept moving!"

Christian waves politely. "Not your fault, trust me!"

On foot now, he sprints beneath the cloud that continues to track him, pouring hail onto his head. A power line above his head snaps, falls, and sheds sparks around him. Christian zigzags off the main road, deeper into a residential development, cutting across yards toward Dee's house.

As he passes a forsythia bush, a swarm of bees emerges and chases Christian. He dives into a nearby kiddie pool filled with small children, who scatter.

"Sorry!" Christian says as he emerges from the pool.

Clutching their mother, the small children watch Christian run in a serpentine manner into the distance, the bees and angry cloud in pursuit. As he crosses the final intersection on his way to Dee's house, he is abruptly lifted sixty feet into the air, as if a parachute on his back had just opened. Rising above the treetops, Christian now floats at a brisk pace of twenty knots toward the downtown area.

Strangely calm, and somehow certain that Dee must have plans for him other than dropping him from the sky, Christian surveys his town: the high school, the grocery stores, the restaurants, houses, and dog parks. The town has grown taller since he and Sloan moved here twenty years ago. There are new apartment buildings, and even a hotel. Christian wonders why Ari chose this place and not some big city like New York, where she would certainly have had an easier time disappearing and meeting men more interesting than himself.

Christian now descends at a forty-five-degree angle. He lands with a hard but not injurious thud on the sidewalk, directly in front of the wine bar. The door opens, and he is sucked in past the barstools to the back of the bar.

"Maybe Zeus wanted this to happen?"

CHAPTER FIFTY-THREE

Dee sits on a throne at the far end of the bar. Above the throne is a neon sign in the shape of a grapevine, purple and blinking. Lenny stands behind the bar, wiping glasses, inspecting them, and setting them on the shelves. The bar area is dark and empty except for a vaporous mist that gives the whole scene the feel of a dream.

Christian sits on the floor before Dee. As he looks up, he notices that Dee's pupils are large and square, like a goat's. With a gasp, he realizes that where Dee's feet should be there are cloven hooves.

"I didn't get what I wanted from you," Dee says in a voice that sounds to Christian as though it were doubled. "You cheated me. I gave you everything. I gave you the erection you used to impregnate my wife."

"I know things have gone differently than you wanted," Christian begins, trembling. "But please don't hurt Ari. It's not her fault. Do whatever you want to me, but please don't take it out on Ari or our . . . our . . ."

"Our what?" Dee says.

From the bar area, Lenny raises a wineglass to the light and says, "I believe he's referring to their forthcoming child."

"I should kill him right now," Dee says. "Lenny, why shouldn't I kill him?"

"You have to show Zeus that you can change; that's why," Lenny replies. "He needs to know that you can care about mortals again."

Dee narrows his eyes, inspecting Christian. "He's the worst excuse for a mortal I've ever seen."

"Exactly, Zagreus," Lenny says. He steps out from behind the bar. "He's precisely the kind of mortal you need to care about again. Not a brilliant man. Not a brave man. Just an average man."

Dee roars and begins to transmogrify into a bull, sprouting horns and a long snout. Christian averts his gaze and covers his ears against the sounds of cartilage and muscle stretching.

Dee bares his teeth and clops down from the throne. He approaches Christian.

"You steal my wife and ask to be the father of my wife's child," Dee growls softly. "And Zeus wants me to care about you."

Christian entire body clenches, anticipating that Dee may be about to crush his head like a grape.

"Maybe Zeus didn't want me to keep the deal!" he blurts out as he looks into Dee's eyes. "Maybe Zeus wanted it to happen this way!"

Dee wraps his forelegs around Christian and hugs him close. He rocks Christian side to side, looking now and again at Lenny. "Your wife," Dee says. "She is not like you. She is like me. Do you know that?"

"Sloan is not like you! No one is like you!"

Dee continues, "She is like me, and always has been. And because she is like me, she is going to come with me."

"You're insane," Christian whimpers. "Leave her alone!"

Dee throws Christian behind the bar. Lenny ducks as Christian crashes into the mirror, which smashes into a hundred pieces.

Dee walks back to his throne, gradually transforming back into a man. He sits and massages his forehead, muttering in Greek.

Behind the bar, Lenny helps Christian to his feet.

"I need your help," Lenny says, setting Christian on a bar stool. "Your friend, Mark Apple, is dying. I want you to speak at his funeral."

"Apple's not dying," Christian says as he clutches Lenny's arm to keep himself steady. "He's fine. I mean, he's not fine, but he's not dying."

"That said, will you help me?" Lenny says.

"Do I have a choice?"

Dee roars, raises his right hand, and thrusts Christian through the front door of the bar.

Christian lands on the sidewalk. The door shuts behind him. In front of him is his Ford Fiesta, tires inflated, parked and idling at the curb.

As he wobbles to his feet, he feels the athletic cup slip inside his underwear. He reaches inside his pants. His erection is gone.

CHAPTER FIFTY-FOUR

After being ejected from the wine bar, Christian listened to an urgent message from Mark Apple's wife, Ellen, who told him that Mark had been admitted to the hospital thirty-six hours earlier after his white blood cell count skyrocketed. Ellen mentioned that Mark said he would love to see Christian.

Christian calls Ari as he walks across the parking lot of the same hospital where she nearly died the night before. When she doesn't answer, he texts her indicating that all is fine between him and Dee and to call if she's feeling any craving for ice cream or pickles.

Inside the hospital, Christian ducks into a restroom and locks himself in a stall. He pulls down his pants and removes the athletic cup. Staring at his shriveled penis, he wonders if he is now impotent for life. Christian chucks the athletic cup into the garbage.

———

As he enters Apple's room, Christian notices a musty smell that reminds him of decay. Apple lies in a bed, his arm connected to an IV drip. There is a stuffed animal upside down at Apple's feet, which Christian reorients. The dying man's face is ashen, but he gives Christian a broad smile.

"Hey, big guy! Ellen said you were coming. How are you?"

Apple extends his hand to shake, and Christian briefly worries that if he takes it, he will also get cancer.

"So." Apple smiles. "Quick downturn. They said it could happen. White blood cells. They sound so harmless. They're heroes, until they aren't! Anyway, I'm not really afraid. I just feel bad for my kids. My father left me, and now I'm leaving them."

"You're not leaving them," Christian says. "And your father left because he was a drunk."

"True. And I'll be leaving them because I'm dead. It's better, but they're still getting left," Apple says.

"You've raised good kids," Christian says, trying to keep his voice from breaking. "You should be proud."

"Well, they're not raised yet." Apple gets choked up. "Which is pretty sad, given that I won't see them graduate. Hey"—he switches gears— "you've been really kind to me, and I want you to know I appreciate it."

Now Christian finds himself close to tears.

"That's really quite amazing, since I'm the kind of guy who tormented you in high school, remember," Apple continues.

Christian wipes tears from his eyes. "You've said that before, but it's not true. Anyway, I think we've grown more alike, haven't we?"

Apple nods and tearfully clasps Christian's hand. "I don't think we'll ever be alike. But that's probably why we're friends. You say one thing and I say another, and between us we get to the truth of a thing. Can you say that at my funeral? That we're not alike but together we get to the truth of a thing? That's a good line."

Christian nods. By this point the tears are streaming down his face. "Of course."

Apple sighs. "Little uptick now, because you're here. Feeling pretty good. But all the numbers are bad. My liver . . . All systems are failing. It's like it all went at once. I don't think I really wanted to do the drawn-out endless sick thing, you know? I'd rather be a running back in that great football game in the sky than be shitting myself here on earth."

Christian lowers his head. "I understand."

"I'm guessing you're too smart to believe in heaven, right?" Apple says.

An image of Dee as a bull pops into Christian's mind.

"I don't know," Christian says, looking down. "I wonder whether what everyone believes is what they get when they die. Maybe there are lots of gods and you meet whatever god you believe in and go to wherever place you believe you will go."

"Where will you go, then?" Apple says.

Christian feels a catch in his voice when he speaks. "I don't know."

"A god for everybody, eh?" Apple stares at the ceiling. "I like it."

"Why not?" Christian smiles.

Apple gestures toward a large plastic cup with a straw on the nightstand, and Christian hands it to him. Apple takes a sip.

"Well, I've been a lapsed Catholic at best. A half Catholic, so maybe I get half a god and half a heaven."

"I think you get the full god and the full heaven," Christian says, squeezing Apple's forearm.

There's a long silence, which Apple finally breaks.

"I gotta tell you, pal, I think I'm a few minutes away from shitting myself, so I'm gonna ask you to go now. Nurse!" he yells out.

Christian considers staying out of love for his friend to help with the shitting but is relieved when a nurse rushes in.

"Alright, visiting hour's over," the nurse says. "Thank you for coming."

As Christian approaches the door, Apple hollers: "Hey, remember to say the thing about how we get to the truth together!"

"I will!" Christian calls back.

As he shuts the door behind him, he hears a loud groan followed by the bellow of an athlete in agony: "Fuuuuuck!"

CHAPTER FIFTY-FIVE

Christian walks through the hospital parking lot, wiping tears from his eyes. When his phone rings, he answers it without looking. "Ari?"

"Christian, Stu Sherwater," says the voice on the other end. *"I've been texting you. Can you come to your office now?"*

Christian cries in the car all the way to Glenhaven. He realizes that he hasn't cried aloud in a car for a long time, and that his cry is tight and anemic. Perhaps he would cry in a more manly way had he kept his deal with Dee. A desperate thought crosses his mind—that he should beg Dee to cure Mark Apple. He could offer up his life or give Dee something important in return. But what would he be willing to give? Ari? His unborn child? Christian recognizes with dismay that he would not in fact give up much to save his friend's life.

As he pulls into the high school parking lot, Christian receives a text from Ari:

RESTING. SEE YOU SOON.

─────────────

Arriving at his office, Christian finds Stu Sherwater sitting on his desk.

"You got the job," Stu says. He rises and shakes Christian's hand.

"You're the new counselor. Apple told the board it was his last request, and that was it. You're in."

"Why are you the one telling me this?"

"Because I'm the acting principal."

Christian places a hand on his desk and gingerly sits down in one of the visitor chairs. "God, what is it with this school and promoting jocks?"

"I think they think we can keep order," Stu says. After a long pause, he steps forward and speaks in a more intimate tone. "Look, that thing with your wife . . . Since we're going to be working together. I honestly didn't know she was your wife when it happened, and I'm sorry." Stu speaks in such a way that Christian immediately believes him. "The truth is," he continues, "I wasn't exactly sure who you were until we talked the other day."

"How could you not know who I was?" Christian says, more offended by Stu's second admission than his first. "We played on the same faculty softball team."

"I don't have much of a memory," Stu says. "I just take care of the day-to-day. My business is the swim team and PE. And now," he chuckles, "the school."

"Say you're sorry for fucking my wife," Christian says bluntly.

Stu sighs. "I'm sorry for fucking your wife."

"Again."

"I'm sorry for fucking your wife. Can we be done with this now?" Stu squints at Christian.

Christian shakes his head angrily for a while, unsatisfied. "Say 'I see now how my fucking your wife could have unintended consequences that could negatively affect your life.'"

"I can't remember all that," Stu says.

Christian rubs his temples. Stu sighs again and seems about to leave but then turns once more toward Christian. "Your daughter had quite the swim the other day," Stu says. "I confess I've never seen anything like it."

Christian feels a pang as he realizes that Francesca will never have that swim again. That whatever power he wielded, on loan from a bad creditor, is now gone forever.

"Just don't kick her off the team if she doesn't swim that fast again," Christian says.

"We don't kick anybody off the team. There are no cuts. That's why I like it. It's good for the kids."

Christian feels a wave of admiration for Stu Sherwater and wonders whether Dee is right and everyone in the world is a better excuse for a person than he is. Fatigued, Christian lays his head on his desk.

"All I can say is that she did seem sad when it was over."

Christian looks up to see Stu stopped in the doorway, lost in thought. "What? Who?"

"Your wife," Stu continues. "Maybe not sad. Bored, I guess. Like the whole thing just wasn't good enough. Not just me. Everything. It was fine. I didn't take it too hard."

Christian now feels a wave of empathy for Sloan, whose very nature he apparently suppressed all these years so that his misery could have company.

As Stu leaves, a text from Francesca arrives.

ASSUMING YOU'RE STILL ALIVE, CALL ME.

CHAPTER FIFTY-SIX

"So, Maron is their only son, although it says here that Dionysus had six or seven children. But it's totally vague, since there are like six or seven versions of Dionysus. None of it makes any sense, but why should it? They're gods, so it's all fairy tales anyway, right? Except it's not, apparently."

Francesca sits in the passenger seat of Christian's car in the school parking lot. She holds three books and an iPad on her lap and talks a mile a minute at her father, who nods attentively.

"He's Bacchus in Rome," Francesca continues. "But he's also Liber and Zagreus and Basserious. And Basserious isn't even supposed to be from Greece. He's from Thrace. Is that how you pronounce that? Thracian? Whatever, the point is the whole thing starts *before* Greece. Meaning these people are *more* than three thousand years old. Which of course is impossible, since why wouldn't they die twenty-nine hundred years ago? Or at least have gray hair? And Dionysus was supposedly born from Zeus's testicle. You can't make this shit up."

"Francesca, I have to tell you," Christian begins, with a pained expression, "I think Dee —Dionysus—he did something that made you able to win that hundred-yard freestyle yesterday. Some kind of power. I'm just saying it may not have been all you. I know you were very excited about winning that race."

Francesca laughs. "Are you kidding me right now? Dionysus is sleeping with Mom, and you're in some kind of relationship with his wife—which you've got to understand at this point is probably not a good idea. So I don't think that my 'swim career' is mission critical right now."

"I should also tell you," Christian continues, finding himself unable to look at his daughter. "I think Ari is pregnant. And I think it's mine. I mean, yes, it's mine."

Francesca clenches her iPad so tightly that her fingers turn white. She doesn't move for a few seconds.

"Jesus," she says, finally exhaling. "You could have waited on that info."

"I'm sorry," Christian says. He looks at her. "I didn't want you to hear it from someone else."

"I'd rather hear it from someone else. Pregnant. What the fuck. Okay." Francesca shakes her head.

Christian can see that her hands are trembling.

"So, I would be sister to a half god then?" Francesca says. "A quarter god?" She turns to Christian. "Would that make me a step-god? I can't do the math right now."

Christian understands that his daughter is overwhelmed. He touches her on the shoulder. "Breathe."

She shrugs off her father's touch. "Wow. This is frickin' . . ." She picks up her phone and dials Maron. No answer. She slams her phone down on her iPad.

"Francesca, I'm so sorry for all of this," Christian says tenderly.

"Right," Francesca snaps. "Once again, I'm the sap who deals with shit other people do. They do shit, and I deal with it. That's my role. My destiny."

"That's not true," Christian says.

"*That*"—Francesca slams her fist on her iPad—"is exactly what people who make other people deal with their shit always say. You're just giving me your self-justifying lines right now! Just like Mom gave me her lines earlier, like both of you have given me bullshit lines my whole life!"

Francesca dissolves into tears. Christian impulsively hugs her, and Francesca lets herself be hugged. After a few moments, her phone rings, and she immediately disengages from her father and answers.

"Maron? Listen to me," Francesca says into the phone. "You can't disappear and go to another school. It doesn't make sense. I love you and I want you to stay here and be my boyfriend or whatever you want to call it. I don't care if you're three thousand years old. You're awesome, you're hot, and you're just frickin' . . . great. You can say no, but I'm just putting it out there. Actually, you can't say no. You have to say yes. Say yes."

During the subsequent pause while Francesca listens, Christian clenches his fists in anticipation of Maron's answer, as though he's left his daughter with nothing but the relationship with Maron to sustain her.

"Yes?" Francesca nods. "I'm going to take that as a yes." She turns to her father. "We're back on." Then, back into the phone: "Good, I'm glad. I love you! Fuck it. Bye."

Francesca hangs up the phone and turns to her dad. "So, you're going to have this baby, right?" she says firmly.

Christian doesn't know what the right answer is and tries to equivocate. "I don't know."

"Dad, you can't abort a fucking god!" Francesca shouts. "I want a sister. Or a brother. You and Mom are obviously going to die young at your current rate of stress, so I need to have some kind of family to have Thanksgiving with when I get older."

"Okay, okay," Christian relents, realizing that he is committing without yet being certain of Ari's position.

Christian's phone rings, and he answers it instinctively as a way of removing himself from the conversation. Francesca watches her father's face fall. "Thank you," Christian says as he lowers the phone.

"What happened?" Francesca says.

"Mark Apple died."

"I call upon loud-roaring and reveling Dionysus,
two-natured, thrice-born Bacchic lord!"

CHAPTER FIFTY-SEVEN

The mood is both somber and strangely bright at the afternoon funeral service for Mark Apple at Midwood Presbyterian. Somber because a middle-aged man with young children has died. Bright because the life-size cardboard cutout of Apple as a high school football player next to his casket has generated an unending stream of spirited, nostalgic stories about the greatest running back in Glenhaven history.

In the cutout photo, seventeen-year-old Mark Apple holds the ball in his right hand and defends with his left, a toothy grin shining through his face mask. Christian suspects that in the grieving limbic brains of some of those present, the teenage Mark Apple in this photo is more real than the dead Mark Apple in the casket.

Apple died the evening of Christian's visit, surprising his young doctor but not the veteran nurses, who told Ellen what Mark had told Christian, that he'd rather be a running back in heaven than bedridden on earth. It was also rumored that Apple's final wish was for his funeral to happen as soon as possible, to avoid prolonging his family's misery.

Christian scans the room. The crowd is large, and he knows many of those present. Stu Sherwater sighs and looks at his watch by the memorial table. Brittany May, Jenny Templeton, and Tina Lowry smile at Christian and wave. Laura Hartwood, once again her cheerful, willowy self, chats with her friends in the foyer. Other people Christian doesn't know, contemporaries of Mark Apple, slap each other on the back and laugh, which Christian finds mildly offensive. Laughing at the funeral of an eighty-year-old is one thing, but a forty-year-old?

Mark's wife, Ellen, sits in the first pew with her head bowed. She wears a black veil and sunglasses. Strangely, her children are not present. Christian wonders if the grief felt by the kids is too great, or whether Ellen's grief is too great to allow them to be present. He wonders about the Apple marriage. *Was it a good one? Would it have lasted?*

A trim, white-haired minister ascends the dais just as a commotion erupts near the entrance. Dee and Lenny enter at the door, arguing in Greek. The minister steps down, folds his hands, and waits. Lenny catches the minister's eye and gives him a friendly thumbs-up. It seems to Christian that they know one another. As Lenny and Dee seat themselves, the minister smiles and steps up once again to the dais.

Christian notices nothing supernatural about Dee's presence today—no shapeshifting, no cloven hooves. In fact, Dee looks almost frail behind his dark sunglasses.

The minister clears his throat. "Today, we celebrate the life of a good husband and father, and a truly great football player, taken too early," he begins sonorously. "Please open your hymnals to page 274, 'Going Home.'"

An organist starts the intro as all stand and sing:

"Going home, going home,
I'm just going home.
Quiet-like, slip away,
I'll be going home."

Christian recalls this tune, and it breaks his heart. He fights back tears.

"Work all done, laid aside,

Fear and grief no more."

As the song ends, the reverend raises his hands to the sky. He bows his head, and the congregants bow theirs as well. After a moment, the reverend looks up with alarm. It appears that he cannot lower his arms, which remain aloft, like a referee signaling a touchdown. Some in the congregation laugh, imagining that the reverend is paying oblique homage to Apple the football hero. One congregant even mutters, "Touchdown," generating giggles.

Christian reflexively turns toward Lenny and Dee. Lenny points at Christian and then toward the dais. He mouths, "Now."

The reverend turns a beseeching gaze toward Christian, and the latter tentatively makes his way toward the pulpit. Christian tries in vain to make the exchange seem planned by shaking the reverend's elevated hand, which results in more laughter from the audience. The reverend shuffles offstage, his arms still in the air.

At the lectern, Christian looks out over the crowd. His only thought is to make certain that he tells the story he promised Mark Apple he would tell, about the synergy of their discussions, when suddenly he feels a wave of dizziness and disorientation, similar to the one he felt entering the orgone box at his karaoke performance. His mouth opens, and he hears the following words come out:

"I call upon loud-roaring and reveling Dionysus, primeval, two-natured, thrice-born, Bacchic lord!"

Christian stops, wide-eyed, and looks toward Lenny, who makes the "keep it rolling" gesture. There is a growing murmur in the room.

"Savage," Christian continues, his voice breaking, *"ineffable, two-horned, and two-shaped. Ivy-covered . . ."*

The congregants look at one another. Ellen Apple raises her head and peers with a dead look over her dark sunglasses.

"You take raw flesh, oh great one," Christian continues, his voice high-pitched. *"And you have triennial feasts. Come! Be with us!"*

"Loud-roaring and divine!" Lenny shouts from the audience.

"Ichos! Ichos!"

Christian catches a glimpse of Dee's grinning face right before the lights in the sanctuary go out. A collective gasp rises from the congregation, followed by a shuffling of chairs. The fire sprinklers in the ceiling come to life, and a liquid rains down onto the congregants.

As the substance from the sprinklers dribbles onto his lips, Christian recognizes the milky drink Dee forced him to take before the karaoke show. He hurries off the dais and through the turbulent crowd to Lenny and Dee.

"Is this what you're doing?" Christian cries. "Drugging people and putting words in my mouth?"

"It's required that a mortal give the invocation for our ceremony," Lenny says brightly. "It seems appropriate that it's you, after all we've been through together as a group."

"What ceremony? This is a funeral!" Christian turns to Dee. "I don't think Zeus will approve of this!"

Dee grabs Christian by the shoulders so hard that Christian fears his bones will break.

"You insipid creature," Dee says, not entirely without sympathy. "You are truly unreachable, aren't you?"

"He's right, you know," Lenny says to Christian as Dee moves toward the exit. "Even after everything that's happened, you still haven't learned how to live, to just simply be. But we will change that tonight. Come!"

A chant arises from the congregation, louder and clearer with every repetition.

"VoHe! VoHe! VoHe!"

Lenny wolf-whistles and catches the attention of the confused minister, who has regained control of his arms.

"Reverend! Your child's questions!" Lenny shouts, waving merrily. "They will be answered tonight!"

"Are these people on some kind of drug?"

CHAPTER FIFTY-EIGHT

Francesca arrives, breathless, across the street from the Presbyterian church, having responded to a text from Maron asking her to meet him there. She sees a black hearse and four black SUVs outside the main entrance. The hearse drivers lean against their cars, smoking cigarettes and laughing. Francesca checks her phone for another text from Maron and then types.

Here. Where r you?

Her head jerks up at the sound of breaking glass. Colored shards from a stained-glass window above the main door to the church cascade to the ground. Moments later, another window is smashed, also from the inside. Sounds of laughter and chanting rise from within, as well as the same ululations Francesca heard the cheerleaders and the women on the street making.

She raises her phone and voice-texts her father. "Are you in there? I'm outside."

Francesca feels an urge to run into the church to rescue Christian. But a competing urge tells her to wait for Maron, who might actually know what to do. A dirgelike rhythm of handclaps, foot stomps, and improvised percussion rises along with the chant. The front doors of the church burst open.

"VoHe! VoHe! VoHe!"

The cardboard cutout of teenage Mark Apple appears first, held aloft and waved by the silver-haired minister. Next comes Mark Apple's casket, borne atop the shoulders of four burly men. For a moment, Francesca hopes the pallbearers will turn toward the hearse like they're supposed to, the hearse will drive to the cemetery like it's supposed to, and they will bury this guy like they're supposed to. But somehow, she is not surprised when the pallbearers turn in the opposite direction and begin dancing the casket down the sidewalk.

Next to emerge from the church is Mark Apple's wife, Ellen. She is seated atop another makeshift bier held aloft by four more men. Ellen rises halfway out of her chair and shrieks. The sound is awful, more catlike than human. Ellen looks to the left and to the right and then lets out another shriek, baring her bright-white teeth against her black veil.

Maron appears. "I'm sorry I'm late."

"What's happening?" Francesca says.

"This," Maron sighs, "is called a *pompe*. It's a procession."

"Where are they going?" Francesca cranes her neck in search of her father. "The cemetery is miles in the other direction. Why is that woman shrieking like that?"

Maron rises onto his tiptoes. "I don't think they're going to the cemetery." He peers toward the crowd. "There's Lenny."

"Lenny's your father's partner, right?" Francesca says. "He's the nice one, right? Tell me he's nice."

"He's nice," Maron replies.

The last trickle of congregants emerges from the church. Francesca notes that there are in total forty or fifty of them. She recognizes many people but doesn't see her father. The marchers flick their heads backward in unison to the first beat, then take a slow step forward on the second, third, and fourth beats. The dance looks exactly like the one Francesca saw the cheerleaders doing at Lime Ridge.

"Are these people on some kind of drug right now?" she says to Maron.

"Yes," Maron says. "Here comes my father."

Dee emerges from the church, ten paces behind the last of the congregation. He lowers his sunglasses and stuffs his hands into his pockets. To Francesca, he seems only vaguely interested in the goings-on. Directly behind him is Christian, who is chattering angrily in Dee's ear. Dee waves him away with his hand.

"Dad!" Francesca shouts. She begins to move across the street, but Maron stops her.

"Not now," Maron says.

Christian continues to harangue Dee, until the latter finally raises his hand and lifts Christian into the air. Ten feet above the sidewalk, Christian's feet pedal uselessly like a cartoon character running off a cliff.

"Oh my god." Francesca covers her mouth. "Is he going to kill him?"

Dee closes his hand, and Christian drops into the bushes.

"He's not going to kill him," Maron says.

"Why does he hate him so much?" Francesca says.

"He doesn't hate him," Maron says, turning to her. "I think Zeus wants my father to learn to love your father."

"Hey, anything's possible!" Francesca says.

Christian scrambles out of the bushes and rushes after the procession, trying again to get the attention of Dee. Watching him, Francesca finds solace in the fact that her father appears animated and engaged. Her worst fears since her parents' separation have involved watching her father sink into despair, playing his guitar into headphones in the Divorced Dads Apartment Complex while drinking one can of Coors Light after another.

"So what's a *pompe*?" Francesca says, trying out the word.

"It's a procession for the *mystae*," Maron says. "Those who are about to become initiated."

"Initiated? Into what?" Francesca cries.

"Into the cult of Dionysus," Maron says. "But that's not important."

"Being in a cult isn't important?"

"It's not that kind of cult," Maron says. "They don't have to do anything in return. It's only for their benefit."

"Isn't that what all cult leaders say?"

"My father has basically ruined the initiation ceremony by mocking and perverting it," Maron says pensively. "I guess he's trying to kill it, but he won't admit to it. He's like an apple that's going bad slowly. And Lenny can't stop it. I hope today is different, but I'm not optimistic."

He faces Francesca, grabbing her shoulders. "I can take you there, but you have to promise to listen to me, not freak out, and do exactly what I say."

"How about two out of three?" Francesca says, grinning. "Because I may have to freak out."

Maron kisses her.

CHAPTER FIFTY-NINE

"Where did you get this car?" Francesca asks as she and Maron drive slowly beside the procession.

"I borrowed it."

Francesca frowns. "You're not helping your bad-boy reputation by stealing cars." She looks ahead. "Why are they going to the high school?"

Maron sighs. "I don't know. Somehow, I'm not surprised." He turns to Francesca. "And I *am* going to return this car."

Francesca playfully slaps the dashboard. "Nah! Let's be Bonnie and Clyde. We can start robbing banks next. We'll hide the money in Zeus's testicles." Francesca looks in the rearview mirror. "God, these people have been dancing and singing for more than a mile."

The procession has accrued gawkers and hangers-on. Ellen Apple, still seated atop a bier, has lost her sunglasses, veil, and wrap, and now only wears a black bra. There are red scratches on her shoulders and chest, which must have come, Francesca imagines with a chill, from her own fingernails.

Christian, at the rear of the procession, has managed to engage one of the congregants in something close to a conversation. He gestures wildly.

A police car brings up the rear of the parade, its red siren twirling silently on top. Francesca guesses that somewhere along the way the cops assumed someone had authorized a parade, so they have joined as an escort.

As the marchers approach the entrance to Glenhaven, Ellen rises again in her chair and chants.

"Kiklêskô Dionyson Eribromon, Euastêra,
Prôtogonon, Diphuê, Trigonon, Bakcheion, Anakta
Kissobryon, Taurôpon, Arêion, Euion, Hagnon,
Ômadion, Trietê, Botryêphoron, Ernesipeplon!"

Ellen's tremulous voice, along with the fact that she is speaking fluent Greek, sends another wave of chills through Francesca.

"What is she saying?"

"It's a tribute," Maron replies. "To my father."

"Why does everything have to be about your father? Why can't anything be about you or your mother?"

"Well, he's Dionysus," Maron says.

"So? You're Maron."

Maron laughs. "My mother used to be a big part of this work. But she got sick of his bullshit. And now Lenny thinks that . . ." He stops.

"Lenny thinks what?" Francesca says.

Maron looks guiltily at Francesca. "Well. I think that Lenny thinks your mother is . . . I'm not sure. Some kind of answer."

"What kind of answer?"

Maron pulls the car over to a curb and parks. "C'mon, we need to get out and get ahead of them." He jumps out of the car and opens Francesca's door.

As the two hustle down the sidewalk, Francesca quizzes Maron.

"What do you mean, my mother is the answer? To your father being an asshole? Or something else?"

"We really have to get ahead of them." Maron grabs Francesca's arm, and the two of them sprint past the congregation. As they reach the end of the bridge that leads into the school, Maron turns to her with a serious expression.

"So, remember what I said?" Maron begins. "Starting now, whatever happens, the important thing is to not freak out."

"I told you, that's a big ask," Francesca replies.

At that moment the sky goes dark and just as quickly brightens, as if the entire outdoors just experienced a power surge. Francesca presses her hands to her temples and moves her jaw like a diver trying to equalize pressure.

"What just happened?" she begins. "My head . . ."

"Just breathe and trust me. And don't look over there," Maron says.

Francesca looks over there and sees that while the mystae continue to stream by them toward the high school, the hangers-on now behind them appear to be frozen in time on the other side of the bridge.

"Maron." Francesca takes a step forward. "Those people over there are not moving. They're not moving at all!"

On the far side of the bridge, a teenager is mid-wheelie on his BMX bike; an elderly woman is stuck halfway through a sneeze; a cop has a sandwich raised to his open mouth; a young girl up a light pole holds a cell phone over her head.

Francesca pulls out her phone. "Why do I have no signal?" Her head feels cottony. When she speaks, it's as though her words are trailing her speech by a half second. "Why don't I have a signal, Maron? What's happening right now?"

Maron takes both of Francesca's hands in his and looks into her eyes, speaking softly.

"Those people on that side of the bridge, they're on pause, like on TV."

"Pause?" Francesca says with a hysterical giggle.

"They're *outside* of time right now. Just for a little while."

"Outside of time?" Francesca laughs again.

"And we're inside of it," Maron says. "Meaning that no time is passing on the clock, or on your phone. You don't have a signal right now because there's no time for a signal to move from here to there.

Does that make sense?

"No." Francesca shakes her head rapidly. "Not at all."

Maron squeezes her hand. "That's okay. You're calm; that's all that matters. Let's go."

"I'm not calm!"

The two follow the procession as it heads deeper into campus toward the football field.

Death...

CHAPTER SIXTY

As Maron and Francesca mount the stairs toward the football field, Francesca smells the familiar odor of char from the outdoor grills mixed with the faint odor of bleach from the restrooms. To her, this is the smell of high school.

"Let's sit in the bleachers," Maron says.

Climbing up the steps, Francesca notices that the forty or so congregants have lined up along the near sidelines of the football field. Ellen Apple rises on her platform and resumes her Greek chant.

"Kiklêskô Dionyson Eribromon, Euastêra,
Prôtogonon, Diphuê, Trigonon, Bakcheion, Anakta."

Dee jogs toward midfield, clapping his hands in all directions like a motivational speaker. "Line up!" he shouts.

"Let me down!"

Francesca hears her father's tinny voice coming from down the field. Christian is thirty feet in the air, clinging to the left fork of the goalpost like a koala.

"Did your father do that? He's going to fall!"

"He won't," Maron says. "Remember, my father does not kill people."

"Pentheus may beg to differ," Francesca says. "I read the CliffsNotes of *The Bacchae* earlier today. Villagers torn limb from limb."

Maron groans. "That's a story. Anyway, it was the women who killed Pentheus."

"Right," Francesca says. "Because Dionysus made them do it. That seems to be his MO. I'm assuming your father enchanted the moms or whatever, and the cheerleaders at the game?"

Before Maron can answer, a loud whistle comes from the field. The four pallbearers hustle Mark Apple's casket forward and lay it at Dee's feet.

With his right foot, Dee kicks open the casket, exposing the former principal's corpse. Silver coins glimmer atop Apple's eyes.

"What are the coins for?" she asks Maron.

"They're to pay Charon, the ferryman. He takes souls to the land of the dead."

"Right. That guy."

Dee removes the two coins from Apple's face and presents them, magician-like, to the crowd. He closes one fist and waves his hand. When he opens it, one coin is gone. The congregation applauds politely. He flips the other coin high into the air, and it lands squarely on the fifty-yard line, on top of the Spartan logo.

Dee squats to inspect the result. "Heads!" he yells to the crowd. "We receive!"

"Receive?" Francesca stares at Maron.

Maron huffs with frustration as below Lenny storms across the field toward Dee.

"I'm not taking part in this!" Lenny shouts. He slaps Dee hard across the head. Dee ducks away from Lenny and turns toward the congregation.

"All of you from here to there," Dee shouts, pointing, "you're on offense with me. The rest of you on defense. Let's go!"

He blows his whistle and runs in place, raising his knees high in the air, as half the congregation rushes forward to join him. This group includes the minister, who sets the Mark Apple cutout down next to Mark Apple's casket.

"This is like one big roofie event," Francesca says. "Everybody's drugged, no free will anywhere."

"It's not like that," Maron responds, peeved. "It's for their benefit. The drug is only a facilitator."

"Isn't that what guys who drop roofies into girls' drinks say?"

Maron shakes his head. "People used to prepare for weeks to participate in the ceremony. There were parades and festivals, and everyone gladly drank the *kykeon*. Because they'd heard about it from their friends and parents and grandparents. They knew it was important. It connected them to their ancestors."

"What does any of this have to do with football?" Francesca says.

"I think the football part is for me," Maron says, squinting at the spectacle below him. "Maybe he thinks it's what I want. He's been so crazy lately that I'm not sure he even knows what he wants."

On the field, Dee shouts, "Where's our ball!? We can't play football without a football, can we?" He tiptoes like a cartoon villain toward Mark Apple's open casket. He yanks Apple's body up into a seated position.

"It's not exactly the right shape," Dee says, twisting Apple's lifeless head back and forth. "But it'll do in a pinch!" With a hard jerk, he snaps Apple's head from its body.

Francesca drops into her bleacher seat and covers her mouth. "I'm going to be sick."

Lenny stomps toward the bleachers and raises his fist toward Maron. "I'm done with him, Maron. Done! He's lost, completely lost!"

"Huddle up!" Dee shouts as he places Apple's head on the fifty-yard line. "We're running a flexbone slot with a Y action double split. Or maybe a Y-bone slot with an X action split." He turns toward the casket and shouts: "Apple! It's your big night; get out here!"

The headless Mark Apple rises from his casket.

Francesca, who has just now risen to her feet, once again sits and covers her mouth.

"Are we still inside time?" She pulls out her phone and then shoves it back into her pocket. "When do we get back to time?"

Maron touches her shoulder. "Just breathe. There's nothing to be afraid of."

"Red twenty-two. Blue sixteen! Hut! Hut!"

At midfield, Dee takes the snap of Mark Apple's head and tosses it underhand to Mark Apple's body, which catches it and begins stumbling forward. The minister and the offensive line form an inept blocking wave in front of Apple, who shuffles along, head tucked under his arm.

Dee claps and wolf-whistles in approval. "Go, mystae! Go!"

Lenny, meanwhile, has snuck up behind Dee and pulls him by his hair to the ground. The two begin fighting, slapping and kicking.

Apple staggers past the line of scrimmage and moves slowly downfield. The defense trudges after him. As Apple reaches the twenty-yard line, a thick fog rises, which eventually swallows him up.

"Where did that fog come from?" Francesca says, jumping from her seat.

Suddenly, a trumpetlike sound is heard from the fog at the far end of the field. Maron rises as well.

"What's that noise?" Francesca says.

"That's a salpinx," Maron says in a hushed voice.

The horn sounds again, and a silence falls over the field. Dee and Lenny have stopped fighting and have turned toward the fog.

"What's a salpinx?" Francesca says.

"It's a Greek horn."

From the fog an object gradually emerges.

"Holy shit," Francesca says, shaking her head in disbelief. "That's Craig Entwerp's golf cart. And that . . . that's my mother!"

Craig Entwerp blows the salpinx with one hand as he drives the golf cart with the other. Beside Craig is Sloan, who is dressed in a long white gown. She wears a wreath of grain stalks around her neck, and there are colorful flowers in her hair. In the back of the golf cart, where the clubs go, Mark Apple stands hunched slightly forward. He hangs onto the cart with one hand while holding his own head with the other. Running breathlessly behind the cart and struggling to keep up is Christian.

Francesca starts past Maron toward the stairs, but he stops her.

"No," he says. "Let's stay here for now."

On the field, Dee strokes his chin. Then he shrugs, turns toward the bleachers, and raises both hands. Francesca feels herself being lifted into the air. She grabs Maron's hand as he, too, rises. The two are pulled at high speed toward the football field, where they drop at Dee's feet.

"What the fuck," Francesca says, brushing herself off as she gets up.

"I thought you might want to be here to say hello to your mother?" Dee says to Francesca. "It seems she's the new sheriff in town."

Dee turns to Maron. "I can see she where this one gets her—"

Before he can finish his sentence, Dee is blasted twenty yards downfield. Francesca turns and sees Sloan standing beside the golf cart with her left hand raised.

Dee struggles to stand and is blown back another twenty yards as Sloan raises her right hand.

"Mom?" Francesca says.

The mystae take a step toward Sloan and begin to chant, louder than ever.

"Ichos! Ichos! Ichos!"

Sloan turns toward the crowd and extends her arms. The congregants roar with approval and join Sloan to create a circle. The chant becomes deafening.

"Ichos! Ichos! Ichos!"

"Amazing," Lenny says, awestruck. He turns to Francesca. "Go to her," he says. "It's why you're here."

Francesca turns toward Maron. He nods.

"Yes. Remember, nothing to be afraid of."

Francesca steps forward. The circle parts for her, and she joins hands with the group.

"Beautiful indeed is the mystery given," Sloan chants as giant purple clouds speed in from the horizon. Francesca notes that her mother's voice sounds like a chorus of her mother's voices.

"For us," Sloan continues, "death is no longer an evil but a blessing."

There is a loud rumbling, and Francesca feels the astroturf beneath her move. Soon, the entire area upon which the congregants stand begins to sink.

"Maron!" Francesca turns and looks with alarm at Maron. He and Lenny simultaneously give her a thumbs-up.

Craig Entwerp appears at Francesca's side. "Drink this," he says, handing her a large mug. He bows officiously and backs away into the growing darkness as the disk of ground they occupy sinks further below ground level. Francesca searches for her mother's gaze and finds it resting upon her lovingly. She quickly drinks the fluid, which tastes like alcoholic milk.

Immediately, Francesca feels dizzy and lightheaded. She looks up at the sky and realizes that she and the group are now fifty feet belowground.

From above, fat snowflakes descend.

Francesca stares at her arm. A snowflake lands on one of many brown age spots that have begun to form on her skin. She looks across the circle at her mother, whose smiling face now shows deep creases, and whose hair is turning quickly gray. Francesca looks to the other side of the circle and sees her father, whose hair is now white. He is stooped over with hands on his knees. Christian waves amiably at his daughter through the falling snow.

Francesca lifts her right hand and watches the skin on her arm slough away, revealing first cartilage and then bone. The wet snowflakes melt as they touch the white bones of her hand, which she can no longer feel. She wonders how she is so calm.

Francesca's legs collapse beneath her, and she drops into the snow. She turns again toward her father, whom she now recognizes only because of his location, and because his skeletal hand is still raised in greeting toward her. All around him, skeletons of the other mystae crumple into the snow. Sloan is seated cross-legged in the snow, her bony arms posed in a supplicating gesture. The last remaining bits of flesh fall from her body.

Francesca looks at her exposed ribs and sternum and, below, her white hips and femur bones. She is now a skeleton, indistinguishable from every other skeleton in this dark, snowy realm.

A peace rises within her as she lays her white skull into the snow. She raises the index finger of her bony right hand and looks at it until it, along with everything else, disappears.

―――――――――――――

"Cah coo cah cah."

Francesca hears the sound of one baby cooing, then another and another. For a long time, she listens, unable to imagine whether she is dead or alive or in any state of being at all. It crosses her mind that if she is in a place where babies coo, perhaps she is in heaven. Only when the sweet smell of baby poop tickles her nose does it occur to Francesca that she might actually be alive somewhere.

Feeling her own eyelash brush the top of her cheek, Francesca gently opens her eyes.

The snow is gone and the air is warm. All around her, giant black flowers have sprouted out of the green astroturf. Dozens of naked babies crawl in all directions. Francesca looks to the place where she last saw her mother—and sees Sloan fully naked and sitting cross-legged. Sloan is the same age she was this morning.

Only now does Francesca look at her own hand and see that it is tiny and pink, the hand of an infant. She inspects her tiny toes, her extruded belly button, her puckered kneecaps, her white thighs. She tries to speak, but no words come forth, only the same cooing sounds she hears from the other babies.

Rolling onto her knees, Francesca crawls on all fours toward her mother. During this trip, which feels endless, she looks around and wonders which of these babies is her father.

Climbing onto Sloan's thighs, Francesca raises her gaze. Her mother strokes her head and gently guides Francesca's mouth to her breast. As Francesca begins to nurse, her consciousness fades.

———————

Francesca opens her eyes. Sitting up, she no longer sees babies but instead children on the astroturf, along with some teenagers and young adults. She looks at her forearm, now longer and downy with hair. She flexes her hand and spreads her fingers.

Francesca discovers her father in the same location he was in earlier, clutching at his full head of red hair with one hand as he stares at the other. Christian appears to be about twenty-five.

The plot of astroturf rises. The purple clouds retreat as the late-afternoon sky gets larger and larger above them. By the time the congregation reaches the level of the football field, Francesca notices that all are present in the same form, and at the same age, they began the evening with—middle-aged, old, and, in the case of Mark Apple, dead.

Francesca rushes to her mother, who hugs her. Craig Entwerp, standing by, hands Sloan an oversized paintbrush, which she gives to Francesca.

As a gentle rain falls from the cloudless sky, Francesca runs from black flower to black flower, swiping them with her paintbrush. The giant flowers turn bright colors: purple, green, yellow, and red.

On the sidelines, Lenny nudges Dee. "Persephone painted flowers after Demeter liberated her from the underworld."

"I'm familiar with the story," Dee replies.

"Clever for her to evoke Persephone," Lenny continues, grinning from ear to ear. "Perhaps an audition?" He rises proudly to the balls of his feet.

"I think she's already got the job," Dee says flatly.

Lenny nudges Dee. "Don't be so glum. You're not done."

"Done?" Dee says, turning to Lenny. "Of *course* I'm done. I'm being replaced, and you know it."

"Replaced?" Lenny scoffs. "What do you mean, replaced? The entire point of your Mysteries is that no one gets replaced! There was never anyone to begin with, including you, so who can replace whom? All that matters is continuity! The community! Don't you remember your Heraclitus?"

On the field, Sloan raises her arms toward the sky. The entire congregation, all completely naked, accompanies her in song. Lenny dances forward and joins them.

"VoHe! VoHe! VoHe!"

Maron appears next to his father. No words are spoken for a long time. Finally, Dee speaks without looking at his son.

"I'm guessing you like the girl?"

Maron smiles as Francesca leaps from flower to flower. "Her name is Francesca," he says. "And yes, I like her a lot."

There is another long pause, during which father and son continue to watch the scene before them.

"You have tests coming up?" Dee says, finally.

"Tests? You mean, for school? Sure, I have a few."

"What subjects?"

"Algebra," Maron begins. "Spanish, economics, history of religion."

"Religion?" Dee says. "What religion?"

"We're studying early Christianity. Roman Empire and the end of paganism."

Dee says, "A difficult time for me. What do they say about me in religion class?"

Maron smiles. "My teacher says a lot of early Christianity comes from the mystery religions. She says the whole 'I am the vine' thing comes straight from Dionysus."

"She used my name?"

"She did."

Another long pause.

"Perhaps you can teach me algebra and economics?" Dee finally turns to his son. "I have no knowledge of either."

"Lenny never taught you?" Maron asks.

"He would say we never had time."

"Maybe now you'll have a little more time," Maron says tentatively. "To learn algebra . . . and you know, hang out."

"Ichos! Ichos! Ichos!"

On the field, four pallbearers load Mark Apple's casket onto a bier as the congregation begins to move. Francesca waves at Maron.

"Go," Dee says. "Be with her."

As Maron starts forward, Dee stops him. "We'll start with algebra? Then you can tell me about economics?"

"Sure," Maron replies. "Tomorrow?"

"Tomorrow," Dee says.

Maron runs off. Lenny approaches Dee and begins massaging his shoulders. "You did it, Agrios."

"I did nothing. It all just happened."

"Exactly," Lenny says. "It all just happened."

"You know this man?"

CHAPTER SIXTY-ONE

Sam Kepler is the first clerk to arrive at the Home Depot at the north end of Glenhaven. Wandering the aisles, he finds three, then seven, and eventually forty middle-aged and elderly naked bodies slumbering in the lumber section. They are draped across stacks of plywood and two-by-fours, tucked into fetal positions atop wainscoting and clapboard. After moving close to one elderly man to confirm that he is breathing, Sam steps back.

Sam's heavyset supervisor arrives, says, "Jesus Christ," and steps back to join the clerk. For a while both men stroke their chins and say nothing. Then the supervisor says, "Jesus Christ" once more and dials 911.

During the ten-minute wait for the police to arrive, more clerks in orange aprons arrive. One pulls out his phone and takes pictures. The supervisor grabs the phone and demands the clerk's password, and everyone waits while the supervisor struggles to delete the photos.

Finally, two police officers arrive. The first one, wearing sergeant's stripes, parts the crowd with his hands.

"How many?" The sergeant opens a small notebook and flips to a blank page, as if this weren't the first call for sleeping naked bodies in a home improvement store he's had today.

"I counted forty-one," Sam the clerk says, stepping forward and back.

"Forty-one," the sergeant repeats, jotting down the number. He creeps toward the racks as if entering a potential ambush, one hand on his holstered pistol. His younger partner stays ten feet behind him, moving forward in the same defensive crouch. The clerks look at one another and snicker.

The sergeant sniffs the first body he reaches. He waves his partner forward. The sergeant pokes a trim, silver-haired man—the minister from the Unitarian church, who squirms and giggles without opening his eyes.

The sergeant delicately pokes the minister in the chest once more.

This time the minister opens his eyes. The two men stare at each other for a long time. "Can I see some ID?" the sergeant says.

Other naked bodies begin to stir on the racks. Some stretch, some yawn. The sergeant unconsciously reaches for his gun, and the younger officer deftly moves the sergeant's hand away from it.

"You!" the sergeant yells to one of the Home Depot clerks. "Get some of those orange aprons for these people. As many as you can find!"

The murmuring, yawning, and chatter among the congregation grows as they climb down from the racks.

The clerk returns with a large bin of aprons. He and two other workers hand them out, politely shielding their eyes from the nudity. Some of the naked people take the aprons; some decline.

"Tell me how you got here," the sergeant says to the minister.

The minister squints at his surroundings. "I don't know."

"I understand this group was at a funeral yesterday. My condolences," the sergeant continues, flicking a page of his notebook. "Do you remember where you went after the funeral?"

The minister turns and listens to his fellow congregants, who are murmuring. "The high school?" he says, turning back toward the sergeant. "We went to the high school?"

"Okay, you were at the high school," the sergeant replies. "What happened at the high school?"

"Well," the minister says thoughtfully, "I had questions from my childhood that I had long ago given up finding answers to. Last night, many of those questions were answered."

The sergeant nods. "I appreciate that," he says. "Can you tell me what specifically happened at the high school?"

Francesca and Maron arrive, breathless.

"Hello," Francesca says to the younger officer. "I'm looking for my father."

The sergeant answers his cell phone. "Correct, forty-one naked people. Don't send the paddy wagons. There are some older people here. Send the nice vans. Rent a couple if you have to."

Maron spots Christian, grabs an orange apron from a bin, and ties it around Christian's waist.

The sergeant follows Maron with his notepad. "You know this man?"

Francesca steps forward. "He's my father."

"Wow." Christian looks in awe around the cavernous warehouse. "There's a lot of wood in here!"

He raises the apron to wipe his eyes, nearly revealing his genitals in the process.

"Can you tell me what happened at the high school last night?" the sergeant asks Christian, turning another page and licking his pen.

Christian yawns so hard that the sergeant yawns in response. "Well, I guess what happened was that I was afraid. And after, I wasn't afraid. And after that I wondered why I was ever afraid. You know what I mean, Captain?"

"I'm a sergeant," the sergeant says.

"I was afraid of a lot of things, like my penis," Christian continues. "And I always thought that people were out to get me. But mostly, I think I was afraid of dying, Captain."

"Sergeant."

"Because dying is supposed to be the worst thing. Because you can't come back. But that's only a problem if you were here in the first place. Do you know what I mean? Like, you're a captain—"

"Sergeant."

"And I'm a guidance counselor. But what if I'm not really a guidance counselor and you're not really a captain—"

"Sergeant."

"What if those are like characters we play on TV? You play the captain, and I play the guidance counselor."

"Dad, we should go." Francesca tugs on Christian's arm.

"What happens when somebody turns off the TV? Who are we then?" Christian steps forward.

"I don't know," says the sergeant, bored, flipping another page in his notebook. "You tell me."

"I can't!" Christian says, his eyes wide. "That's just it. I can't tell you. No one can tell you. Not even the smartest person. You have to see it for yourself. And we saw it for ourselves, didn't we, honey?" He turns to Francesca.

"Dad," Francesca says, looking at Maron for support. "We really need to go."

"But you saw it, didn't you?"

Francesca nods, tears welling in her eyes. "I did, Dad."

Christian turns to Maron. "Your father, Maron, he's . . ." Christian searches for the word. "He's . . ."

"An asshole?" Maron smiles.

"Yes!" Christian shouts, grabbing Maron by the shoulders. "He's definitely an asshole. But I see now what he was trying to show me before! It wasn't about the Hammer."

"What's this about a hammer?" says the sergeant. "Who had a hammer?"

"Can we take him home now, please?" Francesca reaches for her school ID. "I'm his daughter, and he needs his medication."

Christian steps forward and pulls the sergeant into a long embrace. "I love you."

Outside, television news vans have arrived, and a few cameramen maneuver for position. The congregants, some in orange Home Depot aprons and some wrapped in blankets, appear like hostages or prisoners as they file out of the building. Some are escorted by relatives, some by police officers.

"Where are your clothes?" shouts a reporter.

"Why are you naked?"

"Miles! It's David! Do you need a ride?"

Miles waves to David, letting go of his apron, which causes the crowd to gasp and the cameramen to swerve their cameras to avoid recording full frontal nudity.

Maron opens the car door for Christian, and Francesca ushers her father into the back seat. Christian pauses halfway into the car and puts his hand on his daughter's shoulder.

"I'm worried I'll forget everything," Christian says. "You'll remember, won't you?"

Francesca nods. "Yes, I'll remember. I promise."

CHAPTER SIXTY-TWO

"You guys are so great," Christian says as Maron and Francesca lead him up the stairs to his apartment. "So great."

Once inside, they lay him on his bed, and no more than a minute passes before Christian is asleep and snoring.

As Francesca and Maron open the front door to leave, Ari enters carrying a bag of groceries. She rushes to her son and hugs him and then, to Francesca's surprise, hugs her too.

"Is he in there?" Ari asks.

"Yes," Francesca says. "He's exhausted and he just went to sleep."

Ari takes forty dollars out of her purse and hands it to Maron. "The two of you, go have some fun. Get some food. Go to the movies. Enjoy yourselves. I'm going to stay with him until he wakes up."

Inside the apartment, Ari eases into Christian's bedroom. For a long time, she listens to him snoring. Then she takes off all her clothes, crawls into bed, and spoons him.

"Is that you?" Christian murmurs, his back to Ari.

"Yes," Ari whispers.

"You're here," Christian says softly. "You're with me."

"Yes."

There's a long silence, during which Christian falls asleep and wakes again.

"Are you really going to grow old and die?" Christian says, finally.

"Yes," Ari replies.

"Will we die together?"

"No," Ari says. "One of us will die first."

There is another long silence.

"Every part of my skin feels like a little person," Christian whispers. "Every one of those little people are really happy to be touched by you right now."

"Good," Ari says, nuzzling her chin against Christian's neck.

"There's something else," he whispers.

"What?"

"I'm getting an erection. A little one."

Ari laughs. "Just a little one?"

"A teensy one," says Christian. "But it's mine."

———

Downtown, Francesca holds Maron's hand as they wander lazily amid the tide of pedestrians. Francesca looks on in amazement as people move in all directions, dogs sniff lampposts, cars honk their horns, and clouds pass overhead.

"I'm sorry," she says happily, "but this all seems pretty pointless."

Maron raises a finger to his lips. "Shh. Don't say the quiet part out loud."

The two of them laugh. Francesca skips merrily. "Well, I for one appreciate everyone's effort."

"I also appreciate their effort," Maron replies.

"I appreciate it when a person comes up and taps another person on the shoulder," Francesca says.

"I appreciate children playing in the ocean," Maron says.

"I appreciate how leaves are almost symmetrical but not quite."

"I appreciate your eyes," Maron says.

"I also appreciate my eyes." Francesca twirls around a lamppost.

"I appreciate the sun."

"I appreciate the sun too," Francesca says.

"I appreciate your ears," Maron says, circling her.

"I appreciate my ears too." She bats her eyelashes.

"I appreciate babies with food all over their faces."

"Oooh," Francesca laughs. "Getting a little ahead of ourselves, are we?"

"What do you mean?" Maron says, blushing.

Francesca leaps onto a patch of grass. "I appreciate this dead grass," she says. "I *really* appreciate this dead grass."

"I appreciate dead flowers," Maron replies.

"Yes." Tears fill her eyes. "And I appreciate dead people. Making way for other people."

Maron caresses her cheek. "It's not pointless at all, you know."

Francesca kisses Maron. "I know," she says.

"There is only one way going forward."

CHAPTER SIXTY-THREE

Lenny approaches Sloan's front porch. "If I ask you for a cigarette, don't give me one," he says.

Sloan sits against her front door, smoking.

"No need for me to resume bad habits now, when we are just getting started," Lenny says.

Sloan's hair is wild, but her face is clear and bright.

"I would join you on the ground," Lenny continues, sitting on a bench, "but sitting on concrete is not something I do."

Sloan takes a long pull from her cigarette.

"I don't want to watch my daughter die," she says, finally.

Lenny sighs. "That's what you're thinking about? That's a long, long way off."

"But I'll be around for it," Sloan says.

"You'll feel differently about such things by then," Lenny says.

"Such things," Sloan laughs. "You amaze me. How is it that you're so happy all the time?"

"If there were a good alternative, I would try it. Besides, how could I not be happy after last night? You were revolutionary."

Lenny groans as he maneuvers his way down onto the patio next to Sloan.

Sloan closes her eyes and listens to the birds singing and lawn mowers buzzing.

"I suppose I never had a choice," Sloan says, finally. "Does anyone?"

"Does anyone what?" Lenny replies.

"Have a choice about who they become, who they are, what they do, how they die?"

"If you want me to answer that question," Lenny says, "I can only do it by barking, or passing wind, or dancing a jig."

"I'll take the jig," Sloan says. "Do the jig."

With difficulty, Lenny clambers to his feet and commences a surprisingly deft Irish clog dance.

"Can you do that *and* fart?" Sloan says.

Lenny lets out a big fart and dances a few more steps. Sloan laughs.

"What about the bark!"

Lenny barks twice and then howls at the sky. Sloan laughs again, and Lenny reaches for his back. He settles gingerly back onto the patio.

"Don't make me do that again!" he says.

Sloan laughs, takes another drag of her cigarette, and closes her eyes. A twin-engine plane passes overhead. Sloan focuses on the Doppler shift as the plane drifts away.

There is a sudden bustle in the hedgerow as Dee, in the form of the little white goat, trots into the front yard. The goat stops to pee and then steps brightly forward. Sloan sets down her cigarette. Rising to her feet, she walks into the yard, picks up the goat, and holds it to her face.

The goat nuzzles its snout under Sloan's chin and politely licks her cheek before wrapping its little forelegs around her neck. Sloan pulls the goat away and holds it six inches away.

"There is only one way going forward," Sloan says. "Understand?"

The goat once again hugs Sloan with its little forelegs.

From the porch, Lenny reaches for Sloan's still-burning cigarette and takes a drag off it, closing his eyes with pleasure as he exhales.

Sloan chucks the goat to the ground and gives it a half-hearted kick in the ass. The goat morphs into a fully naked Dee. Dee raises his arms and howls at the sky. Purple clouds roll in, and rain begins to fall.

Sloan lifts her chin toward the sky, letting the rain soak her. She grabs at her breasts, then throws her head back and roars so loudly that Craig Entwerp's car alarm goes off and two nearby streetlamps explode.

New life!

CHAPTER SIXTY-FOUR

Epilogue I

Ari waddles across the labor and delivery room in her hospital gown, her butt half exposed. As Christian watches her, he thinks of his many humiliating trips to the urology office during which he wore a similar smock.

Since Ari and Christian arrived at the hospital a few hours ago, Ari's cervix has dilated to six centimeters. The nurses have been coming and going, while Christian, to keep Ari occupied, has been singing to her with the new acoustic guitar he bought himself.

"You are my baby mama," Christian sings to no particular tune. "I have other baby mamas, but you are my favorite one."

Ari rolls her eyes at Christian. She winces and breathes rapidly. When she cries out in pain, Christian jumps to his feet and yells for the nurses, repeatedly pressing the call button.

"Hello, hello," Christian yells. "Things are happening! Come in here, please!"

Moments later, the labor nurse enters and examines Ari.

"I'm gonna guess it was your singing," the nurse says as she lowers Ari's gown. "Getting there." She pats Christian on the shoulder and leaves the room.

Christian rushes to Ari's side and holds her hand. "How do you feel?"

"Like killing you and everyone else," she says through gritted teeth.

Christian squeezes her hand. "You can't kill me. I'm your ride home. Does this feel different from Maron?"

"Are you fucking kidding me?" Ari bellows. She grunts and squeezes Christian's hand so hard that he yelps in pain, just as the doctor reenters with the labor nurse and the obstetrics tech in tow.

"You're not the one who's supposed to be in pain," the doctor admonishes Christian. She sits at Ari's bedside as another nurse enters the room. "I think we may be getting ready to do this thing. What do you think, Ari?"

Ari nods, gritting her teeth.

Christian sits back on his chair to give the nurses room and hugs his guitar close. A brief image of his daughter's birth crosses his mind, when Francesca appeared in the world—a little girl with sticky eyes and a shock of red hair.

"Yo, Dad!" the doctor shouts. "Put down the guitar and get over here."

Christian rushes to Ari's bedside and grabs her hand.

"Baby on the move," the doctor says. Christian glances toward the back of the room, where the labor nurse seems to be explaining something to a medical student, who looks like a child in a mask.

"Moving fast, wow! Good pushing!" the doctor yells like a spin class teacher. "Give me two more like that!"

Ari screams, and Christian watches as the baby's head, then body, emerges. The doctor gently guides the newborn fully out of the womb.

"Good work, Mama! He looks fantas—"

Suddenly the pink, slimy baby wriggles out of the doctor's hands and scampers up Ari's belly. The infant immediately begins suckling on Ari's right breast.

"Oh my god!" the doctor yells. "Cut the cord! He's nursing!" she shouts to her assistant, who first clamps and then cuts the umbilicus.

The doctor and the nurse each take an uneven step back as the baby boy, after having suckled for a few moments, *stands up* on Ari's belly. Though covered in afterbirth, it's clear to Christian the boy is *grinning*. The baby looks quickly from one person to another in the room.

When the baby's sticky eyes finally land on Christian, he squats, raises his little arms, and leaps into the air. Christian instinctively catches him.

The medical student drops to the floor in a faint.

The baby grabs Christian's face in its two slimy hands, looks at him squarely, and razzes Christian's cheek.

The obstetrics tech, who has been staggering about looking for a chair, doesn't find one and falls to the ground.

The doctor, still upright, fishes for her cell phone, which drops to the floor.

The baby now places his feet on Christian's chest and leaps again back toward Ari. The doctor lunges forward to catch him, but the baby lands easily on the side of Ari's bed and swings itself like a monkey onto Ari's chest.

Finally, the doctor loses her equilibrium and slumps into a chair.

Ari and her son gaze at each other. Christian has never seen this particular expression on Ari's face. Since he met her, he has seen Ari amused, angry, sad, and cynical, but he has never seen her joyful. Christian's heart rises.

The child purrs against Ari's face like a kitten and then resumes suckling at her breast.

The obstetrics tech has managed to revive the student nurse. With the help of the doctor, all four of them shuffle toward the door.

"We'll give you . . . a moment," the doctor manages, her voice shaking. "But we would like to look . . . check in soon. Okay?" Her voice trails off as they exit.

Christian strokes Ari's sweaty forehead. The baby boy, nursing away, opens one eye toward Christian and then closes it.

"I thought we were all mortal now," Christian says.

"We are," Ari replies.

"Okay," Christian says, playfully. "But he just—"

"Shh," Ari says, her smile wide. "Look at our boy."

Christian smiles at the boy, his boy, who looks like any baby boy, blissfully attached to its milk-giving mother.

"You don't mind if he's different?" Ari says.

"No, no," Christian responds. "We're all little snowflakes, each unique unto ourselves."

"Christian Orr, psychologist," Ari says. She smiles at him.

"That's me," Christian says as tears well in his eyes.

An hour later, after having shooed the doctors away multiple times, Ari finally lets them examine her and the baby. Christian takes the opportunity to sit in his chair. Hugging his guitar, he feels sleep overtaking him.

As he drifts away, Christian recalls his trip to the cafeteria earlier in the morning, when he went to buy coffee for Ari after the nurses refused to give it to her. In the atrium, Christian saw a small boy with red hair like his own holding his mother's hand. The boy's mother was involved in an animated conversation on her cell phone. The boy's gaze wandered the atrium aimlessly until his eyes landed on Christian. The boy smiled, pointed a finger gun at Christian, and fired. Christian covered his heart, widened his eyes, and staggered backward. The boy laughed.

From her bed, Ari looks over at Christian, whose eyes are now closed. Christian smiles, raises his index finger, and mutters, "*Pew!*" Ari watches him fall further into sleep, a long string of drool falling from his mouth and attaching itself to the body of his guitar.

Flowers in Astroturf.

CHAPTER SIXTY-FIVE
Epilogue 2

The football field at Glenhaven High became a minor tourist attraction in the months following the night when flowers appeared in the astroturf.

Local arborists searched in vain for any sign of soil or substrate by which such flowers could grow. Xylem and phloem were not found in the stalks of the flowers, which, when cut, quickly grew back.

Eventually, as the football season loomed, and under pressure from the football-loving community, the field was excavated. Class 2 road base was spread at a four-inch depth, and a brand-new layer of astroturf was laid.

Francesca and Maron visited the football field many times, before and after the turf was replaced. They came on game nights and quiet nights when the stadium was empty. After their children were born, they brought them too. On nights when no one but her own little family was present, Francesca would occasionally see the astroturf sprout anew with tall, colorful flowers. She knew then to look for her mother.

"Grandma is here!" Francesca would say as her children ran onto the field. From among the tall flowers would appear Sloan, who, as the years went by, began to look more and more like her aging daughter.

Francesca and Maron never asked Sloan about her life with Dionysus. They treated their visits with Grandma as any young couple with children would, enjoying the brief respite from parenting and appreciating the feeling of being a part of something greater than themselves.

Francesca and Maron spent more time with Ari and Christian and their son, who was named Alexander. The couples babysat for one another, vacationed together, supported one another during hardships, and grew old together.

When Alexander became a teenager, Ari overruled Christian and let him play football. Ironically, Alexander's supernatural abilities had begun to wane almost from the moment he left the maternity ward. By the time he entered elementary school, Alexander retained no trace of unusual strength. As a moderately athletic sophomore on the junior varsity football team, Alexander spent most of each game on the sidelines, which suited him, and his worried father, just fine. Occasionally he turned to wave at his proud parents.

Sloan kept watch over all the members of her family and grew to love her new role as Lyaeus, liberator from care and anxiety. She detested the epithet "sexy Dionysus," which was used sarcastically among the gods to describe her. To his credit, Dee never seemed to resent the constant praise that was heaped upon Sloan, whom he referred to as his "last wife." Dee even regained some measure of affection for mortals, even if this was mostly directed toward his grandchildren, whom he showered with whatever good luck he could purchase from Zeus.

Sloan found a way to be present at the elementary school graduations of her grandchildren. She observed Halloween trick-or-treating and rarely missed the school events she had missed during Francesca's childhood.

In the end, Sloan did watch her daughter, and her grandchildren die, as well as their children and grandchildren. On those terrible days, Dionysus would rouse from his torpor and do for his wife what she did for the world. On those days, the two of them danced and drank and sang and screamed until the sun went down and sleep overcame them both.

Made in the USA
Middletown, DE
10 June 2025

76824735R00203